CRIMINAL PURSUITS: THIS IS ME

CRIMINAL PURSUITS: THIS IS ME

Edited by
Samantha Lee Howe

In Aid of
The Pink Ribbon Foundation

First published in 2025 by Telos Publishing Ltd,
139 Whitstable Road, Canterbury, Kent, CT2 8EQ, UK

Telos Publishing welcomes feedback
feedback@telos.co.uk

ISBN: 978-1-84583-245-2

British Library Cataloguing in Publication Data. A catalogue record for this book is available from the British Library.

CONTENTS

ABOUT THE PINK RIBBON FOUNDATION

Lisa Allen

Cancer touches all of our lives in some way, and breast cancer remains one of the most common and devastating forms of this disease. The Pink Ribbon Foundation (Reg. Charity No. 1080839) is proud to stand at the forefront of the fight against breast cancer, providing vital financial support to charities that offer care, education, and hope to those affected.

As we mark our 25th anniversary in 2025, we reflect on the journey of a small but passionate team – just four of us: Jonathan, Angie, Liz, and myself. With minimal infrastructure and a strong commitment to efficiency, we ensure that the maximum amount of funds raised goes directly to those who need it most.

The impact of our grants is felt across the UK, enabling frontline services and helping countless individuals facing the challenges of breast cancer. But none of this would be possible without *your* support. By purchasing this book of short stories, you are making a real difference. We are especially grateful to Samantha Lee Howe for championing this project and curating the powerful stories within these pages, and to each author who generously contributed their words to our cause – thank you for your talent and kindness.

We also want to take this opportunity to remind everyone – regardless of gender identity – to #KnowYourNormal. Regular self-checks of your breasts or chest are essential, because early detection really does save lives.

To learn more about the work we do and how you can get involved, please visit:
www.pinkribbonfoundation.org.uk

Find us on Facebook and Instagram:
@pinkribbonfoundation

With heartfelt thanks

WAITING

Michael Wood

Day One

The building was twelve storeys high, and he was sitting right on the edge of the roof looking down at the bustling city below. It was a cool day, the sky was filled with grey clouds, rain was accumulating, threatening to fall. A stiff wind was blowing.

From behind, he heard the sound of a heavy door opening, the steel scraping hard on the concrete of the roof. He risked a glance back over his shoulder and saw a female uniformed police officer walk out. The wind whipped up her blonde hair. She looked pale. He turned back to look at the view of the city melting into sprawling countryside ahead of him.

The police officer's shoes crunched the gravel as she approached, slow steps. She didn't want to frighten him, make him jump and fall. That wouldn't look good on her record. She cleared her throat.

'Hello,' she called out. He barely heard her, her voice struggling to find volume against the wind up here. 'Hello,' she tried again. 'I'm PC Silver. Rebecca. Bec. Can I ask your name?'

It was a while before he answered, almost as if he hadn't noticed she was there.

'Stuart. Stuart Appleton.'

'Hello Stuart. Do you mind if I sit down here?'

He shook his head.

PC Silver didn't sit down on the ledge beside him. It was clear by the tentative way she approached the edge of the building and lowered herself to the floor that she was scared of heights. The last thing she wanted was to sit down with her legs dangling below. As she rested along the raised ledge, she breathed a heavy sigh of relief. She was out of view of how far above ground level she was.

'Do you want to talk?' she asked.

He looked at her. Stuart wasn't an ugly man. He wasn't handsome either. There was nothing about his appearance that made him stand out among a crowd. He was plain, ordinary, unassuming. His dark brown hair was greying at the temples and receding. He was trim, though softening slightly around the middle as age seemed to dictate. He was an everyman.

'I've nothing to talk about,' he said in a flat monotone.

'There must be something you want to say. I'm guessing you're up here because you're planning on jumping.'

PC Silver was struggling to keep her hair from blowing wild. She was fighting a losing battle every time she tucked it behind her ears.

He nodded.

'So, why do you want to jump? What's brought you here?'

He swallowed hard. 'My business has failed,' he said, simply, shouting a little to be heard over the wind.

'I'm sorry to hear that. What business were you in?'

'Web design. I was in partnership with my brother.'

'What happened?'

'My brother emptied the company account and did a runner. I've got bills to pay and no money to pay them. I've got customers wanting their work done and I can't do it because I'm having to move out of the office and sell the equipment,' he said, rubbing his nose with the back of his hand.

'I'm so sorry. I know he's your brother, but what he's done is fraud. Have you reported him to the police? We can look for him.'

He turned to look at her, tears in his eyes. 'It's not going to bring my money back, is it? It's not going to give me my clients back and restore the name I spent ten years building up. All that's gone. Ruined. I've defaulted on my mortgage. Every time the phone rings or I get an email, it's someone else demanding money I can't give them.'

PC Silver fell silent. She didn't know what to say.

'I've done everything right,' Stuart continued. He sounded in agony. Not physical pain, but mental and psychological torment. 'All my life, I've done everything right. I listened at school and got an education. I went to college and university. I worked for a company I hated for years to get experience before setting out on my own. I've paid my taxes on time. I've never cheated anyone. I've never ever had so much as a parking ticket and now look at me. I'm on the brink of bankruptcy and failure.'

'It's not your fault, Stuart. None of this is your fault. You can start again.'

He sighed. His shoulders relaxed. 'I don't have the energy to start again. I'm fifty-two. I should be comfortable. I should be planning for retirement. I shouldn't be starting again. I shouldn't have to fucking start again,' he screamed into the wind.

'Stuart, please, I know everything is looking bleak for you right now. To be honest, if I was in your position, I don't know how I'd react. I might even be sitting where you are right now, but I know it isn't the answer. Killing yourself is never the answer.'

'I've nothing left,' he said, clearly agitated.

'Are you married? Children?'

'I was married. It ended. Years ago. We didn't have children.'

'Parents? Family? Friends? You must have friends.'

'You find out who your friends are when you're in the shit. It turns out all I had were acquaintances. They weren't real friends at all.' He shuffled on the ledge and edged closer.

'Stuart.' PC Silver reached out to him. 'Stuart, please. I can help you. I promise. I don't know much about the business world and bankruptcy, but I'm sure there are things in place that can help you. Creditors will understand. Your clients will understand if you're honest and open with them.'

He caught a scent of her fragrance as the wind blew in his direction. She smelled of flowers. It was sweet. There was something else in her scent, too. Fear. She was scared. Of being up here or of him jumping?

'Look out there, Bec,' he said, pointing to the view. 'Take a look.'

Reluctantly, PC Silver lifted herself up from the roof and peered over the edge.

'What do you see?'

'Buildings. The moors in the background. I see life.'

'I see money. I see selfishness. All people are interested in is themselves. As long as their lives are going well, as long as they have money in the bank, they don't care about others. They pretend they do. But it's all about profit. Look at governments and big businesses. They say all the right words to get you to vote for them and they promise they're going to bring jobs to the area and boost the economy, but eventually, the truth is revealed about how corrupt and underhand they are. The only thing people care about is themselves and fuck everyone else.'

His words, angry and powerful, were screamed out across the landscape, carried on the wind, and lost among the buzz of life continuing below.

'I'm not like that,' PC Silver said, quietly. She turned her back, once more, on the view, but moved closer to Stuart. 'There are around fifty people in my police station, and none of them are like that. We became police officers because we want to help people, because we want them to feel safe. Last week, I was called out to a burglary of an elderly woman in a bungalow on the outskirts of town. Whatever they couldn't steal, they broke. Her house was a mess. I stayed with her and helped her to tidy up. The neighbours all came round with emergency pieces of furniture she could use until her insurance money came through. The woman next door invited her around for a meal that night and a family across the street gave her a bed for the night and said she could stay with them for as long as she wanted to. Her sister called from Dorset; said she was getting the first train in the morning and invited her to move back down there. Everyone rallied round and helped her. She had offers from the entire neighbourhood. I admit, I get jaded in this job. I see some sights that shake me. But what I saw that night restored my faith in people. There are good people still out there, Stuart.'

He turned and looked her in the eye. 'Not in my life, they're not. I've looked for them.'

'That's because you have the wrong people in your life. You need to find different ones.'

'I'm too old to be searching for new friends,' he said, dejected.

'No, you're not. Mrs Boswell, the woman who was burgled, she's thinking about moving all the way down to Dorset and she's in her late eighties. If she can make a complete lifestyle change, why can't you?'

'I can't. It's too much. I don't have the fight in me anymore.'

PC Silver tucked a stray hair behind her ears. 'It's not about fighting. There's a way out of all of this, Stuart, trust me. What's happened is none of your doing, but you can declare bankruptcy, move somewhere else, start again. You've just said your friends weren't your real friends, so you've nothing to tie yourself to this city. Move. Head north. You've got the qualifications, work for another web design company, or do something completely different. Go travelling. Go to Dorset,' she smiled.

Stuart laughed. For the first time, he let out a genuine laugh.

'This doesn't have to be the end, Stuart,' she said, reaching out and laying a comforting hand on his arm.

He looked down at the hand on his sleeve, followed it with his eyes and looked at the smiling face of PC Rebecca Silver. Her eyes were big and hopeful. She seemed to genuinely want him to live, and not just because it was her job to see a successful end to this particular task.

'I don't want to be up here.'

'I know you don't. I don't want you to be up here, either.

For a start, it's bloody freezing,' she chuckled.

'I didn't pick the best day to do this, did I?'

'I tell you what, come downstairs with me, now, I'll get us a cup of tea and something to eat and we can make a list of all the things you need to tackle, and we'll set things in motion.'

He turned away. Defeated.

'Stuart, I'm not the type of person who's just going to see you safely to the bottom of the stairs and let you walk away. I'm going to help you. I'll find you a solicitor who deals with this kind of thing who'll be able to give you some advice. I've met plenty in my job. Someone is bound to know an expert in this. I also know the vicar at St Giles's, and he has people stay overnight in the church occasionally, for emergencies. If you end up losing your home, he'll let you stay there for a few nights. I'm not going to abandon you,' she said, squeezing his arm firmly.

Stuart looked back. His bottom lip wobbled, and a tear fell from his eye and blew away on the wind.

'Come on. Swing your legs back over this side, and let's go for that cuppa. I'm parched, freezing, and I wouldn't mind a custard slice right now.'

It was a while before he moved as he seemed to be weighing up the options in his head. Eventually, he leaned back, and slowly brought one leg, then the other, over the ledge of the roof and back onto firmer ground.

'You've made the right choice,' PC Silver said with a huge smile.

'Thank you,' he said.

Day Nine

The building was twelve storeys high, and he was sitting right on the edge of the roof looking down at the bustling city below. It was a warm day; the sky was a pale blue with whispers of fluffy clouds floating calmly. A gentle breeze was blowing, but given the time of year, it was a chilly breeze, and took the edge off the spring temperature.

From behind, he heard the sound of a heavy door opening, the steel scraping hard on the concrete of the roof. He risked a glance back over his shoulder and saw a male uniformed police officer walk out. He removed his helmet to reveal a shaved bald head. He took a deep breath, probably to psyche himself up. He turned back to look at the view of the city melting into sprawling countryside ahead of him.

The police officer's shoes crunched the gravel as he approached, slow heavy steps. He had obviously had the same kind of training as PC Rebecca Silver last week. He came forward with caution so as not to frighten him and cause him to jump or fall. PC Silver had been difficult to shake off. She was a woman of her word, and she contacted him on a regular basis to make sure he was surviving and sticking to the plan they had both sat down and drawn up together. That was a very long afternoon. He told her what she wanted to hear and hoped she would soon leave him alone, yet she persisted. PC Silver was a saint in the making. She was also like a dog with a bone, and she refused to let him go.

The police officer cleared his throat. 'Hello.' His voice was deep, masculine, and quiet. 'I'm PC Jeffrey Rice. Are you all right?'

He didn't say anything.

The footfalls of the police officer were strong and confident as he came closer. Whatever fragrance he was wearing wasn't as subtle as PC Silver. He almost sneezed when he caught of a whiff of it.

'Can I ask your name?' PC Rice asked.

He sighed. 'James. James Todd.'

'Hello Mr Todd. Am I OK to sit beside you?'

James shrugged.

PC Rice reached the edge of the building and lowered himself carefully to the floor. Like PC Silver, he obviously wasn't a fan of heights as the moment he could no longer see how far above ground he was, he visibly relaxed.

'Can I call you James?'

He nodded.

'What's brought you up here today, James?'

James didn't say anything. He continued to look out at the view. He was starting to like this view. Eventually, he turned to look at the PC who seemed to be younger than he first thought. His face was fresh, clean shaven, no circles beneath his eyes, no crows' feet, and no sagging around the jawline. He suited his uniform, was tall and broad shouldered. He spoke with a local accent and James guessed he'd grown up on these streets, dreaming of becoming a police officer since he was a small boy.

'Do you ever think you're just not cut out for this life?' James asked.

PC Rice didn't know how to answer that. He opened and closed his mouth a few times but couldn't seem to choose the right words.

'No. You probably don't. You're only young. I've lived. Unfortunately. I've been through so much horror that I'm taking it as a sign that I simply shouldn't be here.'

'I don't believe in any of that. I don't think there's a sign from somewhere in the ether giving us messages or warnings. Some people simply have a run of bad incidents happen to them. It won't last. It can't.'

'Oh, believe me, Jeffrey, it can.'

'Do you want to talk about it?'

'I'm tired of talking. If I was prepared to talk, I'd be in a therapist's office, not on the edge of a roof.'

PC Rice shuffled closer. 'Can I tell you something?'

James nodded.

'Did you hear in the news last year about a machete attack on the Warren Hill Estate? I was there. I was one of the first on the scene. I watched as that man attacked two of my colleagues. I had to stem the blood flow to my partner on the side of the road while the ambulance arrived. How he survived is anyone's guess. When I went into that flat and saw what he'd done to his family, well, I lost it. It was a horror film. I couldn't cope. I didn't sleep. I didn't eat. I was ready to leave the force. My sergeant told me to go to a therapist, which I did. I lasted one session. It wasn't for me. But I found a group in town run by a charity. It's for men to get together and just talk. Nobody judges. Nobody offers opinions. We just sit around and chat about what's on our minds. Believe me, it helps. After that first meet, I felt loads better. I was going every week. Now, I go every month. Therapy isn't for everyone, but talking is. We can't go through life keeping everything locked inside.'

James looked PC Rice in the eye. For a man so young, he was incredibly wise. He liked him.

'I got married at a ridiculously young age. I was twenty. I loved Alice to bits. We had a child, Garrett, the following year. Two years later, Alice was pregnant again. When she was six months gone, she and the baby were killed in a car crash in Dorset.'

'Oh my God. That must have been horrible. I'm so sorry,' PC Rice said, genuinely meaning it.

'When Garrett was five, he was diagnosed with Leukaemia. It was three years of chemotherapy and radiotherapy before he was given the all clear. Two years after that, he was diagnosed with a brain tumour. There was no cure for that. He died six days after his twelfth birthday.'

'Bloody hell.' Rice said. He looked down at the floor and shook his head.

'A year later, my sister was murdered while on holiday in Egypt and my Mum died of breast cancer three months later. My Dad never got over losing his wife and daughter so closely and took his own life. I really was completely alone in the world.

'I decided to move. Make a fresh start. I came here. Don't ask me why I chose this place. I've been asking myself that question since I arrived. I got a job with Benedicts. You're probably too young to remember them. They went bankrupt within three months of me joining the company. After that, I couldn't find work anywhere. I was unemployed for over a year before I got a job with the council. I've been with them ever since and hated every single fucking moment of it,' he said, bile and vitriol behind every word.

'The best thing that came out of working with the council

was that I met my second wife, Ruth.' He glimpsed at PC Rice who saw he was listening to him with rapt attention. 'We married within a year of dating and had twins. They ran in her family, apparently. Talk about a massive shift in lifestyle. We were living in a grotty two-bedroom flat with two screaming babies. Looking back, they were the happiest times of my life.' He bowed his head and fell silent.

'You have good memories to look back on. That's important. When times are hard, you need to remember the happy times. They help you through the bad ones.'

'Ruth left me for one of my best mates,' he said, turning to Rice. 'She said I was dull and life with me was boring. Those were the words she used. She took the twins with her. They're all living happily ever after in San Francisco. I haven't seen my kids for nearly a decade. They don't know who I am anymore,' he said, his words choked with emotion.

'Oh God, James, I'm so sorry.'

'Nothing ever goes just slightly wrong for me. It goes nuclear.'

'I know it must seem like that at times, James, but the world isn't against you or anything. You're not being singled out as some kind of test to see how much shit a person can cope with. Yes, I'll agree with you, you have suffered more than your fair share of horror, but there will be pockets of happiness in your life you can look back on and smile.'

James shook his head.

'We always focus on the negative. I've got this colleague at work. Well, she's just become my boss now she's been promoted, but whenever she watches the news and the lead item is a good news story she always says there must be no news today if that's what they're leading with. She sees the news as being something to report all that's wrong and bad with the world. When it's not. All the bad stands out because we remember it so much when we should be remembering all that's good.'

James turned back to look at the young PC. He seemed to believe his own rhetoric. Was it the innocence of youth and, despite the horror he'd seen in his work, the reality of life had yet to jade him? Or did he really have everything sorted out in his head so early in life? If so, good for him.

'I'm dying,' James said. 'I found blood in my… well, I don't need to give you all the gory details. I went to the doctor. He sent me for a test. Then I had more tests. Next thing you know, I'm being given a time frame and told to put my affairs in order.'

Once again, PC Rice looked stumped for something to say.

'Bowel cancer. To begin with. It's spreading. Very quickly, too.'

'I'm sorry,' Rice said.

James shrugged.

'Is there nothing they can do?'

'I don't want to linger in agony. I don't want to die alone in a hospice. I'm taking control. I'm grabbing life by the collar and looking him in the eye and showing him that despite everything he's done to me, I'm having the last laugh,' James said. He stood up with determination and took a deep breath as he looked down at the city below.

Rice jumped to his feet.

'James, please, don't do this,' he said, panic evident in his voice. 'Trust me, this is not the way to go. Yes, you might be successful and kill yourself, but there are so many things that could go wrong. You may end up in a vegetative state and be confined to a bed for months, years. And what about the people on the ground, below you. Look at them. They're going about their lives. Think of how they'll react when they see you come hurtling towards them. And what if you hit one of them? They could be seriously injured. James, please, listen to me,' he said, grabbing his coat sleeve firmly. 'I shouldn't be telling you this, but there are easier ways to do this without hurting and involving other people. If you're serious about taking charge of your own death, especially as you're ill, then…' he swallowed hard and looked uncomfortable. 'There's… I… I know what you can do. I know some people who might be able to help.'

James looked down at him. 'What are you talking about?'

'I've seen what happens after people have taken fifty

paracetamol and a bottle of vodka. It doesn't look good. There are stronger drugs you can take to make sure you just fall asleep and … that's it. Please, don't jump.'

They maintained eye contact for a long while. James looked into Jeffrey Rice's eyes and saw a young man who wanted to do good in the world, who wanted to be the best police officer at every incident he attended. In this case, he wanted to do what was best for a dying man rather than what the police handbook told him he should do.

James held out a hand. Jeffrey took it and helped him down off the ledge.

'Thank you,' James said, genuine tears in his eyes.

'You're welcome,' Jeffrey said with a helpful, and relieved, smile.

Day Thirteen

The building was twelve storeys high, and he was sitting right on the edge of the roof looking down at the bustling city below. It was a warm day; the sky was a pale blue with not a single cloud. A sharp breeze was blowing, taking the edge off the spring temperature.

From behind, he heard the sound of a heavy door opening, the steel scraping hard on the concrete of the roof. He risked a glance back over his shoulder and saw a male uniformed police officer walk out. He removed his helmet to reveal dark brown hair, trimmed almost military in style. He took a deep breath and stepped forward.

The man on the edge of the building couldn't take his eyes from the police officer as he approached. He sighed, then turned back to look at the view of the city melting into sprawling countryside ahead of him.

The police officer's shoes crunched the gravel as he approached, slow heavy steps.

'Hello!' he called out.

His voice was loud and confident. He reached the ledge,

hitched up his trousers and sat down, his back facing the view. Heights obviously didn't bother him like they had his two predecessors.

'I'm PC Adam Maltravers. What's your name?'

He took a few deep breaths to control himself. He looked down at his hands, they were balled into fists, the knuckles white. He could feel every vein in his body throbbing, blood was gushing through his brain like a tsunami.

'Victor,' he said. He didn't give his surname.

'Victor. Do you get called Vic?'

'No,' he replied.

'Fair enough. Victor it is, then. Do you want to tell me what you're doing up here?'

'I'm going to jump.'

'I gathered that. Why?'

Victor turned and looked at him. PC Maltravers was a slim man somewhere in his thirties, Victor guessed. He was good looking in a plain kind of way. Nothing stood out about him as being remarkable, but his eyes were sparkling, smiling, despite the dangerous situation he'd found himself in. His nose was slender, his lips full and red, his jawline was firm and there were holes where both ears had been pierced at some point. He gave off an air of someone fun, happy, good to be with. He probably didn't have a care in the world and took every day as it comes. Good for him. The stressors of adult life had yet to catch up with him. Mortgage repayments, bills, food prices, cars breaking down, the roof leaking, babies draining your bank balance, school uniforms, Christmas presents, a decent holiday every year, taxes. More money going out than coming in. When did the worry stop?

Victor turned away.

'Mate, listen, nothing can be so bad that *this* is the solution,' PC Maltravers said.

'I'm afraid it is,' Victor spoke into the wind.

'Tell me what's going on. A problem shared, and all that. Sometimes things don't look so bad when you say them out loud.'

Victor didn't say anything.

'Look, I'll level with you, mate. I'm not a trained psychologist or anything. I think therapy is a load of shite, but I do think that talking to people helps. You can't bottle things up or you'll go mad. Now, right here, I'm all you've got. I apologise in advance. I'm usually better at giving out advice when I've got a pint in my hand, but if you tell me what's troubling you, I'll definitely try to help you. I promise,' he said, placing his right hand over his heart.

'My marriage has ended,' Victor said, softly.

Maltravers sighed. 'Mate, no woman is worth killing yourself over. Trust me.'

'I have to sell the house because I can't afford to buy her out. She wants half of everything, which is fair enough, I suppose, but that means half the business, too, and I can't afford to buy her half from her either, and I certainly don't think we can work together. So, that will need to be sold, too. I just don't understand why I have to lose things because she's ending the marriage.'

'That's shit, mate, I'm sorry. Is it… I mean… are you sure it's over between you?'

'She's found someone else. She's been seeing him for over a year. Can you believe that?' Victor turned to Maltravers. 'Over a year she's been with another bloke, and I didn't know. Do you want to know why?'

'Why?'

'Because I was too busy working. I was too busy working every single day of the week to keep our heads above water. What was the point?'

'Look, Vic,' he said, scooting up the ledge, closer to Victor. 'I know, from your point of view, it looks like everything's shit. You've done nothing wrong, yet you're having to lose your home and your business because your wife has found someone else, but that's no reason to kill yourself. I bet, right now, you're thinking why can't things stay as they are, but do you really want to be with a woman who's going to cheat on you? I bloody wouldn't. Can't you see this as a fresh start?'

'A fresh start?' Victor asked, incredulously.

'Yeah. I mean, you said yourself you were working every day of the week. That's not normal, is it? You need some downtime. You need a life. You were obviously working yourself into an early grave. Can't you see this as a sign that your current life wasn't working and you should do something different, something life-affirming, something fun?'

'Fun.'

'Yes. Life should be about having fun, shouldn't it?'

'Should it?'

'Of course.'

Victor looked PC Maltravers up and down.

'I'm guessing you're one of these people that treats life like it's all a game.'

He smiled and his face lit up. 'Life is a game, mate. None of us gets out of this alive, so we might as well make the most of things while we're here.'

Victor nodded slowly. 'And screw anyone who gets in our way,' he said, almost to himself.

'Precisely. Your wife did the dirty on you. I really am sorry to hear that. She sounds like a complete bitch. But you're better off without her. Get yourself a good solicitor and I bet you any money you won't have to give up your business. You're the injured party in this. Play on that.'

Victor swallowed hard. 'I love her.'

'Love doesn't last forever.'

'But it hurts when it ends.'

'I wouldn't know about that,' Maltravers said with a snorting laugh.

'You've never been in love?'

'No.'

'I'm sure women have fallen in love with you.'

He shrugged.

'I'm guessing you're the type of bloke who drops women before they get too close.'

'I only want to see one toothbrush in my bathroom,' Maltravers winked. 'Look, Victor, I'm freezing my nuts off up here and I'm going off shift in an hour. You don't want to do this; I know you don't. So, why don't we go downstairs, warm ourselves up, and I'll stand you a pint when I've finished? What do you say?'

Victor thought for a moment.

'No. I don't want to do that. I want my wife to know that she drove me to my death. I want this to be on her conscience for the rest of her life.'

PC Maltravers's face suddenly paled.

'Oh, Victor, you really don't. Come on, mate, don't do this,' he said, his voice low and shaking.

Victor stood up and faced forward. He was ready to jump.

'Victor, what are you doing?' Matravers asked, standing up alongside him. 'Please don't jump, mate, please. How are you going to know your wife's hurting if you're not here to see it? Surely there's some other way you can get back at her. Surely, making a success of yourself again and living a better life than she is will show her.' His words were falling over each other as he spoke rapidly, knowing that time was running out. 'Vic. Victor. Be the bigger person here. You're angry. That'll pass. You want revenge? I get it. I do. But there are other ways.'

'Other ways?'

'Yes. I know I shouldn't be saying this, but... go and find this bloke who your wife has been seeing, give him a few home truths, give him a punch to the gut if it'll make you feel any better. But not this, Vic, don't do this.'

Victor didn't say anything. He didn't move. He didn't blink. He didn't breathe.

'I'll come with you. We'll go and see him together. If you love your wife this much, if you want her back so badly then we'll tell him to back off. We'll... I don't know, but we'll do something. Do you know where he lives? Who is he?'

Victor turned, slowly, to PC Adam Maltravers. 'It's you.'

Victor smiled as he grabbed Adam by his jacket and stepped off the roof of the twelve-storey building, taking his wife's lover with him.

About the Author:

Michael Wood was born and raised in Sheffield. A former journalist, he is the author of the bestselling *DCI Matilda Darke* series of novels set in South Yorkshire and in 2024 he launched a new series featuring forensic psychologist Dr Olivia Winter. He is also the author of several standalone thrillers. He currently lives in Newcastle where he spends his days either writing crime fiction or reading crime fiction.

https://michaelwoodbooks.co.uk

STRAIGHT TO HEAVEN

Bryony Pearce

'Are you sure you want to do this, babe?'

Lyric is sitting shotgun, hair glinting in the sunlight that reflects from the car mirror. She's the most beautiful woman in the world. Of course, she says I am. I'm not. But I am damned lucky.

'It's not like I have a choice.' I stare at the house at the end of the driveway. The house at the end of the street, at the end of the town, at the arse end of nowhere. I clench my fists.

It looks pretty ordinary for a hellmouth.

Lyric squeezes my hand. 'There's always a choice,' she whispers. 'You could wait till after my tour is over. We could do it together. Or hire someone to take care of this for you.'

The air in the car is heating up. When we'd stopped, I'd turned off the ignition and that shut down the AC. I tug my collar away from my throat. Sweat trickles down the valley between my breasts. I reach over and open the window. It descends with a hiss, and I gasp as air fills the car. Air that is filled with the scent of childhood summers: the lavender in the front garden, now overgrown; cloying honeysuckle; cow-shit from the fields. I swallow. Then I get out of the car and stand still. There is a buzzard wheeling overhead, the hum of bees. It's otherwise quiet.

No wonder Dad cut and ran; there is nothing of him here. Nor can I look at this place and say: 'this is who I am'. It is an alien dimension.

Lyric helps me take my suitcase out of the boot, separating it from her own, against which it was nestled. I wasn't sure how many days to pack for, but I aimed for three. I'll get this done in two if I can manage it. To make sure I stick to the plan, I only put in three pairs of pants, three pairs of socks, three sets of nighttime medication. The case is light.

As Lyric puts my case on tarmac so hot that it's steaming, the front door opens, and a nurse appears. She strides towards us, visible sweat stains under her armpits, her expression fixed somewhere between regret and relief.

'You must be Litha,' she says, but she looks between the two of us, not sure who to hold out her hand to. I sense she's about to turn towards Lyric, with her blonde curls and welcoming smile: Lyric who looks like a daughter anyone would want, and I decide to avoid the awkwardness that would ensue. I thrust out a palm, take hers', shake it.

'That's right,' I say. 'And you're Carla.'

She nods. 'I'm so sorry about your mum, but it's beyond time.' Her eyes tell me she's wondering why she's offering the platitude to someone who has never visited. Never even asked for an update. Disapproval radiates from her. I drop her hand.

'She's ready to go?' I frown as I look around, as if Carla is hiding Mum, with her suitcases and an ambulance behind the pines at the side of the road.

Carla hesitates. She looks at me; at my dark jeans and darker hair that I wear straight and shoulder length, at my biker boots, at my fingers so be-ringed it seems I'm wearing knuckledusters. Then she sighs. 'St Anthony's called - there's been an emergency. Your mum's room won't be ready until tomorrow, and they can't send the ambulance until the morning.'

The sun's heat drains from the day. 'Are you serious?'

Carla nods.

'I'm only here to sort things for storage and prepare the house for sale. You'll have to stay.' I am already turning my rings, one after the other. Lyric grabs my hand and squeezes it.

Carla shakes her head. 'I'm sorry, but I'm on a flight out this afternoon. It's been arranged. I can't just …'

Lyric gives her an understanding smile. 'You certainly

can't. Litha can manage one night alone with her Mum.' She looks at me. 'Can't you?'

'I've left instructions on the fridge,' Carla says. 'Her medication, how to get her to sleep, what happens if she has an episode. How to calm her. She'll sleep most of the time.'

'Most of the time.' I echo, as the world shifts beneath my feet.

'And you can call me if you have to,' Carla says, already edging towards her car, a red Toyota parked just inside the gate. 'But I'll be in the air from six, for a couple of hours, so ... '

'Right.' I raise a hand, releasing her from her obligation.

Carla pauses, fingers on her car door, looking back at me. She's middle-aged, her skin soft and starting to wrinkle at the edges. She squints into the sunlight. 'She's a good person, your mum,' she says. 'Never gives me any trouble.' She climbs inside. 'This might not be as bad as you expect.' She starts the car, giving me no time to answer.

My teeth sink into my lip, and I cling on to Lyric as Carla pulls onto the road and gathers speed, her wheels throwing up dust.

Lyric pulls me close. 'I'll stay,' she says. 'I'll cancel the hotel, head over tomorrow, or the day after, let my agent smooth things over.'

I let her words hang there between us for a moment, wondering what it would be like if I was that selfish. Then I shake my head. 'She's right, it's one night, how bad can it be? Go.'

'You don't want me to come in first? Meet her?'

I laugh, bitterly. 'You want to meet the woman who told me not to come out to anyone else, who threw out my clothes and burned my magazines -'

Lyric pressed a kiss to my forehead, silencing me. 'It was a long time ago. Maybe she's changed her mind. It's a different world now, after all.'

I lean into her. 'She is the reason I could never be myself. Lyric, she drove away the only person in my life who knew who I was and accepted me.'

Lyric tightens her arms around me. 'Litha,' she says. 'Your dad could have contacted you any time after he left. His silence is hardly on her, is it?'

My jaw flexes. 'Who knows what she told him, threatened him with?' I look at the house. 'You don't know what it was like, hiding who I really was. You do that long enough and it's almost impossible to find yourself again.'

Lyric gives me a gentle shake. 'Remember who you're talking to,' she says, and she steps away, leaving me cold, despite the heat, and heads for the driver's seat. She climbs in and pokes her head out of the window. 'Now, kiss me and tell me you'll miss me.'

A grin forces itself onto my lips and I bend to press them against hers'. 'I'll miss you,' I murmur. 'More than you know.'

'I'll be back in a fortnight,' Lyric reminds me, and I nod. Then I straighten, neck prickling. A woman is standing in the living room window, watching, one hand on the glass. Sun glints from the pane, masking her eyes, but her mouth is a single, flat line: Mum.

I give her my back, and watch Lyric drive until the car is out of sight, then I pick up my case. The hairs on my neck stand on end, telling me Mum has not moved. I think about simply walking away, calling a taxi, and heading up the road until I reach the next house, the one that had once belonged to Mrs Kettering, and asking them to pick me up there. Then I kick a stone into the verge and turn. Mum still stands, although her hands are by her sides now. Her hair is in a long, neat plait and her eyes are hooded.

For a moment I'm a terrified fifteen-year-old, and my secret self is choking me, like her hands are around my neck. I'm wearing a denim skirt and a pink t-shirt, my hair down my back. I can even feel the weight of it. I have to touch the ends flying loose around my shoulders to remind me that this is not who I am any more.

I exhale and head for the front door. The grass in the front garden has browned, died back. The flowerbeds are filled with weeds. Things have changed.

I only have to spend one night with her. I'll put her to bed and start packing.

How bad can it be?

Carla has left the front door ajar so that it opens at a push onto a hallway, familiar from years of bad dreams, and indeed, a nightmarish disorientation overcomes me as I step inside, out of the sun. The flagstones are dirtier than they once were, the rug worn under my boots and curling at the edges. To my right looms Grandmother's coat stand, dark spines curling towards the ceiling. It has not moved; even the Barbour hanging from it is the same, though tattier. I would almost be unsurprised to find my own mac hanging under it.

Ahead of me is a clock, as tall as I am, counting out the seconds with a heavy, slightly uneven tick, just as it counted out every moment of my closeted childhood. As I watch, it whirrs and clanks, the second hand reaches the hour, and it bongs ponderously: once, twice. Had Carla kept it wound, or was Mum still doing it every day? Coming down the stairs, inserting the key and turning it, before doing anything else. I glare at the yellowing face. Like everything else here, the clock would be sold the moment Mum was out. If it didn't sell, I'd send it to the tip. I certainly wouldn't be winding it tomorrow. Tonight, it would tick its last tock.

To my left was the door to the kitchen, with Carla's instructions, and everything I needed to make Mum comfortable. As if she'd ever cared for my comfort. Off the kitchen would be the door to the cellar, which had always contained the old chest freezer, overflow from the kitchen cupboards, boxes of holiday decorations, outdoor toys and junk Mum didn't want to throw away. Everything in there could go in the skip, most likely. I'd hired one. It was due to arrive once I'd sorted through some stuff.

A few pictures hang on the walls: an old school photo of me, wearing my hair in a ponytail, my lips pulled into a fake 'cheese' that shows my crooked front tooth, eyes lifeless. Another picture of me was taken the day I got my GCSEs: yellow sundress, blue converse, clothes chosen by Mum. She'd dressed me as if I was a doll. I touch the glass with trembling fingertips. I'd come out three months earlier and a few days after this was taken, Dad would leave, in the middle of the summer holidays.

There is not a single photo of him on display. Not even an old wedding picture, or one from his army days. It is as if Dave Summerfield was never here. Why does she keep the old me, framed, as if preserved in amber, and not him?

The stairs are in front of me. I could go up and put my case on my old bed, assuming I still have one. Carla would have been using one room, Mum the master. Was mine still *my* room, or had it long ago been turned into a home gym, craft space, office? I didn't want to find out, not yet. I wasn't sure which would hurt more: teenaged me laid bare or wiped away like a stain.

I was delaying the inevitable. To my left was the door to the living room, to Mum. There's been no sound, but I know she's there, waiting. I put the case down and twist my rings. I'm an adult now, I remind myself. Then I go to meet her.

For a moment, with the sun behind her, turning her into a silhouette, time stands still, and nothing has changed. She looks *exactly* the same. My heart thuds until she steps forward, out of the light and I see more clearly. What I had taken for a long dress is a nightgown. Her hair is no longer the same shade as mine, but a flinty pewter. Her shoulders have developed a hunch and wrinkles loosen her face. The biggest change, however, is in the eyes. Where she had once looked at me with disappointment, even, at times, despair, she looks at me now, with confusion.

'I don't know you,' she snaps in a voice brittle with fear. 'Where's Carla?'

'Carla must have told you,' I say as gently as I can bring myself to. 'She's had to go. I'm here for tonight.' I pause, but she says nothing, only wraps her arms around herself, eyes darting as if seeking escape. 'It's me,' I say eventually. 'Litha?'

I say it like a question, as if the fact that my own Mum doesn't remember me, erases my own existence.

'Litha,' Mum says it like a prayer. But she isn't looking at me, she's looking at another picture, one above the mantel. In it I'm eighteen. About to leave myself, one foot out of the door. I'm wearing my hair defiantly short, black jeans, the start of my ring collection glinting on one hand.

Then she turns back, and her eyes have hardened. 'Litha's gone,' she says emphatically. '*You* aren't Litha. You're an imposter. A straw woman.' She retreats towards the fireplace. 'You look nothing like Litha. It's in the eyes.' She points at mine, and I am chilled.

There is a smell here. I've only just noticed it, so it can't be that strong, but once I do, I can't get it out of my nostrils. It's awful. Is it just the smell of sickness, or has Mum soiled herself? Do I need to clean her up? I can't do that! There *are* limits, aren't there?

I edge closer, but the smell doesn't intensify. Nor though, does it abate. It's ingrained in the atmosphere, hanging in every molecule. I want to wipe myself clean.

There's a chair in front of the television. Unfamiliar. It has buttons and a power cable. Mum sits in it now, her eyes flickering towards me.

'I've nothing worth stealing,' she says in a wheedling voice. 'I'm just an old lady.'

'Not that old,' I snap, thinking that she isn't. Sixty-four isn't that old. She should have had more time.

Maybe it's like that Roald Dahl quote, didn't he say something about ugly thoughts and how they change you? Maybe she rotted herself away from the inside.

She shrinks in the chair, and I see tears on her cheeks. 'I'm sorry,' I sigh.

This isn't Mum. Mum isn't here. Not really. I can be kind to this shell that has replaced her, can't I?

'I'm your new nurse, just for one night, then you're going somewhere really nice.'

Mum stiffens. 'I'm not going anywhere.'

'Alright.'

I clamp my teeth together. What's the point in arguing? Tomorrow, I'll help to get her on the ambulance. I was going to start packing things up today, but if I can't do that in front of her, I can save it for tomorrow. Perhaps today I can pull together the important documents, things that need to be saved, filed.

First thing is to check when she needs her next medication, her meal and so on. I leave her in her chair and head towards the kitchen.

Mum catches me before I reach the door. 'What are you doing? Stop, thief!' She drags at my shirt with surprisingly strong fingers. 'Get out,' she shouts. 'Get out of my house!' She slaps me, a ringing thump that knocks me sideways.

'Jesus!' I clutch my burning cheek and whip around. She stands staring, defiant, reminding me of the picture of myself above the fireplace, then she races for the front door. I let her get a few steps, then go after her, putting both arms around her waist, unsure if that is the right thing to do.

'Mum,' I say. 'I'm not a thief. It really is me, it's Litha. You have to calm down.'

Am I doing the right thing? Saying the right thing? I have no idea. I need to read Carla's instructions. I should have done that first.

I reach past her struggling body and snap the lock on the front door. Then I swing her round and half carry her back to the living room. She's wailing and thrashing like a toddler; she's hurting me. I dump her in her chair and stagger back. She glares but remains in place. Her plait is barely intact, loose hair sticks to her lips and the sweat on her cheeks.

She licks her lips and looks around, fixating on the window. I follow her gaze. The window is double glazed, she's not getting out that way either.

'Mum,' I say. 'I have to go in the kitchen. I won't take anything. I'll make you a cup of tea, how about that?'

She nods, as if I'm her captor and she can do nothing but

appease me. I retreat, watching her all the way.

'Litha,' she calls suddenly. 'Remember, I like it with lemon?'

I pause, one hand on the kitchen door.

'No milk.' Her voice is stronger now. 'And not too hot, a splash of cold water.'

I am slammed back into my youth, the words familiar as a mantra. 'Not too hot, a splash of cold water.' She said it every time, as if I was congenitally incapable of getting it right.

'Yes, Mum,' I say, and my heart ticks louder than the clock as I enter the kitchen.

The windows are all closed, and the smell is worse in here. I hold a hand over my mouth and wonder if something has crawled under a cupboard and died, or gone off in the fridge. Surely Carla should have found the source and dealt with it? Wasn't that her job?

Sun beats through the glass and onto the Belfast sink and the breakfast dishes on the draining board. These, at least, are clean. I read the instructions on the fridge. Carla has been very clear: times, medications, techniques. Mum is at least capable of wiping her own arse. The real problem is apparent from the soot stain on the wall above the oven and the singed wallpaper, peeling from the wall.

I put on the kettle and start going through drawers, looking for keys, paperwork, receipts anything worth saving. She used to have an 'important documents' folder, in a drawer under the tea-towels.

I find it and flick through: Birth certificate, Marriage, National Insurance card, her parent's death certificate, a copy of the deed to the house, an old EHIC card, an out-of-date passport, my red book of vaccinations. My GCSE certificates.

I put the folder on the side, and, just as I am about to close the drawer, I see something else under the blue towel, something bright and cheerful: primary colours, smiling teenagers. Marketing material of some sort? A take-away menu? Rubbish. I might as well start a pile. I pull it out and stop, staring, my fingers going numb, as if I am holding a block of ice.

Straight to Heaven

My eyes flicker across the rest of the pamphlet. For the parents of gay and lesbian teenagers ... Jesus loves you and your child ... a choice that can be unmade ... therapy ... boot-camp style training ... mixed-sex social calendar ... six-week course ... some hard decisions.

I turn the pamphlet over. There is an address, a telephone number, and beneath that, scribbled in black pen, a date, a time and a goddamned booking reference. I realise that I've stumbled when my hip hits the marble edge of the work surface. I put out a hand to keep me upright. The date I should have been picked up to go to *Straight to Heaven*, is precisely one week after Dad left. That's *why* he must have left. Why Mum didn't go through with it, most likely.

The kettle clicks, shocking me. Steam has filled the corner above it and heated the air further. Moving automatically, I make her tea, my hands trembling.

I knew she hated what I was, but it had mainly been quiet little comments, poisonous barbs that twisted under the skin.

'Why not wear that pretty dress, Litha?'

'He looks like a nice boy, don't you think, Litha?'

'Why do you have to make so much of this, Litha? People don't need to know.'

I'd felt like a plant endlessly pruned away from the light. She'd been stifling. But really, she'd hated me, and *this much*?

Why hadn't Dad taken me with him? Protected me?

I turn the pamphlet over again. *Straight to Heaven*.

Her medication is on the side, carefully measured doses. I look at the tea.

Mum is sitting on her chair, staring at my photograph on the mantel. When I walk back into the living room, she starts. 'I thought I'd dreamed you,' she says, frowning. 'Litha.'

Her voice is steadier, and her eyes clearer. She seems sad.

'You remember me now?' There is a dangerous edge to my voice. I put the tea on the side table next to her. 'Just how you like it,' I say. She doesn't pick up the cup.

I take the pamphlet from my pocket and hold it in front of her. 'Do you remember *this*?'

She turns her face away and I fight to stop myself from catching her chin, forcing her to look.

'Do you know what they used to do to kids at those camps, twenty years ago? What they'd have done to me, trying to make me into someone I'm not, someone I could never be?' She stands, suddenly, panic in her eyes and I grab her arm. 'You're going to listen to me, you poisonous bitch.'

I shake her but she squirms free, knocking the tea onto the carpet. It soaks in, dampening the soles of my boots.

I think she's going to go for the front door again, but this time she scuttles towards the sideboard, muttering under her breath, making placating gestures, as if I'm the one who has already hit her.

She yanks at one drawer and then another, throwing out papers, tablecloths and old pictures. She soon stands in the middle of piles of detritus, a dumpster diver picking at the backs of drawers with her fingernails, looking for whatever she thinks is in there. I watch for a long minute, listening to the clock ticking, as sweat dampens the underwire in my bra and sticks my hair to the back of my neck. I'm angrier than I've ever been. Angrier than the day I realised Dad wasn't coming back and wasn't going to answer my messages. Angrier than the day I strode out, a single rucksack over my shoulder, and never looked back. I screw up the pamphlet in one fist, letting the edges of the paper cut into my fingers.

What am I expecting from her? An apology? It would be meaningless. My heart pounds hatred through my veins and at the same time, the smell reaches into the back of my throat, sickening me. I thought I might be getting used to it by now, but it is like one of those air fresheners that changes scent every so often, so you can't push it away.

Finally, Mum finds what she is searching for. She

straightens, holding out an old phone. It's unfamiliar; not Dad's, he had a Blackberry. It could be hers', perhaps she replaced the Nokia after I left.

I don't move. She steps closer. 'See,' she says. 'See!'

I grit my teeth. 'Why would I want an old phone? Jesus.'

She keeps thrusting it at me, in my face. I knock her hand to one side and the phone bounces on the carpet. She shrieks and goes after it on her knees; it's that important.

I clench my fist around the pamphlet and the need to punish her races through my veins like a drug.

Why am I waiting for tomorrow? I'm going to take everything important to her and burn it as she watches.

Then I think of Lyric. She'd be ashamed of me. I start to unclench my fist. This is ancient history. This is not who I am any longer. I'm better than this.

Mum turns around and peers at me. Her eyes grow wide. 'Litha, my *God*, what are you wearing? You want everyone to know? You look like a butch. Go and put on a skirt, right now!'

'Seriously, Mum?' I snatch the phone from her and shove it in my pocket. 'Fuck you!'

I dash to the mantel and snatch the photo in its wooden frame. It'll burn, just like everything else, it'll burn.

I race around the room, as Mum wails and chases after me. Anything she tries to protect; I gather in my arms and carry to the garden. I toss it all in a pile on the overgrown lawn, then go back for more. Mum is picking things up and bringing them back in, but I'm faster than she is, and the pile grows. Eventually she stands, her arms around the picture she has saved, that first one, watching me.

I go into the bedroom and take her bedding, her clothes, the pictures of her parents and grandparents in their gilt frames. I head into the bathroom; I'm even burning her toothbrush. Grandmother's coat stand. The fucking clock. That isn't easy to drag into the garden, but I manage. It's not so hard when you don't care about damage. It dongs and clangs and finally I smack it into the doorframe, where there is a crunch, and it stops ticking as if time itself has been suspended. I dump it on the pile.

Then I move into the kitchen, panting and opening drawers, I can't burn the dishes, but there's a tea towel she used to love, printed with a drawing I'd done aged six. That's going if I can find it. Maybe it's long gone to rags. I open another drawer to find a collection of junk and old cables.

The phone is pressing against my thigh, too big for my jean pocket. I pull it out. *There's a matching charger.*

I could throw it away. or dump it on the bonfire I'm building. But a part of me is curious. Whose phone is this? Why did I need to see it? What was so important that she remembered it, when she has lost so much else? I plug it into its charger. I'd like to know the value of what I'm going to destroy. Is it another picture, a text from Dad, a precious memory, a message from a lover, perhaps?

After a minute, the charging light flashes and I turn away, to find Mum standing in the doorway, sweat beading on her forehead and tears on her cheeks. She's still holding the picture of me, as if it's the most important thing in the world.

The lie of her holding it close, renders me breathless with rage.

It's time to find a match. I can't light a bonfire without one. There are none in the kitchen; she's almost burned the place down more than once. Carla would have got rid of everything capable of starting a fire, and I'm not about to start rubbing two sticks together. I pinch my nose; the stench is making it hard to think.

The cellar door catches my eye. There were candles among the Christmas decorations; Dad would light them with long, waxed matches from a box he picked up in a bar in Salzburg.

I go to the door. It's locked, but I remember a bunch of keys clattering onto the floor. I search among the scattering of things that won't burn. I've been a tornado. I find the keyring under the wok.

'Please,' Mum is muttering. 'Stop. Please. No. Stop.'

She's hurting now, and that stokes the blaze in my chest. How many times did I plead for her to listen to *me*. To see *me*. I unlock the cellar door, slam on the light, and start down the stairs.

The heat and the stench hit me like I've run into a wall. I gag and cover my mouth. Whatever it is, it's in here. Dead in a corner, probably. I force myself to keep moving, pushing my feet down one tread and then another as if I'm pushing through a physical barrier.

The Christmas decorations are in boxes behind the freezer. I'm going to have to grab them and take them upstairs to find the matches. In fact, they can go on the bonfire too: the ornaments I made as a kid; Grandmother's glass beads; the antique angel, blonde and pretty and probably straight as hell, it can all burn.

I reach the freezer. Here, I can barely breathe. I take shallow breaths, trying to inhale the scent of my own skin when I do, but all I can smell is rot, as if it's me decaying more with every moment I spend here.

The light on the freezer is off, and there is no hum. That's where the smell is coming from: all Mum's old meals, steaks and stews, defrosting in the dark. I wonder if it was the heat that has tripped the old machinery. Maybe it's only happened in the last two or three days, and that's why Carla hasn't dealt with it.

I stand over the freezer, hesitant to take my hand from my nose to pick up the boxes. Should I empty it and remove the source of the smell? The house won't sell, stinking like this. Like rot and sickness and something dead. A short and horrible job, but worth doing?

'Fuck,' I whisper and then I open the lid.

When I see Dad's body, defrosting on top of the Findus Crispy Pancakes, there is a part of me that isn't at all surprised.

I call the police and, in a voice deceptively calm, I ask the dispatcher to send someone over. They say it'll be half an hour, or thereabouts. It's a busy time of year. Anyway, it's not an emergency. He isn't getting any deader.

As I put the phone back in my pocket, my chest is tight, my limbs trembling. I'd always thought Dad was out there somewhere, in a two-bed terrace with a neat little garden, perhaps with an allotment to grow his beans, working for himself, doing a Sainsburys shop at the weekend. I'd pictured him looking for me on social media, keeping up with all the curated details of my life, which I put online mainly so he could see them. So much wasted bragging.

But … some part of me mourned him years ago. Some part of me knew that if my dad could have spoken to me, at some point over the years, then he would have. When I got my first real job, when I got engaged, he'd have called, if he could. I stifle a sob.

Why did she do it? Was he trying to stop her sending me to that camp? Was he going to leave her and take me with him? Did she plan this, or was it a spur of the moment thing? I couldn't look at his body, couldn't bear to try and see if there were injuries. His fingers curl damply over the fish-fingers.

'Oh, Dad,' I whisper.

Somehow, I manage to pick up the nearest box of Christmas decorations and carry it upstairs. I have half an hour to set that bonfire and watch Mum scream. Watch her pay, for everything.

With every step upstairs I feel freer. The guilt for what I was doing lifts from my shoulders. I shake my hair back from my face and drop the box on the kitchen floor. Like a child, Mum is watching me through her fingers. Does she remember what is down there, why she didn't want me to find those keys, open that door? She has to, doesn't she?

I dig through the box, locating the candles, the matches. As I stand, the old phone beeps. It has switched on.

I don't care, not really, but I'm moving on automatic when I pick it up.

'What's in here that's so important?' I say as I flip open the screen.

The phone is so old that there's no lock screen, no smiling family picture. There is an unread message notification flashing on the screen though, and I click it. The phone is from the days when there were character limits to messages. I have to scroll down to see the whole message and those it joins to. A whole chain.

Dave. Your kid's fuckable, so I'm happy to do this if you can guarantee no comeback.

Leave your door unlocked on Friday and get Maggie out of the house. She can't know, obvs.

By the time I'm finished, your little dyke will love dick so much you'll have a different problem on your hands.

I'll send her straight to heaven my own way. Lol, right!

I read the messages once, twice, three times, four. Then I drop the phone, but the words are still going round in my vision as it bounces on the tile, screen cracking.

My dad. He was arranging for some mate of his down the pub to … to …

'Wear a skirt, Litha,' Mum whispers. 'Don't let anyone know.'

I stare at her.

'Don't let *him* know,' she mutters, looking at the photograph she is holding, rather than at me. 'Make him forget you ever told him. Tell him it was a phase. Wear a skirt, smile at the boys, isn't that a nice-looking boy, Litha?' She stares into the distance, and I exhale. The smell, since I opened the freezer, has intensified. It's like he's in here with us.

'Keep it to yourself,' she says. 'There's no need to make such a big deal of things. How about this nice dress?' She's picking at her nightgown with bird-like fingers. 'Have a whiskey, Dave,' she says. 'You deserve a nightcap, that's right.' She gazes unfocused at the open cellar door. Then she looks at me. Really looks at me, her eyes clear as if she is seeing me for the very first time. 'What could I have done otherwise, Litha?' she says in a stronger voice. 'What else could I have done?'

It takes both of us, wearing bright yellow marigolds and two of Mum's aprons, to move his body out of the freezer, into the garden and onto the bonfire. I pour a bottle of Jack over the corpse, then I light three matches and toss them onto his chest, one after the other.

The heat haze wavers above the fire, making everything unreal, it crackles as smoke blackens the heavens and the glass front of the clock snaps with a sound like a gunshot. The heat and the stench of burning, rotting meat forces us away from the blaze. I tug at Mum's hand, and she comes, clutching at me, as if she is never going to let me go.

Dry-eyed, we watch for hours, as the bastard burns to unrecognisable bones and sirens finally shatter the quiet.

I hold Mum's hand, finally understanding that she had always known who I was, always loved me, always protected me: from him. And later from what she had done. She had let me go, so that I could be myself, unfettered, so that I would never have to hide again.

About The Author

Bryony Pearce is a multi-award-winning novelist and short story writer. She has written a mixture of thrillers, paranormal adventures, science fiction and horror, for Mid-grade, Young Adult and Adult readers. Her most recent novels are based on Greek mythology: *Hannah Messenger and the Gods of Hockwold*, for readers aged 9-12, and *Aphrodite*, for young adults.

In addition to writing her own novels, Bryony teaches creative writing at City University (London) and works as a consultant and mentor in order to help aspiring authors achieve their dreams.

She lives in Gloucestershire and has two teenagers. Consequently, she spends a lot of time at the side of sports fields, listening to concerts and being creative in car-parks.

For more information about Bryony Pearce, please visit her website: www.bryonypearce.co.uk

Or follow her on X or Instagram @bryonypearce

ALL THE DOORWAYS OF DEATH

Preston Grassmann

The sky had a wounded look, a long bleeding gash stretched over the high mountains in the east, a red-orange light that spilled down the hillsides and the quiet brick lanes of the campus. The cool wind scattered leaves over well-cut lawns and broad ivy-league courtyards, carrying the sounds of distant doorways.

She quickened her pace as she passed the inverted 'T' of the old chapel, its central tower covered with a scaffold for renovations. Beneath it, she could see a stained-glass cross over a scene of resurrection, and a sign that read Lux et Veritas – *Light and Truth*. A group of college boys were sitting on the steps leading to its entrance, talking about women and their frat-night party plans. She stifled a sudden urge to laugh – give them a few years to learn about the verities of Life and Death.

She reached into her pocket and pulled out the bronze sobriety chip. She flipped into an open palm. TO THINE OWN SELF BE TRUE. The words surrounded a pyramid and a single 'I,' representing one-year of sobriety.

It had been a year since the incident, and she couldn't help but see that single line as the 'I' of an indeterminate self, an opened doorway leading to different versions of her life. Who was she, after all? Drugs and alcohol had never been able to answer that question.

She entered the hall and tried to focus on her breath, the

ponderous echo of her steps, the quickening pace of her heart. She heard voices from the rooms ahead, muted conversations, a professor's lecture punctuated by chalkboard scribbles. These were all quotidian elements in a world she no longer knew, containing a self that wasn't hers anymore.

She still had the chip in her hand, and she clung to it now, as if it was the coinage for a ferryman bound for a Stygian shore. She only hoped he would accept such a modest fee when the time came.

The dead were so much closer now, and they whispered from the shadowed spaces of the hall, guiding her through the doubts and the hesitation. *It won't be long now. You'll find yourself when the time comes. We'll help you through it.*

The PTSD Workshop was scribbled on a sheet and taped to the door. An odd place for this, she thought, with its antiseptic floors and white walls, a few half-familiar equations left behind on a chalkboard in the corner. Inside, the desks were islands, heads staring down at pages in silence as if in prayer. As she entered the workshop room, a few of them looked up, but most of them were still gazing at the internal spaces of their traumas.

Her own face was covered in a mask, the scars on her neck concealed with a scarf. She felt exposed, like a creature pieced together out of ill-fitting parts. But she pushed forward and found a vacant chair close to the front of the classroom.

The doors were opening wider, and she felt their presence in the room, rising over the sound of sliding chairs, the unzipping of bags, the murmur of voices.

She took a deep breath and looked around her. It hadn't been that long ago that she sat in a very similar room, but now it felt like something foreign and unfamiliar, as if it belonged to another person's life.

Some part of her felt the sudden urge to leave, to go out and find the nearest bar, to escape from this place and never look back.

If you fail us, you fail yourself, she heard them whisper.

'Is this your first time here?' a woman said next to her. There were scars on her cheek, not unlike her own, and her calloused hands were folded on her desk.

'It is,' she said. The space between them felt like a chasm.

The woman leaned over to shake her hand. 'I'm Nicky.'

'Carla,' she said, wishing that was true. Perhaps it would be when she was done.

'This is my third time here. They say it's always harder at the beginning, but it doesn't really get any easier. Are you planning to read something today?'

'That's the plan. It's taken me long enough to get it down.' She'd been avoiding it for as long as she could. But when she finally began to put words on the page, she started to find something of herself again, an 'I' among the gathered voices. It also gave her a chance to understand how deeply their shared traumas bound them together – the living and the dead.

Nicky offered a smile. 'I'm glad I'm not the only one. It took me a year before I could share it.'

She watched the last few members file in, nervous glances cast around the room as they searched for seats. Some sat in their chairs with a ponderous unease, while others seemed almost eager to start. As the hour struck, most of the seats were unfilled, spaced between them like defensive walls, barriers against their own traumas. Next to her, Nicky sat with a rigid posture, alternating between her phone and the workshop manuscript she'd placed on her desk. It was clear she wanted to be anywhere but here.

A silence hung over the room, like an indrawn breath held, like a respite in between storms. And then she could feel it expelled all at once as the door opened and the murderer made his way into the room. She could feel their anger surging, their words jostling for purchase with every step he took.

Here was the source of so much trauma, the centre-point of all the pain that she and so many others had endured for so long. And here he was, leading a workshop on PTSD.

When she looked up at him, she felt a flood of heat on her neck, the scar pulsing beneath her scarf. She felt the one-year mark of her coin again, the 'I' bleeding outward.

The voices clamoured around her, like a river in flood.

She floated in that river too, joining their rage.

'Welcome everyone,' he said, turning his gaze through the room.

It wouldn't take long for him to recognize her, she thought. Would he notice her green eyes first, the distinct sound of her voice?

He placed a bag on the table and took off his coat. Without looking, she could see his smile broadening, a knife edge arcing downward. 'I'm Dr Lanius, for those of you who are new to our group. Many of you have prepared an introduction. I'd like to have you read them today, if you can.'

He didn't seem to recognize her as he pushed forward with his introductions. She was suddenly aware of the silence around her, as if the dead had stopped to listen to him speak. She held her breath, knowing this was just the calm moment before the sky broke and left its flood.

'I know it can be hard,' Dr Lanius said. 'But no one's here to judge you. Externalizing is a large part of dealing with trauma.'

She took the manuscript out of her bag and placed it on the desk. This was only a small part of that 'externalized' pain, but it was important because it was hers. This was her way back to herself, as it was for all the others she'd lived with over the last year. Their collective pain needed to be spoken through her. Knowing that gave her a share of confidence she wouldn't have had if she'd been alone.

When the readings began, Dr Lanius leaned back in his chair and gazed at a fixed point in the room. But she saw the change in his face as they spoke about their traumas, the way he'd lean forward and narrow his eyes, as if placing them in some internal catalogue of atrocities.

When it was her turn, he focused on her with a renewed intensity.

'Are you ready to share something with us?' he asked.

'I am,' she said.

The 'I' became a doorway, a slash against the sky, a pillar that gave her strength as she prepared to read. She could feel the stoked fires of rage, the river in flood. Aware that he was still watching her, she looked back at him, a rock in the surging rivers of her own memory, and felt the dead make their way forward. Their whispers became screams, breaking around her to flood over him with their currents, and from them came their own tales of atrocity. It wasn't long before Dr Lanius faltered, his expression breaking in the strain of a new awareness. He realized he was in waters he couldn't tread.

'Have you … been here before?' he asked, struggling to find the shoreline.

'No,' she said, simply, turning to the first page of the manuscript. She continued staring at him as his breath quickened in panic, as he gripped the pen more tightly and clutched at his desk. His hands flailed as if searching for something to hold onto. There were no lifeboats on this river, no escape from the currents of this dreaded oath.

'I feel like we've met before,' he said in one breath.

'I don't think so,' she said calmly. Whoever she had been, that wasn't who she was now.

'We should let her read,' Nicky said next to her, anchoring her back to the moment.

She turned to look at Nicky and saw a part of herself there, a part she'd lost and had to find again.

Taking a deep breath, she began to read.

Beneath an interstate, I slip between states, and emerge into a new awareness. There is only pain at first. Each passing car above me is the downward arc of a knife, a blade cutting through the world. I blink through it, an infant trying to view the space around me for the first time, aware of my own dependencies, my inability to breathe. I feel the panic all at once, the sudden need for someone to hold me up, to protect me. I see a group of vagrants huddled over a trash-bin fire, like blind witches over a cauldron, empty eye-sockets and toothless mouths. Are they sharing a single eye? I call out to them from my place in the half-dark ruins, but my voice falters.

That's when the voices come. She's with us, *someone says from somewhere high above me.*

And she can hear us, another says in my ear.

The pain surges as I turn to face them, but no one's there …

nothing but the junkyard ruins of the city, all its rejected and left behind. My neck burns, and I feel something warm spilling down my arms, bloodied wounds reopening as I move. A deep maroon drips between my fingers, as if the sky has bled out over me, as if the womb of my rebirth has left me here alone, motherless. The memories jostle through the pain, until I fix on the scene, remembering how it began, the car that dropped me here.

And yet, I'm not alone. We're here to help you. Get up, *one of them says.*

Another whisper from somewhere above me: Don't give him the satisfaction of your death.

And then I see the doorways, slashes of dusk-coloured light, like wounds against the shadows. I remember the knife held against my throat, eyes like grey green shards, as cold and sharp as the blade. I remember the deep slashes against my face, the cut across my neck that should've killed me, how much I bled before I was thrown out here, left alone to die in this interstate junkyard. They show me their bodies through the doorways, a gallery of atrocities framed against the horizon. A body in an alleyway, a courtyard, on a desert trail, all bled out in the same way. The anger surges and lifts me back into myself.

She stopped reading and noticed Dr Lanius staring around the room, a mouse in the cage of a hungry cobra. His face was drained of colour, his jaw was tensing.

It wasn't long before others began to take notice. They watched him glance at the door, at the ceiling, through the windows, as if he was trying to find something that wasn't there.

But Carla knew that it was.

She turned back to the manuscript and continued:

Death is full of doorways, but none of them are open to me now. It's only life and the living that offer hope for justice, that will lead me away from the pain.

I ask them who they are and what they want, speaking through cracked lips, with a voice that comes in faltering whispers, but I already know.

We are the ones who didn't live.

Beneath this Interstate, I slip between states. The sirens come, and the ambulance takes me away. The police come and ask their questions. They offer their promises of justice, their sympathies, their assurances. As time goes on, they talk about leads and new investigations, about progress, how hard the force is working to find the man who did this to me. But nothing is found, and it isn't long before those doorways close; before justice falters and life falls apart. Friends and family are frightened by this new version of me, this rebirth with its parentage of unfamiliar voices, with this new selfhood searching for a new 'I'. But the voices never leave me, and I can't tune them out and forget what happened anymore. I can't free myself of what they've revealed and so I give in to their purpose and the chance they've given me. I give in to their pleas and queries, and when they offer clues, I let them guide me. I let them take me through the evidence of their own deaths and provide details the police could never have found, tying all the clues of his identity together among the false names and professions. A lawyer, a professor, a war correspondent, all fragments of a life constructed for these murders.

The dead lead me to the sites of their own deaths. In the alleyway, the courtyard, the desert trail, I see each scene as it happened, experience the pain of all his victims. I hear their stories, so many lives cut short, until I find the last clue I need to piece it together. Some of doorways have never closed…

'I'm … sorry,' Dr Lanius said, his words choked loose from a stoppered throat. His hands were shaking as he began to put his paperwork back in his bag. 'Something's … wrong,' he said. She could hear the quiver in his voice: 'I'm … not … feeling well … so we'll have to end a bit early.'

I'm afraid things won't get any better. She reached into her coat pocket, opposite the coin, and pulled out her blade - a doorway, a slash against the sky, a pillar of strength.

'You're not going anywhere, Dr Lanius.'

She held the blade in front of him, a proclaimed 'I' finally asserting a selfhood. There were cries in the room, pleas and panicked voices calling for her to put the knife down, but his next words silenced them.

'I didn't have a choice,' he said. 'You don't understand. It's like there's a part of me that isn't me. … I never meant to hurt them.'

'But you did,' she said, moving closer. 'You've caused more pain than you'll ever know.'

'You don't know the kind of suffering I've been through' ...'

She looked around the circle, watching expressions run through a convoluted maze, horrified at Dr Lanius's confession.

'We've all suffered. Nothing can ever excuse its cause,' she said.

'Please,' he said, pushing himself up from his chair. He held one hand out in a plea to hold her back.

'We all have choices,' she said, remembering her own choice on the day she almost died, and the oath she promised to carry out.

As Dr Lanius reached for the door, he slipped and struck his head on its handle. 'How ...' he exclaimed, putting his hand up to the fresh wound on his forehead. He tried to stand up, but he was pinned to the ground. The dead, she knew, had found a way into the world through her words and they were here, holding him down. 'Who are you ...?'

'I'm everyone you've ever hurt,' she said.

The others in the room had been through enough to understand. Words alone would never be enough to end the kind of trauma she had to face. They also knew that something beyond their understanding was in the room with them, a presence they weren't prepared to comprehend. In acknowledgement of both, they began to file out of the room. Nicky, the last to leave, put her hand on her shoulder and said: 'Do what you have to.'

When they were gone, she stood over Dr Lanius, a rock rising from the surging river.

'I don't know who you think I am,' he said, 'but this won't solve anything.'

'You're wrong about that,' she said, kicking him away from the doorway. She took off her scarf and her mask, revealing her old wounds, the crosshatch of her scars. She pointed her knife at him.

He turned around to face her.

'How did you ...?'

'I had some help,' she said.

She thought of the interstate again; the day she emerged

among the ruins of herself. The dead had raised her from that infancy, had given her a purpose. But now she was ready to be on her own, to live beyond the wreckage and find out who she really was.

As the blade hung there in front of him, the dead spoke, their voices cutting through the room.

'This is for all of us,' they said, and watching the blade take its arc, she saw the 'I' that she would soon become.

When she was finished, she placed her one-year coin over the single, closed eye of Dr Lanius, and read the words one last time - TO THINE OWN SELF BE TRUE.

ABOUT THE AUTHOR

Preston Grassmann is a Shirley Jackson Award finalist. He is a regular contributor to *Nature* Magazine, and has published work in *Interzone*, *Strange Horizons*, *Apex*, *Shoreline of Infinity*, and many others. His recent books include the BSFA nominated *Multiverses: An Anthology of Alternate Realities* and the Bram Stoker Award and BSFA longlisted *The Mad Butterfly's Ball* (co-edited with Chris Kelso). His forthcoming fiction includes *War in the Linear Heavens* (PS Publishing), a collaboration with Paul Di Filippo, and 'The Translator', due to be published in *Weird Tales*. He currently lives in Japan, where he is working on a series of mosaic stories with Dempow Torishima.

KILLER QUEEN

Steven Smith

When I was a very young man my father asked me, 'Would it surprise you to know that so many people wear a mask? Never forget to look behind the face they are showing you.'

These were wise words spoken right before his untimely death.

Why am I telling you this?

Think: That sweet old lady in the green overly-worn coat is pushing her basket along the road. So often I have seen you offer to help her, her soulful dewy eyes so full of kindness look up at you with gratitude. Her hand trembles as she lifts it to wave 'thank-you'. She looks fragile. Innocent. Trust me, you would kick her basket away and spit on her if you knew what I know. She's wearing a mask, like so many people you may know. Those same frail hands have committed atrocities you couldn't even imagine. Some years ago, she found God. Then she took a job in an orphanage. I leave the rest to your imagination.

We so often see what we want to see; it makes life's journey so much easier.

Now, it is important for your hands to stop shaking. Take some deep breaths and try to become centred, a little calmer. You can do this. Listen to my voice, and sit down at the desk. Open your lap-top – please no dramatics or attempts to run. Just do what I say, and it might just be all ok.

There now see! Your breathing is becoming more consistent. Look at the screen, click on the blue file marked KHD. Please do not get hysterical. Yes, it is your daughter. She is all fine for now and you can keep her that way. No tears. I can see you are frightened and struggling to catch your breath. Close the file now; do it or you'll leave me no choice but to hurt her and really, once you get to know me, you will realise it is not my usual style.

It will be several hours before the injection wears off and you can talk properly so stop trying before you damage your vocal cords.

Listen, I will tell you, my story. This bit should be easy, after all you have written about me before in not such glowing colours in that vile column you pen for the tabloids. Here is your chance to get the real story and the 'exclusive' you people live for. Let's begin, shall we?

Don't worry, I'll turn on the recorder since you are struggling to move.

If 'The Emperor's New Clothes' was written today, the boy that shouts out, 'He is naked!' would probably be cancelled or banned for life from social media. This is an era where people like me flourish; we walk among you letting you see what we want you to see. Spin is everything and the truth isn't that important.

I have to tell you it is quite fascinating taking someone's life from them. Just as they are about to take their very last breath and their body goes limp, I feel a rush of power as they give up hope. I choose to release them from Death's arms, and they stare with surprise into my blue eyes. It is beautiful to see the relief flood over them, I pity them. Almost. There is an indescribable look on their face as they register you have shown this mercy. I delight in their mistake; my whole body starts to shiver with excitement. Killing brings you such energy!

Of course, there are the ones that simply make too much fuss. All the pleading, screaming, and thrashing about. To be honest that is why you need to take time to plan a victim's demise. But the best laid plans of mice and men as they say… that is why you always need a knife. Do not stab in the chest, it takes time to die that way. The best way is a deep slice across the throat and that has the added advantage of cutting the vocal cords and stopping that awful howling that may attract attention. I particularly like it when they choke on their own blood and eventually drown.

One of the many things I loathe is how we rush to put people in boxes. That ignorant belief that all serial killers must have had a terrible childhood and tortured animals. Far from it, my love for creatures rather than man could not be greater. One of my victims had two small Pomeranians and it briefly occurred me to spare him because I thought he couldn't be ALL bad if he was a dog lover. But when he put on a Kylie Minogue album and said he was going to slip into something more comfortable, I knew it was my job to make sure it was in fact uncomfortable. He just had to go. Alerting the police to his demise, so the dogs were not left for long, nearly got me caught but I would never hurt a dog.

Killing is an obsession: once you taste it you just cannot get enough. It is a unique compulsion that has nothing to do with my upbringing, lifestyle or any other addictions. I don't overly drink, never smoke or do anything that is considered unhealthy. Who really needs drugs when the rush of death is so absorbing?

I know what you're thinking: it's morally wrong to take a life. And under normal circumstances, I wouldn't condone it. But many of the people whose lives I take are obnoxious. Really it is a favour to the world that I get rid of them.

Just a minute. I'm checking that your recorder is working. Once you have finished writing this, their names will go down in history depending on how much of my story I share. Just think of Jack the Ripper's victims such as Mary Ann Nichols, who would remember her otherwise? A common prostitute. Everyone's goal is to be remembered surely?

I know what you're trying to ask … where did it all start?

Being incredibly wealthy and educated opened the gates to the world of fame and showbiz which everyone naively inspires to live in. This world, however, stirred me to do something else. Pick them off. One by one. I'm talking about the awful ones of course … the untalented, the influencers, presenters who got jobs because of who they slept with. The lame hangers on – some partners of these so-called celebs – who revel in the money, the fame, the party lifestyle.

There are so many deserving candidates amongst them,

the choice of victims is immense. Just take last Friday when I attended a huge charity ball, where the lovies, the obscenely rich and their entourage were out in force: this is my preferred hunting ground. As an aside, it is preferable to attend without a plus one, who can cause you to leave loose ends or take your mind off your purpose, though on occasions for image's sake you need a date on your arm.

Of course, you must not strike each time, a pattern will start to raise suspicions.

There is a fanfare of greetings and kissing numerous people. Many 'meerkats' – people who talk to you but are looking over your shoulder to see if someone more important or useful to them, will appear.

'You look marvellous darling, have you lost weight?' the Kats will ask. On occasions I have replied, 'Yes, I have cancer', only to have them reply, 'Wonderful I must try it!'

Watching them walk off, I'd like to throw a bottle at their head.

But I digress, back to Friday night. It was time to take my seat and to be honest, I was ravenous that night for a kill rather than food. The man nicknamed the 'Rabbi' arrived and sat down across from me with his vacuous fiancée I thought of as Princess D, not because she had any of the class of royalty, but because he spoiled her and paraded her around like his own personal trophy. Princess D was never out of the toilets at these events snorting half of Peru up her nose. Getting more boring as the night went on, she snuggled up to the grossly overweight Rabbi like a Pomeranian on heat, squeaking the words, 'Baby needs another treat, make a call!'

She was generous in asking if anyone else needed some of the devil's dandruff of course, whilst skimming off the top financially of her 'seemly' kind act.

The Rabbi was a huge (pardon the pun) agent to the stars but like many in the business had a desire to be as rich and famous as those he represented. What was more unforgivable, he was also so vulgar, his language was appalling. He didn't know that I was aware he was struggling money-wise, and had been a naughty boy ripping off his clients and taking from Peter to pay Paul.

Princess D was expensive and so was her cocaine habit.

'Our new maid lives in and brings me tea in bed in the morning,' Princess D bragged almost as soon as I took my seat near them. I smiled, kissed her, and shook the Rabbi's hand who pulled me closer to him and said, 'Come on son I have a bit of business to chat about later.'

What was really going on in my mind was taking a chainsaw to the pair. Cutting his head off first and making her hold it screaming, 'BABY IS GOING TO GET A TREAT!' as I take the saw and cut her into many pieces …

But of course, I gushed about the maid, did not mention the gossip of bankruptcy, and continued to sip my champagne. Luckily my seat was not directly next to either, but one day they wouldn't hear my footsteps and my body would bathe in their blood. When the time was right.

The rest of the table consisted of a wealthy businessman who had been a boxer from Dubai called Muhmad. He was very handsome but despite his best efforts to look like class personified, his image was still that of an ex-boxer who had been polished. Please forgive me really, this is not to be a snob. It is just calling a spade and spade. As my dear old mother used to say, 'You can roll a turd in diamonds but sometime during the evening it will start to stink.'

My mother was a beautiful redhead. You really should think what you write in your column about redheads, it is just one of the things that has led me to choose you.

To continue though, he had brought his incredibly beautiful wife Magda, who spoke three languages, owned a gallery and oozed class and elegance. So often those that would not fit into high society try to marry into it, perhaps in hope that some rubs off on them or acts as camouflage.

Look at Onassis and Jackie Kennedy.

Magda was perfection. Her nails were French polished to just the right length, her hair beautifully set yet natural, her skin glowed. She wore a sheer Chanel gown which was gorgeous. It showed just the right amount of flesh to be seductive but was dripping in elegance, and even her make-up was subtle but stunning. Her greeting was warm, of course I stood to shake his hand and kiss her gently on the cheek. The Rabbi, lacking all class, remained seated whilst Princess D rushed over with a vulgar over the top 'hello' fuelled by cocaine. There is a saying, *Cocaine is not about you and all about me.* So true. There is a skill to greeting and neither the Rabbi nor Princess D had it.

The next to arrive was one of the performers for the charity event, Ella Dayley joined by her husband Frank Hallway, who was also predictably her new manager. They had flown in from Los Angles the day before as they are both big supporters of the cause. Ella had incredible presence, a voice like an angel, and wore her afro embracing all that is beautiful of her culture.

The rabbi mentioned something inappropriate about her last single flopping, adding he liked it – as if anyone cared what he thought about anything.

I wanted to put my dinner knife through his throat.

Instead, with dignity, I interjected, asking about their flight.

'It's an honour to meet you,' I said after a few words of sweet exchange.

She was, I believed, talent personified and would never receive my wrath or my blade but only my worship.

There was one seat left next to me. Looking down at the name card it said 'Sheba B'. How I loathe abbreviations of names.

Ella smiled over at me, 'That's my publicist, you will adore her.'

My eyes glared back at the name card and the fact that she was late. I thought to myself, *Oh, how wrong can you be?*

The starter was served. Being a vegetarian, these events can be tricky, but the spicy three cheese quesadilla was a pleasant surprise. There was a small speech about the plight of the distempered lion and the video followed. Everyone was deeply moved and some in tears, except for the Rabbi, and Princess D was absent having table hopped or gone to the bathroom to powder her nose again.

Passing a tissue over to Magda, she thanked me, but the lateness of Sheba B was starting to annoy me intensely, already hate was crawling out of my pores. Everyone agreed that we had to save the lions; Ella had indeed been to Africa to work with the charity. Turning to my right, I saw that Princess D was returning to the table, flanked by a large woman wearing some kind of pink blancmange outfit that looked like Barbie has vomited on her. As they got closer it was evident that she was American. She practically catapulted herself at me,

'Sheba B, darling,' she said. 'I do not do handshakes give me a hug.'

It was hard not to throw her off me as I reacted to this huge violation of personal space, the bile rising at the back of my throat. There were no apologies for being late, just a comment that she had changed three times and my mind boggled at just how horrific the other outfits must have been.

'Have I missed anything, darlings?' she squeaked, pushing her ample buttocks on the designer chair. Being a gentleman, it was my duty to offer to get her the missed starter. Surprise, this gave her the gateway to talk about my second least favourite subject – diets.

On Sheba's return home Dr Goldenthorn, Beverly Hills' premier plastic surgeon, would be performing a revolutionary treatment on her that would take her down three dress sizes in a month. This made me chuckle as the treatment I had planned in my head would take her down even quicker. As she waffled on, it turned out not to be a gastric band but a balloon that is lowered into the stomach and inflated. Ella assured Sheba that she did not need to lose weight as did Magda. My mouth was sealed as one wished Sheba's had been, but the sisterly union was quiet moving.

Ella politely asked to be excused as she needed to get ready to perform.

Sheba leaned in, 'Gosh I keep telling her to go more Beyonce and ditch the afro.'

My reply that I thought it was 'stunning' got no reaction as Sheba had taken a bread roll, hidden it on her lap and was sneaking bits of it. God, how I wish I had been on a different table.

Lady Tamara waved from across the room and made a gesture for me to call her; she was very nice and we were on the board of a children's charity together. Really if I did not despise table hopping so much, it would have been my queue to move and sit with her as there was a vacant seat, but it would have been a vulgar thing to do.

Biggles, one of the UK'S national treasures was suddenly making a beeline to chat to me.

After kissing 'hello', he introduced himself to Sheba B and waved at the Rabbi and Princess D. Biggles always dominated a room and once was so loud at a wedding he upstaged the couple's vows. He is never on my radar to take down as he unintentionally amuses me.

'I love you gay guys,' Sheba announced, telling how much she was adored in West Hollywood and had even been given the Drag Queen name, Lady Sheba Diamante.

Biggles threw me a look that said she was such a cliché.

'You guys always have such style, those cufflinks you are wearing, my God they are incredible.'

This could have been the moment of salvation for her, but upon explaining they were solid gold with emerald stones, bought for me at an auction at Christies in New York and they had belonged previously to Truman Capote who had worn them to the famous Black and White ball in the 70s, her response was, 'Who is Truman Capote honey?'

It was rumoured that they originally belonged to F Scott Fitzgerald who had found them at a treasure hunt at the estate that was the inspiration for *The Great Gatsby*. However, I could not bring myself to continue with the story. Biggles interrupted with a story about his time in LA and promised to come see her next time he was there.

It was a great relief when the main course was served, and Princess D took Sheba off to the powder room even though that meant the pair would return even more boring than they had been before. Biggles was still giving me a monologue on his lunch with Joanne and the upcoming trip to the South of France.

The vegetarian pot roast served as my main left a great deal to be desired. I was counting the minutes for Ella to perform, and it would be polite to leave. Having ascertained Sheba was staying in the hotel for the week she would just be checking out a little sooner than expected. All together it had been an appalling evening, making me itch to put a certain person out of their misery.

Having studied chemistry at Cambridge it really was of no use to me, well, until my hobby started. There are so many ways to take someone down or numb them for varying periods of time. A small box of chocolates injected with just the right amount of propofol and ketamine for instance, I could see Sheba B guzzling them down and within minutes of digesting them she would be fast asleep with me clutching a key to her room. The stage was set.

Over the years killing has become an art I pride myself in. The first was a little clumsy but ten out of ten for effort. My parents died just before my 16th birthday; nothing to do with me honestly. They were my rocks but they were killed in a plane crash just outside Lisbon, making me a very rich orphan with a need to grow up quickly. My favourite club in the lates 70s was the Sombrero in London's High Street in Kensington. It was the haunt of the likes of Bowie and many of the elite homosexual community – what they called the in-crowd. Even before that, my experience with men had taught me that they could be predatory and, in some cases, just would not take no for an answer. Coming out of the clubs' men's room my body had been pushed back, me struggling while a cloth covered hand engulfed my nose and mouth. It had been covered in the disco drug amyl nitrate, which slowed the brain down, in my case enough to be raped in the cubical toilets.

Back in the late 70's many young men were victims of the predators, who felt safe in their actions knowing their victims were underage, the police were less than sympathetic to homosexual youth, and many boys blamed themselves.

But I had seen his face, remembered his smell and

thereafter, it became my goal to seek revenge.

The gay club scene back then was sufficiently small, and queens love to gossip, so it did not take long to find out everything about him. His usual haunt was Earl's Court, the infamous Coleherne pub, which was the choice of gays who like to play at being macho; leather and rough sex ruled the waves.

Warhol spoke a lot of sense. People's fantasies are what give rise to these problems. If you didn't have fantasies, you wouldn't have problems because you'd just take whatever was there. But then you would not have romance …

They say youth is wasted on the young, but if you are wise beyond your years, it is an incredible weapon and men's fantasies can disarm them, they make mistakes that could take down an empire. Being a fresh face on the scene with just a few changes such as slipping into a studded leather jacket and tight blue jeans – he had no idea what hit him, nor did he recognise me. It took no time in the gay world, so often driven by fantasy to mask the pain of a world that rejected the love of the same sex, to find out my victim had a love of S&M and the art of bondage. Back then security cameras were limited, so armed with my rucksack it took no time at all to persuade him to take me home. He had the perfect house, detached with a blue door garage, I'll never forget. It led to a room just off to the side, which was like a dungeon with a swing and torture devices.

'Let's have a drink pal before we play,' I said, running my hand down the outline of his cock. He swallowed hard. I observed his every move, his eyes were intense, like a wolf about to eat a rabbit.

'It is sexier to get to know one another a little.'

I winked at him. Men with a hard on made me laugh. Even before University, the use of Flunitrazepam or Rohypnol had been no stranger to me.

He eagerly asked, 'You like the room kid?'

Staring at the bag he asked me what was in it, laughing was it my school uniform (he wished). He made his first and last mistake by leaving the room to take a slash. On his return, he couldn't wait to knock the beer back and get started.

'Please show me how the swing works, I'd like to be your boy ...' I teased.

He beckoned me to get in. 'No, show me.'

The fool was only too keen and as he did, dizziness hit him, and he asked me to help him up. Before I pretended to reach out to him, he was flat out. It gave me time to tie him in and gag him like a prize turkey after years of boy scouts' skills and some careful research on human bondage.

I was disappointed it had taken him so long to come round. I had removed his trousers and pants, his legs were lifted and opened just enough it slightly distracted from his eyes, that was my main objective to investigate.

Really, for my first time I should have been commended on my bondage success, as when he did wake no matter how he struggled and shook, the swing harness stayed in place, as did he.

'Remember me from the club?'

He struggled against his bonds, not really listening to me, whilst I removed a cannister from the rucksack, collected my empty beer bottle (no need to leave any evidence) and put it in my bag. I lit the end of the cannister, adjusting the flame so it was just right then, with some pride and a Machiavellian smile, told him he was about to be truly fucked.

My first real killing was clumsy without a doubt, having fantasised about it in my head so much. I hadn't considered that there was only so much pain a body could take, and the flame burning his anus caused such agony, he passed out several times. The smell was appalling and just as I thought it was going somewhere he died of a heart attack.

Clumsy yes, but it did teach me to research more and led me to study at Cambridge.

No-one suspected that a fresh-faced youth could be involved in such a heinous crime, so it was attributed to Colin Ireland, the infamous serial killer who hunted the Queer community and tortured his victims during that period. Though even then my debut performance could have been executed with more style.

In the US alone today, the FBI estimates there are

somewhere between 25 to 50 active serial killers walking on American soil. Triple worldwide with their masks firmly in place most might seem very normal but are just waiting to lower them and strike when the time is right.

That leads me back to why we are here my journalist friend. My carefully crafted mask has for once slipped. No, not because of your column, though clever you to see a connection between the murders and high society.

No, it happened that night with Sheba B.

Really Ella was superb and as always when it came to exit the evening, I slipped off not drawing attention to my departure. All those insincere comments of 'You must stay!', and 'Please let's get together', just make me sick.

The dancing had started and there was a clear path to the door for my get away. The beautiful actress Karen Pilipino had noticed me and really my urge to say hello was tapered by the fact her con artist husband was there, and I could not bear to hear about his latest self-published masterpiece.

Pushing open the door, the hallway was quiet and provided me with the opportunity to take the stairs a few floors down unnoticed and take the elevator the rest of the way to the hotel exit. This was a mistake as on the floor below was Sheba B and Ella's husband Frank Hallway hard at it, there were no cameras in the stairwells. Why she did not use her room, and why the man was poking a hamburger when he had filet mignon at home was beyond me. Either way my visit to her would be sooner rather than later as I hated broken trust.

They had the manners to stop what they were doing and of course my natural etiquette prohibited me from acknowledging either of them. Being from LA LA land she, of course, could not leave it alone. As Frank scarpered her footsteps came behind me,

'Excuse me Honey, do you know where you can smoke around here?'

Perfect. Of all the hotels in London this one did not have cameras on backstair exits. I could not have planned this better.

'Yes, do you mind if I join you? Let me show you the way.

You won't believe the view.' Sheba was slightly out of breath by time we hit the roof. There was some murmuring of 'hope you don't think I am awful' coming from behind me.

'It is not what it looks like,' she said.

It never is, I thought to myself.

When she saw the view, she was blown away.

'Come this way.' I led her around the corner to a narrower edge.

The wind was giving her trouble lighting her cigarette, so I suggested a better, less windy place for her to try, at the far edge. It was a perfect place to push her from, but my timing was slightly out, and she managed to grab my arm as she started to fall. Her grip slipped down my suit jacket to my wrist and the pain was considerable, despite the intense rush of adrenaline. The screaming, the terror in her eyes was simply magnificent but it took all my strength to shake her off my wrist and her final screams left me in ecstasy.

As she landed, I brushed myself off as though ridding my body of her awful perfume. My suit had no tears, no obvious dirt. A perfect result, or so I thought.

There was no time to bask in my success, I had to get a plan in place so the ecstasy was soon replaced by panic on how to cover my tracks. It was a must to return to the event and be seen so people did not think I had left or been gone for long. The dancing was in full force and Princess D was shaking it to the Rabbi, when I walked up to them and whispered in her ear 'How about a line for me?'

She was excited but of course wanted her palms crossed with gold.

Over the years I have indulged when I wanted to blend in, but it is not really my style. However, it meant that when the news broke of the tragic accident, me and Princess D would be in a cubical snorting together.

I rolled up my jacket sleeves and, taking up a straw to inhale, I noticed the gold cufflink from my right sleeve was missing. I stopped in my tracks: a vision of Sheba grabbing frantically at my arm flashed before me.

That was the downside of seizing opportunities rather than following the plan.

I had been careless, had the years taught me nothing?

Planning and following the rules were crucial. My need to feed this addiction went hand in hand with my need to remove offensive people from the face of the Earth. That night there was not a part of me that could control what was needed so badly.

Snorting a line, I turned to Princess D but something in my eyes must have frightened her, my mask was slipping.

'What's wrong?' she asked, suddenly gathering her stash, and turning to leave instead of waiting to see if the coast was clear. She made a beeline out of the cubical.

Do you know something, she was so right. The revelation of losing that cufflink had knocked me off kilter and my hands could have easily choked her; my appetite was insatiable and becoming less controlled.

I left the cubicle and the news must have broken as there was so much chaos outside.

Lying awake that night I wondered, was she clutching my cufflink or was it nearby or had it lodged onto part of the hotel building, or the pavement nearby? Either way, it was not good and perhaps only a matter of time until it was found and awkward questions are asked. My days may indeed be numbered.

Then there is your little column.

That is enough for now, do with it what you like.

Your daughter will never know I hacked into her laptop and was watching her every move. She will be safe, and when the drugs wear off, so will you.

My plans are uncertain, but let's be clear … watch yourself as the next time you wake and feel my presence the outcome may be different.

I commend you for seeing that I was out there, but your names to describe me just don't resonate: *The Café Society Murderer*, *Posh Slasher*, *Upper Class Hacker*, are somewhat pedestrian.

No, my dear, just call me 'The Killer Queen'.

About the Author

Steven Smith, born in Coatbridge, Scotland, grew up in Whitley Bay before spending brief periods in London and Brighton, where his talent for hairdressing began to gain recognition. He later spent eight years in Beverly Hills before returning to London in the late 1990s, where he became a renowned stylist in Knightsbridge.

Steven has worked with numerous celebrities, including Denise Welch, David Hasselhoff, and members of the *Baywatch* cast. He also wrote a beauty column for *The Sun* and appeared on *Lorraine*, where he famously transformed Lorraine Kelly into Elizabeth Taylor.

Now a freelance writer, Steven has authored two books: *Powder Boy*, which explores the darker side of showbiz, and *It Shouldn't Happen to a Hairdresser*, a blend of humour and heartbreak. He is currently working on his third book, *The Hacking*.

Steven also writes a monthly column titled *Tales of a Single Middle-Aged Gay Man*, which explores both the lighter and more serious aspects of gay life, featured in *2shades magazine*. He is a proud patron of Anna Kennedy Online, an organisation dedicated to supporting and raising awareness for the autism community.

https://2shadesmagazine.com
https://www.youtube.com/channel/UC_xrPX1TwpkuSZcnDGMOhAQ
https://x.com/asksteve2c
https://www.comptonmanagement.com/?p=739

BLOWJOBS AND THE DEFINITION OF NOIR

Maxim Jakubowski

It was Paris and we were young.

We'd meet in an old bar by the Place Saint Michel, owned by a widow from the Auvergne, who had adopted our motley Left Bank gang and allowed us to spend hours on end sipping on coffees and the occasional beer and probably deterring better-paying customers from venturing into the joint. She didn't seem to mind. Maybe she thought of us as her adopted family. I found out a few years later, that shortly after we had all departed Paris for our real lives, she had promptly sold the bar to return to her *Terroir* and it had become yet another of the kebab joints that now blight the Latin Quarter.

We never talked much about the things we were studying or learning. No, we conversed about movies, books and women. Or, more specifically, girls. Those we had known, those we had not known in the Biblical sense, those we yearned for, those we had lost.

Two or three times a week we would meet up near the rue d'Ulm and go and see films at the cinématheque. They were the cheapest seats in Paris and, on most evenings, we had no clue as to what we were about to watch. Often, it would be an obscure Mongolian film with Swahili subtitles or worse, but Henri Langlois or one of his minions (many of which would go on to become famous critics, writers or directors) would formally introduce the film and swear it was an undiscovered masterpiece and this was the only remaining print left in the world, one of the thousands of rarities the mad curator had squirrelled away in his vaults, many such illegally, during his notorious career; when we were luckier it was a series of Buster Keaton shorts. To this day, I still kneel at the altar of Keaton's genius. Charlie Chaplin can't compete!

Not all of us in fact were even students. Max was working for a British bank in Paris, Michel supplemented his income from painting and illustrations by working in the music archives of French radio, the ORTF, Marcel was an accountant for a multinational. They were the core of the group. There was also Roland, Philippe, Pascal and his brother. Others drifted in and out on the whim of exams, budgets and a lack of steady relationships. But we had somehow congregated together through a set of common acquaintances and accidental friendships and now formed a distinct group of drinkers, complainants, and dilettantes. There were others on the periphery of our group, who would join us from time to time, then disappear, including a fat pretentious twat who shadowed us like a lapdog, until we managed to insult him away, and to our great surprise actually became famous manning the barricades in May 1968 and even got himself elected as a French MP. He was probably still a twat, but he became a famous twat!

It was then that Maryanne Armshaw crossed our paths.

Max had been walking down the Boulevard Saint Germain on his own, when he had noticed her strolling in the opposite direction with a girlfriend. He'd heard them speaking English together, though with an American accent and had turned round and begun following them on a whim. They led him a merry dance, but he only had eyes for her legs. She made him think of Julie Christie in *Billy Liar*, a film that had made an indelible impression on him, or rather the actress had. Eventually the two girls, after walking miles in circles, from Les Deux Magots down Boulevard Montparnasse, Avenue Raspail and then back north toward the Luxembourg Gardens, decided they needed a rest and sat themselves down at a trendy and expensive café on the corner of St Michel and St Germain. Certainly, one he could not afford. But he was smitten. He found a table close to theirs and ordered an espresso; the cheapest choice. From overhearing their conversation, he found out they had only arrived in Paris from somewhere in the Midwest a few days previously, but the blonde one, who turned out to be Maryanne, was staying on for several months on some course while her companion was only in Paris for another week. Eventually, he got the courage to speak to them, using the fact that he was English ('wow, we're all strangers in a strange land' was his feeble opening gambit; he'd been reading the Heinlein novel just a few weeks ago) as a perfect pretext and offered himself as a free guide to Paris for the rest of their joint stay in the city. The red-haired American girl politely declined, arguing she had already made plans, but the blonde agreed. She told him her name was Maryanne and she was from Cedar Rapids.

Maryanne was a mixture of prudishness and sensation-seeker. She openly admitted she had not come to Paris to study properly, but wanted to live her life. Not that, coming from her native Midwest, she had even seen the Godard film. She was happy to be kissed, felt up in strategic places but couldn't stand the thought of someone, let alone a man, touching her breasts. They were slight; a bit like Jane Birkin's. Max courted her for weeks and never succeeded in getting much further than first base, introduced her to his friends and she became a regular hanger on, after which to everyone's surprise, a week later, Marcel confessed to the others that he had managed to bed her. Marcel was a sly one. No one even knew he had been seeing Maryanne behind their backs. He confirmed, with a wry smile that the young American blonde would allow him to do absolutely everything to her between the sheets, but shrieked to high heaven if his fingers, mouth or tongue ventured within an inch of her nipples. It was frustrating, he admitted, but beggars can't be choosers, and it was his first American girl after all and there were other pleasures to assuredly enjoy with her. She gave great blowjobs, he informed them, grinning.

The problem with Maryanne was that she knew nothing about books, movies, philosophy or politics and remained mostly silent and blank looking when they all met up to draw out their coffees in the bar, which made her something of an uninvolved hanger on. By then, her college friend had returned to America and she was staying in a small rented room by Ménilmontant, to which Max often escorted her back to late at night after all the others had dispersed. Marcel never stayed up late because of his day job and only saw Maryanne proper at the week-ends.

They had all been to see *Gun Crazy* at the cinématheque. Maryanne, who had never watched a black and white movie before had, unlike them all, not been impressed. Why was it a noir movie when it wasn't in colour; why not *Noir Et Blanc*? Why did the characters get up to such stupid things knowing it would do no good, and accepted their fate so easily. They all tried to painstakingly explain to her what the essence of noir was, but she refused to take them seriously.

'You're pretentious old farts,' she complained.

Max, on the other hand, pictured her at night while he was jerking off with her face and slight body to the forefront of his mind, like an image projected onto a silver screen, as the epitome of the femme fatale. American, blonde, slim, unattainable (to him). He was happy to forgive her intellectual failings which he blamed on her youth and sometimes dreamed they improbably became lovers and were fleeing along mythical American highways on some mad mission to get away with the loot, dodging crooked cops and malevolent villains and staying in sordid motel rooms to the loud sound of rock 'n roll music.

She had become the siren of his dreams of noir.

Eventually, Marcel tired of her. No doubt fed up with her bothersome and often noisy protests every time his hand strayed in the direction of her breasts when they were in bed. He was assuredly a tit man and the frustration got to him, even though all her other sexual parts were readily available.

Max was encouraged and began courting her again. He convinced himself he would become the first man to be allowed to kiss her nipples and make her writhe with pleasure. It would be his mission. After all, she had come to Paris to escape the clumsy embraces of American jocks and surely his carefully constructed air of sophistication would win the day.

He drifted away from the group and spent more time with Maryanne. Taking her to movies, reading to her from books he admired. Somehow he felt she was moving in his direction, step by step, fascinated by his knowledge of popular culture, his passions. He liked teaching her things.

They watched *Double Indemnity*, *Rififi*, *The Lady in the Lake*. He even took her to see his favourite film, Louis Malle's *Le Feu Follet*. A movie about the last 24 hours in the life of a man who would commit suicide and wanted to say goodbye to all the women he had known and loved. Max found it profound and romantic. Maryanne found it boring, but after they argued came back to his flat and went down on him for the first time. Oh yes, she was good! Was this the sort of thing girls learned best in American high schools? he asked her, spent, on cloud nine, his trousers still around his ankles. No English or French woman – not that there had been many he hadn't paid for – had been so skilful.

Odd then that she had such a phobia about her breasts!

But he would remember the first time she had taken him inside her mouth forever. A feeling, a warmth he would find unforgettable. He would live on that memory for years. It would return in his dreams, in his imagination whenever he least expected it. To the extent that thirty years later, adrift and between love affairs, the disturbing thought occurred to him of how it might have felt for Maryanne (and all the other women who eventually followed in her path) to take a penis between their lips. Was it pleasurable? erotic? unnatural? tactile? It became a subject of fascination and one day, when his mood balanced between loneliness and grief, he resolved to find out and looked up ads in the personal section of

Craigslist and met another man and agreed to suck him off. He didn't find it unpleasant, nor did it trigger him sexually though he would begin to do so on a fairly regular basis, but that's another story.

'Of course,' Maryanne replied, with a mischievous smile.

'We have special classes about it; it's on the curriculum ...' You couldn't say she didn't have a sense of irony. 'In America we take that part of a girl's education very seriously. A bit like all you Europeans study the essence of noir ...'

She was adamant Max and his friends took certain things much too seriously. Which they did.

He ground her down and she consented to sleep with him.

It lasted a couple of months during which time they lived in a world of their own, no longer seeing his friends – she had none in Paris – and gravitating between bed and movie theatres around the Rue des Ecoles, where a trio of arthouses screened the classics on a regular basis and afternoon tickets were half-price. She enjoyed musicals, Busby Berkeley, Fred Astaire and Ginger Rogers, Gene Kelly, Cyd Charisse, but still couldn't fathom his passion for film noir and its doom-laden stories.

A distant cousin of hers from Iowa was coming to Paris with a group of college friends and Maryanne had planned to spend time with them over the weekend. Max declined joining them as he wanted to see *Pierrot Le Fou* again and it was only playing at the Dragon on Sunday afternoon. It would be their first weekend apart in ages. He had a bad feeling about it.

They were on the phone. He was at work. She was supposedly in her room going through her study papers, not that she had done much in the way of studying since she had arrived in Paris.

'How did it go with your cousin?'

'It was OK.'

'Just OK?'

'Yes.'

'What did you do?'

'You know … the Eiffel Tower, Notre-Dame, a bateau-mouche on the river … Not the sort of things we do together.'

'Good …'

There was a lengthy silence on the line.

'So how was he, your cousin, his friends?'

'Hmm … He's OK, a bit of a jerk. But he came with Justin.'

'Who's Justin?'

'Someone I knew in high school.'

Max felt guilty that the very moment she said that he pictured her practicing her blowjobs on Justin, deducing the fact that this was how she had perfected her oral skills.

'Oh …'

Another silence.

'What is it?'

'Well … on Sunday night, Pete stayed in and I went out to have a couscous with Justin and …'

'And?'

'We slept together… '

'What?' It felt like a knife digging deep into his guts.

'And it was good, Max. He was my first boyfriend, you know … I like you, but it's not the same. We're so different. You're so … European, I'm simpler, you know.'

'I see …'

'It felt like … coming home … I even …' she was hesitant.

'What?'

'It felt just, how can I put it … right … when he touched my boobs …'

They agreed not to see each other that week, and meet up when her cousin and Justin has returned to Iowa.

By then, Maryanne had decided she no longer wanted to be in a relationship with him. Didn't think it was fair on either of them. She was sorry and all that. It's not you, it's me. We think differently. You're a nice guy. All the habitual clichés.

Max was gutted. His mind in a tizzy.

He knew Maryanne Armshaw wasn't special and that deep down they were not particularly suited for each other. Came from different worlds. But there was anger inside of him that rose to the surface. He rang her. Begged for one final meet. A chat, not even a mercy fuck. She reluctantly agreed.

On the day, an hour or so before Maryanne was expected at his flat, he carefully prepared the scene, tidying things up, looking at the place through her eyes.

He took a razor blade and meticulously cut into his wrist. The blood began to run. He'd left a towel on the floor by the couch to absorb it. He hadn't done his homework though, and cut the wrong way. He would carry that small white scar for the rest of his life. He'd prepared an A4 sheet of paper and pinned it to his chest.

On it he had written with a black felt pen 'This is essence of noir'.

Spite? Wit? Madness? He wasn't even sure himself.

When Maryanne punctually arrived, he was woozy and half-conscious.

She screamed when she saw him sprawled out on the couch, with his arms hanging over the side and the crimson stain on the towel below it.

She ran out onto the landing.

An ambulance came quickly and he was rushed to the nearest hospital. He was only kept there two days while the doctor explained how he had botched the job by cutting in the wrong direction. Next time, the disapproving medic said, you'll at least know how to do it properly.

He found out from her landlord that Maryanne returned to America within 48 hours.

Max lived on and began the next chapter in the book of his life, in which he would enjoy some blowjobs (as well as give them). He still enjoys film noir.

About the Author

Maxim Jakubowski is a British writer and editor, active in the fields of mystery thrillers, SF & fantasy and Erotica. He is a past winner of the Anthony, Karel, Red Herrings and David L Goodis/Noircon awards, and former chair of the Crime Writers' Association (and currently joint Vice Chair). He has written 23 novels, the most recent being *The Piper's Dance*, *Just A Girl With A Gun, The Exopotamia Manuscript* and *Manhattan Death Ballad*, and under a pen name authored several *Sunday Times* top 10 bestsellers. His latest short story collection is *Death Has A Thousand Faces* and recent anthologies amongst the over one hundred he has edited are *Black Is The Night, Reports From The Deep End* and *Birds, Strangers And Psychos*. He lives in London amongst his book, magazine, CD and DVD collections; his daughter says he is a hoarder, but he prefers to be seen as a collector.

http://www.maximjakubowski.co.uk

THAT

Caroline England

You know when your heart is broken, raw and bloody and you think it will never mend? When you've been dumped by the boyfriend you first glimpsed at the works party three years ago, and though weeks have passed, you still ache for his arms, his body, his smell? Because his are the only ones that will ever, ever matter? *That*.

When your confidence is at an all-time low; when you speak, you hear stupid, when you look in the mirror, you see ugly.

When you don't know what to do with your pecking, jabbing mind. When the radio's a no, no because there's bound to be a song you once smooched to; when you can't bear to watch a rom-com because it's too bloody happy; when you avoid talking to friends because he's still in your social circle. When every which-way there's a reminder?

When you barely eat because he was the cook. When the vibrant oranges, sleek apples and plump grapes in the fruit bowl, or the supple skin of a buffalo tomato, brings the good times back. When you're alone in the kitchen, yet you hear the sizzle and bubble of rich sauce on the hob, or smell the smoky, piquant aroma of roast garlic, onions and pecans, still in the atmosphere like a phantom?

When you pray to God for it to just stop.

Then December comes around, and despite kicking and screaming in your head, you force yourself to dress to the nines and attend the office Christmas bash because you're on the team and you have to go. Then someone mentions 'the hot new guy', so you glance at the bloke everyone's ogling at. And though he's the unattainable-type with cheek bones to die for and a perfect white grin, he's looking back at you, really looking. *That.*

'Hi,' I eventually heard. 'Is this chair taken?'

I looked up from my glass of cheer. 'No, go for it.'

He sat down beside me and amiably chatted as the festivities buzzed all around us. I couldn't help but notice his lithe frame and blond hair, the dimples in his cheeks, the glow in his eyes. He was undoubtably attractive, yet I couldn't feel it. The mince pies, booze and music, the overly-giddy revellers swaying on the dance floor – other peoples' flaming joy – was dragging me down. Conversation was too much; I just wanted to leave.

'I'm sorry, I'm not very good company,' I said after a while. Then hating myself as I blurted it out: 'I recently split from my boyfriend and-'

'You feel knocked off your axis, sobbing one day, drained the next. Lost, isolated, alone, even though it's self-imposed.'

I lowered my head to hide the stupid tears. 'Something like that.'

'Don't be afraid,' he replied. 'Believe me. Time's all it takes to heal your soul. And the help of a friend doesn't hurt.'

Wistfully said, and too bloody kind. I had to leave the room and as I stood, he caught my hand, a feather touch.

'If you ever need a chat, call me,' he said. Smiling, he shrugged. 'You know where I work.'

I knew there'd be no point even trying to explain my continuing despair to Mum, yet I still retreated to our remote Cheshire farmhouse – and her brisk TLC – like a homing pigeon for the Christmas break. Although it had taken many years of his womanising and alcohol-induced coercive behaviour, she'd finally got rid of my father when I was thirteen. She'd been delighted to replace his oppressive presence at the farm with her feisty sister, Auntie Greta, so when Mum caught me snivelling on Boxing Day, her look was 'all men are bastards; move on, girl'. I tried to see it that way; but in all honesty, I couldn't. I was still haemorrhaging inside, longing for a text or a call from Adam telling me he had got it all wrong, that he missed me and wanted to come home.

My week at Chimney Farm wasn't all bad, though; just like always, I had the animals to talk to, and thank God, the babies were allowed to grow into adults and only died of natural causes these days.

'I know in a weird way you'll miss him,' Mum had said after Dad went. 'But there'll be no more trauma. You know, getting attached, and then … Well, the slaughter has finished, love, I promise you that.'

In fairness, she'd been true to her word. From that day onwards no calves, lambs, hens or other livestock were taken to market or sold to the local abattoir. Instead, they became the founding members of her wildlife sanctuary, which was later supplemented by rescue animals as varied as reindeer, a boa constrictor, parrots, kestrels and a variety of domestic foxes. Though it was strictly supervised for their wellbeing and safety, the shelter was opened to the public, and all the residents were given names, which took some mulling over when there were well over a hundred.

It was good to be back in my childhood bedroom, rise at daybreak and meet the newer – and more exotic – recruits as I helped Mum and Auntie Greta with their daily chores. Yet when I was alone, I sought out the oldies – our Irish donkeys, Bella and Bonzo; dairy cows Peaches, Pippin and Posy, and Heather the horse, to share my grief. Their eyes huge and trusting, they stilled attentively as I poured out my heart.

Our huge sister sows, 'Gilly' and 'Greta', had a different approach. Dad had named them as such when they were piglets. 'Because pigs eat anything,' he'd said with a smirk.

At only nine or ten years of age at the time, I'd awaited

my mum and auntie's reactions to his 'joke' with fearful breath. To my relief they'd shrugged it off rather than risk challenging him.

'Gotta love a porker. They can run faster and squeal louder than most men, for starters,' Greta had commented with raised eyebrows.

'They're social, highly intelligent and can multi-task too,' Mum had muttered with a hint of a smile.

She'd been right, of course. Though Gilly and Greta snuffled, foraged and rooted for food as I sounded off about Adam, I knew they were listening, and when they finally looked up at me with their sharp, flinty eyes, that they understood far more than most humans gave them credit for.

When I returned to the office in the New Year, the Christmas do was still the subject of gossip.

'You and the new guy looked cosy.'

'Only had those baby blues for you! Disappeared once you'd gone.'

'Did he ask you out? Come on, spill the beans.'

'Mr Gorgeous, eh? Don't say you're not tempted.'

I wasn't, I really wasn't. I was too down, too insecure, too broken. I went to work and functioned with a brave, efficient mask, then escaped to my terraced home, managing to force down a baked potato or a banana before bed. Only it wasn't just my home, it was Adam's too, and I'd heard on the grapevine that he'd been seen with a woman.

Undoubtedly prompted by her, his initial, 'I'm sorry, so sorry, you can have everything, stay in the house for as long as you like …' was changing day by day, appearing in a flurry of cowardly texts: he'd paid for the microwave and the toaster himself; the Hoover had been his aunt's; it was his mum who'd bought the Le Creuset casserole set.

Then finally there was the icing on the cake: he wanted to buy a flat; he wouldn't wait forever; if I couldn't raise the funds for his share, I'd have to sell.

For a while I convinced myself his love interest was new. Sadly, my internet stalking told me otherwise. Whether deliberate or not, the woman's Facebook settings weren't private, and when I scrolled through her photographs, a whole trance of cuddly his-and-her pics had been taken a good six months before Adam left.

A broken heart was bad enough, but one mixed with anger, resentment, jealousy and self-pity was worse. Even I didn't know which emotion it would be at any given point. Deep sorrow one-minute, white anger the next. And as time passed, it was the latter which consumed my thoughts. The utter, utter bastard; not only had Adam betrayed me, he'd lied, he'd gaslighted me when I'd suspected something was going on. When I'd tried to address it, his 'I love you, babe, you know that,' responses had morphed into, 'Don't be daft; I'd never cheat on you', to 'That's an outrageous thing to suggest'; moving onto 'You're deluded'. Then finally, 'Your paranoia is doing my head in; I need some space.'

In truth, I'd believed his assurances, which made the devastation, the sheer humiliation, all the more intense. What an idiot; what an astonishing fool I'd been. How good would it feel to extract my revenge and make him suffer ...

As I lay awake each night, I couldn't help the intrusive, sinful thoughts: what would that retribution entail? Slashing Adam's car tyres or shredding his clothes? Spreading malicious rumours about him having a particularly nasty STD? Adding a heavy dose of laxative to his food, or hair removal to his shampoo? Sharing his dick pics with his mum, his granny and work colleagues? Posting dog shit through his letter box?

As the days marched on, my insidious musings turned even darker. Did any of those penalties really equate to the visceral devastation I had endured? Real justice had to have a physical response, to *hurt* as much as he'd hurt me. A mugging at knife point; a machete to his throat; a taser gun to his crotch.

But it wasn't just him who deserved to be punished; it was her too. What could I do to kill both birds with one stone?

At close of business on Maundy Thursday, I heard a voice behind me.

'You look as though you need a drink. Bad day?'

When I turned, it was the hot guy. I hadn't seen hide nor hair of him since Christmas and I'd honestly forgotten he existed.

'No, I'm fine,' I replied, the stock answer.

He titled his blond head and gestured to the car park. 'I'm driving today. I can give you a lift home if you fancy?'

I drew breath, ready to say 'no'. Yet the heavens were a moody mottled grey, the rain was unlikely to let up for some time and I had no umbrella. What was there to lose?

'OK, thanks.'

'What's up?' he asked after ten minutes of silence.

I cried, of course, spilling it all out with the snot and the tears like I had with the animals. And he made it easy; his gaze was on the road and not on me.

Raphael turned out to be a veritable saint, the one solid thing in a swirl of uncertainty. I could see my friends' eyes glazing when I tried to explain how devastated I was by Adam's treachery. Hell, I was even boring myself. But, like a malignant spirit, the bitterness had to come out and Raph gradually exorcised it by listening. At home or at a bar, we'd drink wine, eat meze and chat. He'd comment from time to time and occasionally give advice, yet as he put it, I was really talking to myself. He was respectful too. Apart from a quick hug when we parted, he kept his distance – albeit with the occasional compliment thrown in.

'Good job you're so pretty when you cry,' or 'Adam's a fool. One day he'll wake up and see what a beauty he's lost.' All the nicer because they came when I least expected them.

Like an arid plant given water, my confidence grew. I replenished the fruit bowl, filled the fridge and cooked myself healthy dishes. I smiled at cheesy rom-coms, enrolled at a spin class, and joined a running group. Thrilled to see the pink in my cheeks, I progressed from 5K to 10, and signed up for a half marathon. I replaced the microwave with an all-singing, all-dancing new one, returned the moody Hoover to Adam's aunt along with his tasteless prints, old comics and aeroplane memorabilia. Finally, I negotiated a great deal for his half of the house because I knew he was desperate for the cash. One morning I awoke and my first thoughts weren't of him. Astonishingly, I was fully cured.

I no longer needed to murder him.

It was strange; the moment my heart mended, the very day the scales fell from my eyes and I could see Raphael in a renewed, blinding light, he seemed to pull away. Not unfriendly exactly – we still exchanged daily texts – but the pub dates dwindled, him turning up at my place seemed to slide.

It perplexed me; until then, I'd been sure that he liked me, was even falling in love with me. It was he who'd built me up, chat by chat, to make me whole again. Had I done something wrong? Had he found someone new? Or was I being the paranoid woman Adam had described?

What had I said on the second or third 'date' when he'd gazed at me a little too long for comfort?

'I'm not looking for a boyfriend, Raph.'

A wry self-deprecating smile. 'Nor am I.'

So, then it started again, that constant longing and wishing, desiring and wanting, the mind-churning doubt deep in my psyche from a different type of gaslighting, nuanced certainly, yet somehow more hurtful than before.

Raph had made me feel so very special; there had to be an extra dimension to our relationship. Was he gay, asexual or just shy? Had I done something wrong? Or was it because I was defective, intrinsically not good enough for him?

Just like in the hours, days and weeks after Dad had left, the dichotomy between the need to know why, and the fear of it, was agonising. My sensations of rejection and abandonment became increasingly debilitating; I knew I had to be brave and face it head on.

When Mum and Greta asked if I could mind Chimney Farm for a long weekend, it felt like fate had decided it for me. I'd invite Raph to come with me and find out.

'Fancy a sleep over at Mum's in the Cheshire sticks?' I said on the phone. 'It might involve some mucking out, but I'm happy to rustle us up a feast for dinner.'

'Meet Bella and Bonzo; Peaches, Pippin and Posy. And Heather the horse?' He knew all their names; that was how close we'd been since Easter. 'How could I possibly say no?'

'I have to go for a couple of extra nights, but if you don't object to the vagaries of public transport, I'll collect you from the nearest bus stop on Saturday, then drive us both back on Sunday?'

'Sounds perfect. What can I bring?'

His sweet eagerness was encouraging; I'd been wrong to doubt him.

It was heartwarming to show Raphael around my home, the farm land and outbuildings. Kicking the autumn leaves, we trekked from shed to barn to field, and though I named some of the livestock, others needed no introduction, especially the birds of prey.

'Don't tell me; this is Ghost?' he said, spotting the snowy owl almost camouflaged by leaves. Then turning to the red-tailed hawk in the opposite enclosure, 'And that's Gwen!'

'Very impressive.'

'Beautiful creatures.' He fingered the crucifix around his neck. 'So sad they have their wings clipped, so to speak.'

'Totally agree. They were pets before coming to Mum and wouldn't survive in the wild, though. Their former aviary was tiny, so at least they have room to fly. Not as good as freedom, but the best we can do with the cards we were handed.'

Raph nodded. 'True.' He took a breath. 'What happened to your dad?'

It was the one topic we'd never covered, mostly because it was too complicated to unravel: my father had been a brute and a bully with no redeeming features, yet I'd still loved him and missed him terribly when he went.

'One day I woke up and he'd gone,' I replied. I smiled ruefully. 'Which, I guess, is why I might be a little ... insecure.'

He took my hand. 'Well, you'll always have the constancy of ...'

My heart pumped so loudly in my ears; I almost didn't catch the rest of his sentence.

'... our special friendship.'

The dismay must have been plastered on my face, as he ruffled that halo of silky blond hair. 'Because that's what this –what we – are about, yeah? More a spiritual connection, if you like.'

Though deeply winded and crushed, I managed to hold onto my dignity, thank God.

'Yes, agreed completely.'

Unleashing something inside, the knowing better, actually. High from my peculiar new-found freedom, I smiled and conversed as we cleaned cages, mucked out stables, fed and groomed the inmates. Then with an energy I hadn't known I possessed, I left the wheelbarrow at the back door of the farmhouse and took to preparing our evening meal, a hearty casserole made from vegetables grown on the land, followed by a piquant rice pudding, created with creamy milk from our cows and spices I found in Mum's kitchen cupboards.

Accompanied by a ruby red Claret, me and my confidant ate and chatted and laughed over dinner. Although I was too stuffed to join him in dessert, we finished the night by sharing the best part of a bottle of tawny port, then retired to our beds.

When I awoke at dawn and peered into the spare bedroom, Raphael wasn't there.

Like Dad, he had gone.

Suspending all thought, I spent a good hour cleaning and tidying after me and my guest. Once spotless, I donned my wellies and went outside, methodically collecting fodder from the old chest freezers in the grange, putting one foot in front of the other as I traipsed from paddocks to pens, from enclosures to coops, to feed the permanent residents and say adieu.

I left visiting the pig barn to the last. Breath stuck in my chest, I made my way over to Gilly and Greta's corner stall and peered in. Despite my failure to feed them their usual barley, wheat and soybean mix yesterday, they weren't snuffling the ground, foraging or rooting for food, but asleep on the straw, contented and replete.

Once I'd inspected their cosy nest for any midnight feast leftovers – and only found a couple of perplexing white feathers – I doffed an invisible cap to my father.

'You were right, Dad, they do.'

You know when your heart is broken, raw and bloody and you think it will never mend? When you've lost someone dear and though weeks have passed you still ache for their companionship, their kindness, their laughter. Because their special friendship was the only one that will ever, ever matter? That.

When you don't know what to do with your pecking,

jabbing mind. When every which-way there's a *did one do the right thing?*

Then December comes around and despite kicking and screaming in your head, you force yourself to dress to the nines and attend the work Christmas party because you're on the team and you have to go. Then someone mentions 'the hot new guy', so you glance at the bloke everyone's ogling at. And though he's the unattainable-type with cheek bones to die for and a perfect white grin, he's looking back at you, really looking. That.

About the Author

Dubbed the 'Duchess of Dark Domestic Noir', Caroline England is the author of seven psychological suspense thrillers, including bestseller *My Husband's Lies, Betray Her, The Sinner* and newly released *The Return Of Frankie Whittle*. She also writes gothic-tinged psychological thrillers as CE Rose.

Caroline writes 'scarily brilliant', dark twisty stories that delve into complicated relationships, secrets and the moral grey area. Drawing on her career as a criminal and divorce lawyer, she creates characters who get caught up in extraordinary situations, moral dilemmas and crime. She guarantees a jaw-dropping ending!

https://carolineenglandauthor.co.uk

I SHOULD'VE KNOWN BETTER

Noelle Holten

'He's gone. He's gone. He's gone ...' rocking back and forth, cross legged on the floor I dabbed the back of my hand at the blood dripping from my nose and lip. The crashing of the front door slamming into the wall caught me off guard again. Fear took its familiar choking hold of me. I scrambled across the wooden floor, squeezing my aching body behind the chair, forcing my fist into my mouth. Biting down.

'Jess! Jess! Where are you?!'

My shoulders slumped, the coiled tension leaving my body. It was Cara, my sister-in-law; a friend, not a foe.

Pulling myself up, I turned my face towards the shadows, teased my sweat dampened hair forward until it hung over my face. I didn't want her to see what he had done to me. What he had done to me again.

'Oh my god, Jess! What happened?' She rushed over and gently lifted my chin, tilting my face towards the light. Her fingertips warm. 'Where is he. I'll fucking rip his balls off.' She hissed through gritted teeth as she glared around the room, free hand balled into a fist at her side.

'He's gone ...' My words fell stilted from my mouth like broken porcelain.

'Right then. We're calling the police. They can nab him if he has the nerve to show his face back here again.' She turned away from me towards the landline. I grabbed at her. Flailing.

'No! No police ... please. I just want to forget about it. He won't be back.'

'What the hell, Jess? Why are you *still* protecting him?'

The tears locked tightly inside rushed out of me. Quick. Silent. Tears of upset, tears of sadness. Tears of frustration. Cara didn't understand. She never would. She had the perfect marriage. A husband who adored the ground she walked on. Spoiling her with gifts. Flowers. Tenderness. Love. Kindness. Making her feel ... special. My mother had raised a decent man.

'Hey. I'm sorry. Don't get upset. When Debbie called me, I panicked – didn't know what to expect ... here ...' She pulled a tissue from the box on the table and held it out to me.

Debbie lived next door and couldn't keep her mouth shut if her life depended on it. I sometimes forgot how thin the walls were. She must have heard the argument and instead of coming to see if I was ok, she'd rung Cara. I suppose I should've been grateful it wasn't the police.

Wiping at my eyes, I noticed my tears had mixed with the blood around my mouth and nose and was starting to drip onto the floor. 'Fucksake' I brushed past Cara and grabbed a handful of tissues. 'What a mess.'

Cara glanced around, taking in the room. The overturned chair. Shattered porcelain. 'It's not too bad, I'll tidy it – you just sit down. I'll make us a cuppa first and then start cleaning this place up, okay?'

I hadn't been referring to the room. The broken vase, the spilled tea on the rug in front of the fireplace, or even the shattered picture frame. I let her make her own assumptions. I hadn't the energy to argue and she wouldn't have listened even if I did.

Ten, or it could've been fifteen minutes later, Cara returned to the room with two mugs of coffee, and a half-eaten packet of biscuits tucked underneath her arm.

'How are you feeling now? We should really go to A&E.' She looked me up and down quickly, the pity evident in her limpid eyes.

'I'm fine. It's just a bloody nose – and a headache. I need some pain killers …' I stood up too quickly, my head span. Grabbing at the arm of the chair for support.

'Sit back down. I'll get them. Where are they? Bathroom cabinet?'

'No. Second cupboard right of the sink.' I aimed a trembling arm towards the kitchen and prayed she hadn't heard the panic in my voice.

Cara headed towards the kitchen but turned in the doorway, looking at me with that same mournful pity again. 'I've told your brother. Don't be mad …' Then she was gone.

Why couldn't she just leave things well enough alone? I thought. *Tommy will be out looking for him now and just stirring up more shit. I hope he doesn't come over. The look in his eyes will break me and the shame, guilt, embarrassment, and pain will crash to the surface again. I don't need my big brother here. This isn't a playground fight where he can defend me. He won't understand that I just want to forget … move forward and put this awful chapter of my life behind me. I really should've known better …*

I didn't notice Cara come back into the room until I heard the rattle of a small bottle of pills being shook in front of my face. I took two, gulping them down with a mouthful of coffee.

'Where did he go? Do you know?' Cara said as she lowered herself into the chair beside me. The squeak of leather and hiss of air being released from the cushions a welcome distraction.

I shook my head, then regretted it when a sharp burst of pain tore from my cheek to the top of my forehead. Answering her through gritted teeth as I rubbed my temple. 'I've no idea. He won't be back though …'

'His van is still outside. 'Course he'll be back. But don't worry. I'm not leaving, and Tommy said he'll come by later.'

Fuck … Just what I needed.

'I'm really tired. You can go. I'm just going to have a nap.' I began to tuck my legs under me on the couch. Cara grabbed at them.

'Jess. You can't sleep. What if you have a concussion? I

really think we should call an ambulance or take you to A&E.'

'No! Will you just leave it, Cara? I don't need to go to the hospital. I don't even have a concussion. It's not like … like … this hasn't happened before … I just need to be left on my own …'

I fingered the sore split in my bottom lip as I lied. Lying to Cara, but mostly lying to myself.

Cara sat back, eyes wide staring at me, and I regretted getting so angry, but she just didn't get it. I needed to be alone.

There was a long silence in the flat – a roar of deafening nothing.

'I'm only trying to help …' Cara finally murmured.

'I know.' I reached out and touched her hand. 'I didn't mean to yell, but really, I just want to forget about today … He's gone … and he'll never touch me again.'

I lied again and the atmosphere fell once more into a void of all the things we couldn't say.

Cara was never comfortable with silence, and instead tried to occupy her time by tidying up. Every now and again I noticed her looking at me from the corner of her eye, but I just stared straight ahead. My gaze locked on the window, on the white van outside with PETE'S PEST CONTROL and a picture of a giant rat painted on the side. Reminding me of my wedding night …

The day I became Mrs Flanagan was both the happiest and saddest day of my life. I should have listened to my mother. Pete and I had met in a bar and dated for eight months before he proposed. I was twenty years old; he was thirty and I was smitten. Never had a man loved me so much – he took me out, bought me little gifts, called me day and night telling me how much he loved me.

Love bombing. That's what they call it now. But back then, I didn't know that. I thought, naively like all new lovers tend to be, it was just his way of showing how much he loved me. Turns out

I wasn't the only one he bombed with his love.

We had said our vows, proclaimed our love and he'd kissed me with such passion, I beamed when he said 'I do'. However, at the reception something had already started to change. I thought he was just tired but there was a definite distance. A coldness. I chose to ignore it. I drank champagne, chatted, and danced until my feet were sore. It seems so foolish now.

After the reception, on our way through the hotel lobby, Pete had said he needed to use the restrooms and he'd meet me back in the room, but I didn't want to go into the honeymoon suite on my own. I wanted to walk in as husband and wife, so I hung back in the lobby. Waiting for him. My husband. I was staring out of the big glass windows overlooking the beautifully manicured front lawns of the hotel, when I caught a glimpse of a woman in a red dress heading to the toilets. She had dropped something and as I got closer, I realised it was her key card. She'd need that. I headed towards the toilets but when I entered the ladies, no one was there. Every cubicle door stood wide open and vacant. I'd just leave the key card at reception, I thought, as I fixed my hair in the mirror and put on a fresh coat of lip gloss.

I should have stayed there. Staring in the mirror, at the reflection of a bride. Eyes so bright with hope and contentment. And love. But I didn't. He showed me who he really was that night.

The woman in the red dress was coming out of the gents as I left the ladies, giggling as Pete grabbed her arse from behind before he spotted me. I couldn't speak. I just stared at the pair of them waiting for some kind of an explanation. My mind screaming at me it wasn't what it seemed. *But it was.* I'd just married a cheater. A cheating scumbag rat.

'What the hell is going on?' My voice broke. I threw the key card at the woman's feet. She didn't stick around. She picked up the card, shrugged her shoulders at Pete and brushed by me as if nothing had happened.

'Now don't get your knickers in a twist, Jess.' He walked towards me, palms out. 'She just went into the wrong toilets is all, and we were having a little laugh about it …'

'Do you think I'm an idiot? You grabbed her arse. I fucking saw you! Do you do that to a lot of random girls?' I turned to walk away, and he grabbed my arm. His fingers pinching into my flesh.

'Don't touch me!' I tried to wriggle free, but he squeezed tighter. The pain forcing me into motionlessness.

'Are you calling me a liar? Do you seriously think I'm such a bastard that I'd cheat on you. On our wedding day? What kind of man do you take me for?' He shoved me hard backwards against the wall and stomped towards the elevators. I saw a concierge watching from down the hall and bowed my head.

Maybe I had seen it wrong. Maybe it was all innocent, Pete had always been a total flirt – was I being a jealous wife?

'Pete! Wait …' I dashed after him as fast as my wedding dress and heels allowed. 'I'm sorry. It just took me by surprise … Of course you wouldn't do that to me.'

I was embarrassed I'd even thought it, and wished I could've taken back my accusation.

He held the elevator doors open looking me up and down slowly. His mouth like a hard scar gouged in his lower face. A winter coldness in his eyes. I didn't see it at the time, but it was the first red flag, one of many, that I shouldn't have ignored. But I was young, newly married and in love.

Fingertips on my shoulder. 'Earth to Jess. Hey! You okay? You were miles away. What were you thinking about?'

'Uh. Nothing. Sorry – just … never mind.' I didn't want to talk about it.

Cara nodded as though she understood. 'Where should I put this? Is there enough room in the kitchen bin or should I use the one out back?' She held up the dustpan of broken things she had collected and then poured them into a plastic bag.

'I'll do it.' I went to take the bag from her hand, and she pulled away.

'Don't be silly. I'm already standing.' She headed towards

the kitchen and then called out. 'This one's full. I'll take them both out the back.'

I swallowed down frustration like a bitter pill.

'Cara! Will you just stop! Leave them both in there and I'll sort it out later. Look, I know you're only trying to help but I'm tired. Give me another hour and I'll be right as rain and needing to keep myself occupied, ok?'

When she returned to the living room, hands in the air and brow furrowed I regretted shouting at her again but my eyes still pleaded with her to just go. To give me space.

'I just want to help. What is going on, Jess?'

Had I gone too far?

'I told you. I'm shattered and my face is killing me. I can feel it swelling. That ibuprofen hasn't done a thing …'

'It *does* look like it's swelling up, but if you won't let me take you to hospital I don't know what to say, how about I make us something to eat … I saw some soup on the stove I could reheat that and …'

'Don't touch that fucking soup!' I jumped up, bumping Cara on the shoulder as I pushed past her on my way into the kitchen, grabbing the pot off the burner and dumping the contents down the sink. I began scrubbing frantically at the pot, my hand aching from the pressure as I pushed down and scraped the bottom of the pot.

'Jess! What the hell are you doing? What is wrong with you? You're hysterical.' She grabbed at my arm and used her other hand to wrench the pot from my grip. Water splashed over her shirt. She sighed, placed the pot on the counter. 'I'm worried about you.' She said dabbing at her blouse with a stained tea towel. 'It's soaked through,' she sighed again and turned away from me, starting to walk towards the stairs.

'I'm just going to grab one of your tops, all right?'

Fuck.

I raced past her and blocked the stairs. 'You can't go up there …' My legs shook as Cara cocked her head and frowned. 'There's some clean clothes in the back room.'

'I need the loo.' She placed her hand on her hip. 'Do I have to piss in the back room as well?'

My hands were trembling and I slid them both into the back pockets of my jeans. Out of her sight. 'I'm sorry. It's just a mess up there. That's where the fight started. I just didn't want you to see.'

Cara reached out and rubbed my shoulder. Her touch warm and tender, but also patronising. 'Sweetheart, I've already seen it a few times before. Why don't we give it a quick tidy and then you can put your feet up. I'll wait with you until Tommy arrives – you look exhausted, but until I'm sure you're not concussed, I'm not going to let you sleep.'

I stepped aside and let her pass. Watching her as she made her way up the stairs. She turned, pointing to the left. 'There's a basket of clean clothes here, I'll just grab a tee-shirt.'

I bit down hard on my lip, opening the split in the flesh wider. All I wanted was for Tommy to come and take her home. Then I could do what needed to be done and after that, rest. Lots of rest. I was so fucking tired.

It felt like hours but there was no scream, no shouting, nothing from Cara except the flush of the toilet. I looked up when I heard her footsteps. She stood at the top of the stairs and stretched; her blouse bundled in her hands.

'I'll just pop this in the hamper. Two secs.' She turned and headed in the direction of my bedroom. Everything moved in a thick mist. Slow motion. I scrambled up the stairs. The pain in my face returned and I caught a glimpse of the raw injuries across my cheek and jaw in the mirror on the landing as I yelled for Cara to stop. But it was too late. She had already entered the bedroom.

'Oh my god, Jess! What h-h-happened? He's … Pete's … Oh my god.'

I stared past her at the body of my husband slumped on the floor. Soup or blood or both splashed across the walls like paint. The mug, I'd served the soup in, smashed to small pieces looking like the white teeth of rats scattered across the floor around him.

Then Cara's hands were on my shoulders, shaking me. Softly at first, then harder. I couldn't speak. Pete's eyes were wide open, mouth a bitter grimace and his hands locked in an odd position as if he was reaching out … for me.

'Jess! Tell me what happened.' She led me out of the room, towards the bathroom. I heard the water running from the tap and then something cold brushed against my hand. Now she knows what I really am.

'You're in shock – drink this.' She directed my hands towards my mouth, and I gulped the water down slowly, knowing that the moment the last drop touched my lips, I would have to explain.

When the water was drained, the plastic cup dry, I looked Cara in the eyes, and told her what happened.

I knew he was drunk and angry as soon as I heard the back door slam. The bellowed shouting. It was how it always started.

I was still in bed, exhausted from another restless night. My insomnia had returned with a sick vengeance. I pulled the duvet over my head and ignored him. Pleading silently for him to just stay downstairs. Begging for this time to be different. But my silence was a mistake. One I would be forced to pay for.

He stamped up the stairs. Screaming out the words 'lazy bitch' over and over again like a mantra. He ripped the duvet from the bed exposing me. I was trembling so hard it was as though I was in the midst of a deathly fever.

'Where did you fucking put it, you bitch? Get up and find me those boxes, I have a big job coming up and I need it. I fucking want it now.'

'I'm so sorry. I'm sorry. I don't know what you're talking about?'

I rubbed at my eyes feigning sleep, sat up and reached for my dressing gown. Buying time. I knew what he was talking about, but he called me dumb all the time so that's how I acted. Sometimes it calmed him down. Other times it didn't.

'The fucking rat poison – the boxes from my dad. Stop messing

me about, you dumb little bitch.' He growled the words through gritted teeth. Spittle flew from his mouth.

'I'm sorry, I'll go look now, no need for getting upset. No need to talk to me like that.' He hated when I talked back.

'Get out of my face and find those boxes or I'll be real upset ...' He headed towards the desk, the makeshift office in the corner of the room where he worked on his invoices.

I wrapped my dressing gown around me and slid my feet into my slippers. 'Have you checked the shed?'

'Of course, I fucking did. Are you deliberately trying to wind me up?' He wouldn't even look at me, and I'm glad he didn't as a smirk suddenly broke out across my face. It was like a flower kept in a damp, dark place had finally blossomed. It felt beautiful.

'Okay, I'll have a look around. Are you hungry?'

He grunted as he shuffled through the invoices. 'Yeah. I'll have some of that soup. In a mug, not a bowl and make sure it's not too hot.'

He'd always been a fussy eater. I used to love cooking, until his demands became ever more annoying. His bread had to be sliced a certain way. His food separated on the plate – God forbid if his potatoes touched his meat. I had made a large pot of his favourite soup and baked a fresh batch of crusty rolls for tea last night and hoped he would want the leftovers today.

I was humming when I got to the kitchen. Turning the knob on the oven to medium heat and grabbing a spoon to stir in the special spice I'd be adding today. I opened the cupboard under the sink, pulled on the plastic gloves I used for washing up, pushed aside the bottles and grabbed the last box of rat poison from Pete's dad. I had dumped the others. This poison had been discontinued in 2006 because it contained strychnine, but his father had never destroyed his overstock and Pete still used it occasionally. And I was so glad he did.

I only had one shot. I was banking on the greedy bastard taking a big slug of the soup before the piece of shit realised what I had done. I still hadn't figured out what I was going to do afterwards, with the body, but that wasn't going to stop me.

I dumped half the box of poison into my granite mortar, picked up the pestle and began crushing the pellets into a fine dust. Holding my breath. When I was done I stood back, arms outstretched and dumped the contents into the boiling soup. Stirred until the powder blended with it completely. I ground some black pepper in and then ladled the warm soup into his favourite mug. Removed the gloves, chucking them in the bin – I'd get rid of them properly later, and carefully picked up the mug of soup to take upstairs to my dear, soon to be dead, husband.

He was sat on the bed, talking on his mobile phone when I entered the bedroom. I stood in the doorway, trying to steady my shaking hands while I waited for him to get off the call. I didn't wonder who he was talking to. I already knew. It was another woman - another new piece on the side.

'OK, doll. I'll see what I can …' He turned around and glared at me. 'I gotta go. Speak later.' Tossed his mobile on the pillow. 'You spying on me now?'

I just bowed my head. He needed to drink the soup. I wasn't going to do anything that would make him angry now. 'Here, drink it before it goes cold.' I placed the mug on his desk. He eyed me strangely. Shit. Did he suspect something? Maybe I should have questioned him more about the telephone call. Acted jealous. But he reached for the mug and took a big swig from it.

'Oh, I found that poison you were looking for.' His face went red and then drained of colour. 'Good soup?' I began backing away as his body started to convulse, soup sprayed all over his invoices and the wall. He staggered to his feet. Shit. I turned and stumbled towards the bedroom door when I felt fingers claw deeply into my shoulder. Then he shoved me with such force into the door I heard the cartilage and bones in my nose splinter. Blood sprayed from my nostrils everywhere, I nearly slipped on the now slick wooden floor.

Pete did slip. Fell on his back, right where he dropped the mug of poison. His breathing became harsh. Raspy. His body shaking. I just stared at his chest, willing him to die fast. Not because I wanted him to be out of his misery quickly, I just wanted him dead. Gone out of my life forever.

And then as if by magic, the convulsions stopped. His choked breathing ceased. He lay there frozen in a macabre position, like he was climbing an invisible ladder. But there'd be no stairway to heaven for Pete. He'd be speeding down the highway to hell. Ironic really, considering how he so loved AC/DC.

'That was it. After that I went downstairs, smashed a few things to release the tension, sat on the floor and tried to figure out what I was going to do next. Then you arrived.' I told Cara.

She looked at me blankly for what seemed a lifetime before she pulled her mobile phone from her pocket.

'What are you doing?' The pitch in my voice rose with panic. I tried to grab the phone from Cara's hand, but she pulled away, and held her other hand out.

'Stop it Jess! We have to call the police. What were you going to do? Hide the body? What about when people called looking for him – his sister? His mother? His employees? Think about it. Do you want to be looking over your shoulder for the rest of your life?' She started dialling. 'You can tell them all about the years of abuse. You just snapped. We'll sort this out.' She turned away and spoke to whoever was on the line.

'Ok ...' Prison wouldn't be so bad. At least he was finally gone, and he'd never hurt me ... or any other woman again.

I slid down the wall. Maybe she was right. Maybe we would figure it out, but my eyes kept swaying to the long, sharp piece of broken porcelain on the floor next to my dead husband and back to Cara speaking hysterically into the phone.

About the Author

Noelle Holten is an award-winning blogger at www.crimebookjunkie.co.uk.

She is a PR and Social Media Manager with 7+ years experience, for Bookouture/Second Sky, a leading digital publisher in the UK and imprints of Hachette UK.

Her experience as a Senior Probation Officer for over 17 years, gave her insight and experience to write *Dead Inside* - her debut novel with One More Chapter/Harper Collins UK. It is an international kindle bestseller as well as the start of a series featuring DC Maggie Jamieson. Noelle also writes standalone thrillers for One More Chapter, her latest: *His Truth Her Truth* is out now.

THE WRONG BLONDE

James Grady

Platinum blonde hair. Black rims glasses windshield electric blue eyes. Thick rubied lips. A cheap jacket over a taut emerald blouse. Boring slacks sheath dancer's legs. A fake gold chain, black party purse clunked on that bar's table for two as she plopped into the empty chair across from the all alone man.

Her husky voice: 'So here we are.'

The window behind her in this booze-scented cave glowed a red neon sign:

The Lost & Found Tavern

Their table had 19 replicates positioned through the main floor between the front door and the bar of this oasis. A side room nearer to the *closes-at-10* kitchen held tables for another 30 customers.

The scarred wooden bar ran the length of the main room. Behind its stacked bottles of dream-makers & ache-breakers rose a mirror reflecting souls sitting on stools in the swirl of the wall speakers' streaming music.

Bartender Lorna didn't give a shit if the music was too loud. She streamed songs from way back when she was a child and still safe from their poetry. Ivory letters across the back of her black satin jacket read: '**FUCK OFF**'

The man sitting across the table from the platinum blonde faced the door.

That blonde faced the bar and the mirror that reflected them sitting at that table. The back of his trim, dark brown hair.

His straight spine.

Blink.

She sees his chiselled face. Steel sky eyes. Puzzled lips. Maroon shirt under a scruffy unzipped leather jacket. Black jeans. Lean and *maybe* not mean.

Mark it as 8:09 on a chilly spring Tuesday night.

The blonde lowered her husky voice: 'Aren't you glad to see me?'

'Glad doesn't cover it,' he said.

Frowned: 'But you don't look like your picture on the App.'

'Oh, *her?* She was hunkering in the side room when you walked in six minutes before 7:30. You probably figured to be early. She probably figured to beat you to the punch. Stared. Fidgeted. Kept her baseball cap snug over her bunched-up *sandy blonde* hair and skedaddled out a fire exit door back there. Didn't you hear the RING! of the alarm bell? The music's not *that* loud.'

The Rolling Stones' '(I Can't Get No) Satisfaction' rocked the bar.

'Well … *huh.*' He shrugged. 'Guess I got truly swiped. But where did you come from? I would have noticed you when I came in.'

She shrugged back: 'The side room's got an obstructed corner.'

'But you peered around what blocked the view and saw me.'

'And her checking you out. If it's any consolation, Miss Dating App wobbled for almost 10 minutes past the half hour mark – obviously the agreed show-up time – before she bolted.'

'Took you a while to walk out and sit down here.'

'I wanted to know that you're a patient man.'

'Why do you care?'

'Because I need someone like that to sit with.'

'You could sit with any lonesome guy in here. Except for gay Paul. He tries to keep the next stool open in case his deserved *smart-and* finally materialises.'

'So you know this crowd. Picked the meet-up place.'

'I'm no poseur. Asked where she wanted us to go. Told her my choice.'

'She chose not to show you her turf *until*.'

Server Clarisse braked at their table: 'You two want something?'

Laughed: '*From the bar*. You can't just sit here taking up my tip space.'

The blonde's ruby lips said: 'I'll have a single malt Scotch on the rocks.'

The man told those ruby lips: 'My blood runs Irish.'

Told server Clarisse: 'Bring me a glass of your blended red.'

Added: 'Please.'

Clarisse tapped her mini-iPad. 'Want a couple menus?'

Her male customer asked his lucky date: 'Are we going to eat?'

'Leave the menus,' said the blonde.

Clarisse marched away as the bar's speakers freed the music of 'Jungleland' released by Bruce Springsteen a dozen years before bartender Lorna got the delivery room doctor's slap to cry her way into this life.

'So why are you here?' said the man in the scruffy leather jacket to the platinum blonde who sat across from him at his chosen table. 'You're no random stranger.'

'We're all strangers.'

The tavern door *clunked* open.

An invasion of chilly night air. The bar mirror's image of a handsome silver suited prince of the city striding towards that glass filled the glass lenses over the blonde's blue eyes. She flipped a menu up in front of her face.

The bar door *whunked* closed.

The prince pranced past that *obvious* and thus *ignorable* couple.

Picked his stool at the bar.

Re-arranged the empty stool on his heart side *just so*.

Claimed that stool by putting his car keys on the bar in

front of it.

'Look at me,' said the leather jacketed man to the held-up menu.

The menu laid down on the table.

'What will I see?' said the curious red lips.

'We don't have time for anything but the truth.'

Her ruby lips twitched.

Her blue eyes blinked.

'Let's start with names,' said the beating heart sitting across from her.

He stepped up first: 'I'm Jesse.'

Her red lips released: 'Embry.'

'Is that who'll you'll be in the morning?'

'Who we all want to be in the morning is alive and lucky.'

'Here you go!' chimed server Clarisse as she bent over the table to put a glass of Scotch poured over a lone ice cube big enough to sink the *Titanic* in front of the blonde who oddly gave Clarisse no scent of perfume.

Clarisse put the generous pour of red wine in front of the *'has the street edge to scratch her itch'* man sitting across from the lucky blonde.

Who – *Damn it!* – was not a bitch but told Clarisse: 'Thanks.'

'What can I get you guys from the kitchen?' said Clarisse.

'Could you give us a few more minutes please?' said the blonde's date.

Him picking up his glass pulled both women's eyes. He sipped his wine.

Smiled: 'For the delay, tap in another dollar for a service charge.'

The blonde blurted: *'I'm paying!'*

Jesse blinked.

'Cash,' he said. 'So you can pay in cash. No credit card.'

Clarisse watched the blonde fill her eyes with *him*.

Those ruby lips cupped surprise and admiration.

He got that she got that he got her as their stares softened.

Oh well, thought Clarisse. Sashayed away to *Next!*

The great Richard Thompson song 'Wall Of Death' guitared the air.

'Aren't you going to taste the Scotch you're paying for?'

'In a bit.'

'Or in a *never*. *"Never gonna"* leave a red lipstick DNA stain on the glass. Or fingerprints on it. Me, I'd just *accidentally* knock it off the table to break into shards for the trash. And cash can't be tracked.'

'Who are you, *Jesse*?'

'Who you picked.'

'Maybe I didn't know what I was doing.'

'We only know what we think we know,' his *no bullshit* face told her lake blue eyes. 'And no matter what all that is, we gotta live with what we do.'

Tremor on the table.

Blonde Embry tapped the cellphone on the table beside her drink.

Jesse sipped his red wine.

Her blue eyes rose to lock on the *him* across the table from her.

'Go ahead and answer the text,' he said. 'Or is that not part of your plan?'

'What plan?'

'I wish to hell I knew. But you're carrying the tons of it on your shoulders.'

'Everybody carries weight.'

'Not like whatever this one is. And I'm sorry.'

'What are you sorry for?'

'That I wasn't there to help you pick it up. That I might not be good enough to help you with its *whatever* now. That I'm not sure if I should be on your side.'

Her blue eyes looked at him. Really looked at him. Filled with him.

Music played: Tracy Chapman's 'Fast Car' from the year bartender Lorna got her driver's license to steer down empty streets.

Embry said: 'Sometimes it's too late to help and sorry isn't enough.'

'This *sometime* is now. Tonight. And I'm sitting here. Still.

'Who knows?' he added. 'Maybe we'll get to laugh.'

She twitched some genre of a blood red smile.

He leaned across the table so she'd be certain to hear him under the music.

Said: 'The only thing I'm scared of is that you're scheming while scared *and* scarred as well as savvy. And that you won't let me stand by your side with whatever I can do to help your *whatever*.'

Emotions waterfalled Embry's face.

She tightened her shoulders. Resolve won.

'What you can do for me – all you can do for me – is just sit right there. I've got to go outside now. Alone. I have to vape. Privately. I'll be back.'

'No, you won't. I'm a used up prop. You don't smoke. Not tobacco anyway. You don't have that smell. And you'll keep this *whatever* out of any other cloud.'

He blinked: 'In here. Tonight. You had to see. Know. But not be *seen* seen. Recognised. So sitting with some random guy, ducking behind the menu when –'

Jesse whirled in his chair to face the bar behind him.

Drilled his eyes into the silvered prince of the city commanding a stool.

A glass of water rose in front of the empty stool beside the prince.

Jesse whirled back to face the stranger perched across from him.

'Look,' she said. 'I made a mistake. You're not nobody … I can't let you … I'm leaving. That's the way it was always going to be. Has to be. You stay here. Sip slow *and* have another glass of wine. *Hell*, order the dinner you didn't let yourself have before you came because the idiot *natural blonde* who ghosted you might have wanted to share a meal. You're right, I'll drop cash to pay for this *whatever*. But forget it. Everything. Never think about *if* in another lifetime.'

Her right hand reached for her black purse on the table.

His rocket left hand beat her there/pushed down by her strong right palm.

Gun.

The hard shape of *gun* in the black purse filled his pinned-down grasp.

Her grip and pull were strong.

He was stronger.

Slowly. Oh. So. Slowly.

Their pressed together hands fought/slid the black purse across the table toward him in the sounds of the bar's music they no longer heard.

The purse stopped between them in the middle of the table.

Her left hand dumped her eyeglasses onto the top of a menu. Those lenses did nothing to the view of the menu's listings of cheeseburgers and tater tots.

'Glasses with clear lenses,' he whispered so only she could hear. 'Clothes that aren't you. Dyed blonde hair and beautiful red lipstick to pull glances away from the rest of your face. And that's a burner phone. Embry is all disguise.'

'Not all,' she whispered back.

She shook her head. 'I used to have dark chocolate hair. Just like you. Going blonde … New me goes bold.'

'What about the gun?'

Her blue eyes nailed him.

'The gun is my gotta,' she whispered.

'My *not gonna just take it*,' she said.

'My *stand and deliver justice*,' she vowed.

'What did he do?'

'You know what he did.'

Their muscles gripping the purse agreed to relax – but only a bit.

'Bridal shower. Upscale club 'cross town from this by-the-railroad-tracks real people bar. Two to many glasses of champagne. Bride and besties take the limo for more but I'm done. Gonna call an Uber. *See ya! See ya! Love ya!*'

'But *whoa!* Steady girl. Wobbling after the last wave of their *gone.* Alone now. A stranger's hand steers me to the bar. Empty stool. Wooden bar to press my arm on to let me hold onto the real world.

'A man hunk in a big money suit. Helping me. *"Here. A glass of water. No more booze for you. Sit here until you can better Uber-up."* Sipping, gulping it as the world stops vibrating and he's telling me how cool his car is and other big bucks' bullshit *yeah,* but I figure he's just keeping me company.

'*"Good idea to hit the ladies' room,"* he says. Suddenly I gotta go. He points. I shuffle away. Steadier. Focused. *Whoosh* goes the toilet. I walk out. He's standing there. Holding a glass of water stained by my *all-the-time* pink lipstick.

'Hands glass to me. Bartender and server know it's just water he's carried back to the Ladies and me with one hand. Other hand … Empty.

'Tells the bar I still don't look so good. Not sober. *"I'm fine, I'm fine,"* but the champagne slur's still there so only I believe me. Drink some more water. Just sit here and you'll be OK.

'Then it's … I don't know. Twenty minutes? I'm shuffling and weaving. Dark, it's dark and I'm outside. Swirling. Brain numb. What was in the second glass of water? *Whoa,* he wasn't lying. A fancy gold car 'n' why dropped me in the backseat? Cold again. Keys in my purse. Stairs. Bedroom, my bedroom …'

Jesse felt her tighten her grip on his hand.

On the gun.

On everything.

'Sniper shot memories. What … what he did. Said. A pill. Call it a second pill. The killer pill. Him laughing. Shoving it down my throat. *"Trip time!"* Bathtub. Naked. Him washing … No DNA. No *him* evidence of sex.'

'You didn't have sex with him,' said Jesse. 'That was assault. Rape.'

He knew *she knew* he wanted to raise his hand to comfort her.

But then the gun …

'Second pill was some kind of hallucinogen. Took until the next evening to … to get clear. Get to "hospital" who found signs of *maybe*. Blood tested an illegal party girl hallucinogen. Booze. Got a *maybe* on some other drug. Cops got nothing but a gold car. I didn't remember the make. Sketch artist got an unusable blurry memory of a face but … but missed the stroll, the royal fucking stroll.'

She slumped (held onto the gun).

Took a deep breath.

Heard the him she'd chosen say: 'Have you …'

'Yeah. And *yeah*. Was on my way driving back to my new apartment *slash* studio after my last therapy session in which I had remembered *Mercedes* plus its gold colour that …

'That there the fuck it was! On the passing-through street I was driving. Pulled up to the doorman outside a fancy schmancy high rise apartment building. And *him*. Climbing out of that Mercedes. Turning it over to a valet who I watched zip it down into the "residents parking" basement garage while the doorman tipped his cap at Mr Big walking that royal fucking stroll into –'

'The building where he lived,' said Jesse.

Asked: 'How did you get him to come here tonight?'

'Told him the truth. This *across the river* bar's got a parking lot outside not too close to the railroad tracks. Perfect for protecting a bragged-about car.'

'You scouted this place.'

'I found what I needed.'

'And me,' he said.

'Please don't make me regret that any more than I already do.'

'And here I thought being ghosted by the other blonde was as bad as tonight was going to get,' said Jesse.

'Let me go now,' whispered the blonde labelled Embry. 'Stay here.'

'*Here* is always going to be part of me from now on.' Jesse shook his head. 'The *where & when* are *here & now*. Tell me the rest. All the *how*. *What*.'

Her hand on his shifted –

– his hand locked down on the purse holstering a gun.

'You know it already,' she told him. 'No cop could trust this witness.

'But Google gets you everything. Car license plate to vehicle owner to confirming his address. A LinkedIn profile. Family money. Harvard. Making more money moving other people's millions in and out of dark treasure chests. Never married. And not on any dating apps.'

'At least not as *him*,' said Jesse. 'But his picture …'

She shook her head.

'You name the hook-up or dating App, I joined them all. Plus a few you never heard of. I set up a "prospects" radius of five miles from his apartment building. He's no Batman jumping from rooftop to rooftop to his secret lair.'

'Who is?' mumbled Jesse.

'Found him. His face with a phony name. Profile that implied you'd be lucky to match with him.'

'You used a fake name too,' said Jesse. 'Probably something that sounded like a movie star every guy in this bar except gay Paul dreams about.'

'Thank God for AI,' she said.

'Don't make me think you're insane.'

'Haven't you ever stepped over to the dark side for something that desperately needs to be done?'

He gave her a look that wouldn't tell.

'Oh that profile I posted! Raven black hair. He liked my pink lipstick I always wore *before* so she slathers it on. He targets big breasts. The *wow* pictures of her. The hotshot celebrity ball with her V neck red gown that could almost have gotten her kicked out or arrested if any of that was real. The straining bikini leer. Face down on a beach blanket with the bikini top unsnapped and her barely clad pouty ass saying "*Come on!*"

'Got him to agree to meet where nobody knows them: "so we can be just us". Fits right into his hunter's needs. A place where he's not known. A place down by the river and train tracks. He'd bragged about his car. She told him the truth: The

Lost & Found Tavern has a parking lot. A streetlight drops a protective cone of *see me* over the parked cars. Didn't mention there are no security cameras.'

'That's why he's sitting at the bar *now*,' said Jesse. 'But what's *next*?'

'He's got the glass of water already waiting. That's what he *thinks* is next.'

'But the purse I'm holding –'

'We're holding!'

'– is too small for a brunette wig even without the gun.'

'Call it by its name I learned on the shooting range: Glock.'

'Its name is death.'

'Not if you learn how to aim and hit more choices. Blast a groin. Maybe a knee, too.'

They stared at each other seeing what she'd said.

Jesse frowned: 'So there's no wig to fool him that you're that digital her.'

'The night outside. The parking lot. There'll be a gold Mercedes there.'

Jesse drilled his eyes into her.

'Text,' she said.

'Like the one you just got on your phone.'

'From his burner phone to mine. Asking if my Uber is getting closer.'

She leaned her real world's peroxide blonde hair and lipsticked ruby lips closer to him.

'She's going to text him. She adored everything he told her about his studly gold car – except of course, its make. Text she's in the parking lot, her ass on the front of the only truly hip gold car in the streetlight's glow. Ask him to come out. Make sure she's right before they go back inside amidst people.'

'She – you – put her in the bullseye. He can come out already prepped with that water. Drive her off and nobody could see.'

'But "*she*" will turn out to be some red-lipped blonde he's never met.'

'And the Glock,' said Jesse. 'Are you sure you can live with this?'

She whispered: 'I'm sure I can't live with letting him keep hurting other *hers*. Or him getting away with … with what he did to this *her* named *me*.'

They both knew music was playing.

They both heard nothing beyond their own thumping hearts.

And the other one's breaths.

THE PURSE!

Moving! It's moving!

Two struggling hands slide the black purse across this barroom table …

Embry's hand gets ripped off Jesse's hand that pulls the purse to him.

She slumps back to her side of the table.

He opens the black purse. Nods.

Stares at her as some timeless Roy Orbison song played.

She knew better than to plead.

Refused to plead.

He's a smooth current of continuous motion in their river of *now*.

Standing. A wad of greenback bills from the purse lands on the table.

'Come on,' he says. 'Leave the cash. Bring the eyeglasses.'

She can't think. Can only sense. Carried forward by his current.

She's standing. She's turning. She's following him out the *whunking* door.

They're outside in a red neon darkness.

The parking lot.

Tuesday is a slow night at The Lost & Found Tavern.

The parking lot holds only a few cars.

A gold Mercedes is backed to near the rear wall of the parking lot that abuts a gray shale hill support the railroad tracks to somewhere else, like the *wherever* that a distant chugging ever closer train will go.

'I parked on the street,' said Jesse.

Shrugged: 'I wanted to save an easy parking lot space for my date.'

'I burner phone Uber'd to a café around the corner 'n' six blocks away.'

'No record of you or your digital fake being here.'

'If cops somehow come asking, I can tell 'em they got the wrong blonde.'

'A lot of that going around these days,' said Jesse.

Shrugged: 'You can dye your disguise hair back to brown.'

She shook her platinum head: 'That me is dead.'

Stared at the man carrying her black purse under these stars.

The distant train *Woo*'d closer.

'You've got the gun,' she said. 'The power of *whatever*.'

'If only,' he said. 'But I do got the gun.'

Marched toward the grille of the gold Mercedes.

She hurried beside him.

Wondering … *No*: She couldn't wrestle the purse from him.

He stopped.

She stood an arm's length away from his heart.

Snap! went the opening black purse.

He pulled out the Glock.

Like he's shaking hands with an old friend, flashed through Embry.

She heard him say: 'Here.'

The black purse filled her two surprised reaching hands.

The gold Mercedes' empty headlights stared at them.

He glanced to his left:

Confirmed she was still safely standing there.

Checked further back along the parking lot made by the bar's brick wall jutting out from the sloping hill's elevated train tracks:

The bar's door – still closed.

The front window with its red neon sign faced the other

way.

Bartender Lorna's songs rumbled out to be heard out here in the night.

The train chugged closer to where it would race above and beyond them.

The train's cyclops lone headlight came 'round a not-far-away bend closer, ever closer, to the elevated track above and beyond the gold Mercedes' rear.

'WOO!' whistles that train.

Jesse snaps into the two handed shooter's crouched stance.

BANG! blasts a round toward the gold Mercedes when a second 'WOO!' roars *clackety-clack* past and the bar's music plays out into the night.

Embry staggered.

Jesse bent over to retrieve the gun bullet's ejected copper jacket.

'Don't touch anything,' he warned her.

Step by step Embry closed in to the front of the gold Mercedes.

A bullet-blasted a hole in that windshield.

A bullet hole surrounded by a cracked-glass spiderweb.

A bullet hole smack dead centre over and above the steering wheel.

A bullet ripped the driver's seat headrest through its middle where the driver's face would be.

'He'll get the message,' said Jesse. 'Now his every heartbeat brings fear.'

Embry stared at him with … with … with …

Filled that cone of light with her ruby smile.

Told him: 'Let's be sure.'

She stared at the two golden tubes of lipstick in the black purse she held.

One was yesterday's pink.

The other was today's red.

She chose her tube.

'*Wow*,' he whispered no more than one song from inside

the bar later.

'I got another idea,' he said. 'Come with me.'

They quick-walked out of the parking lot.

Leaving behind the Mercedes with the bullet-blasted windshield …

… artistically streaked with pink lipstick:

Emoji-like, palm-sized snarling faces glared on either side of the bullet hole.

Giant pink letters below the bullet hole:

RAPiSt!

They hurried past the closed tavern's door.

Heard music coming from inside that they couldn't recognise.

Couldn't see gay Paul *finally* getting to smile at the *shy but 'wow' smart and obvious* guy who'd appeared beside him.

Four storefronts beyond Lost & Found they crossed the street to the perpendicular road spilling into its dead end at the Lost & Found's street.

Just up past the intersection's corner, he nodded her to his five years old, sadly still gas-guzzling, dented and dark car's passenger seat with its windshield view of that bar's door and halfway up into the bar's parking lot.

They dropped into that car's front seats together.

Clunked their doors shut.

Jesse tore his eyes from her sitting there.

Gazed at the still-closed tavern door.

Asked: 'Your *come-outside-and-meet-me* text to Mr Mercedes. Is that burner phone already ready to rock?'

'With a picture even you couldn't resist.'

'I want *real*, not a *picture*.' He held out his hand. 'If the message is saved and safe, let me make an actual *human being to human being* phone call.'

She handed him the burner phone to tap and hold to his strong mouth.

'*Yeah, yo, 911?*' said a panting voice that didn't sound like him. *'Like, I just walkn' by 'n' heard a gunshot in the parking lot of that Lost & Found bar down by the river and the train tracks 'n' man I whipped around 'n' feet flyin' hightailing it away from there 'cause I ain't gonna be some innocent casualty bullshit but you oughta roll some hotshots out there right fucking now!'*

Jesse tapped the phone off.

Rolled his car window down.

Embry did the same.

He handed the phone back to her.

'Tee it up. Be ready. Hope.'

She mumbled: 'That's what I've been doing all night.'

'You're not alone.'

She couldn't stop her ruby lips smile he almost couldn't turn away from to watch the bar door and listen to the night outside his window.

They heard the whisper of the bar music but not what it was.

Heard each other breathe.

Felt each other's *there* there.

Knew the chill of the night.

Stared at the Lost & Found Tavern.

From off in the distance: The soft wail of police cars' sirens.

Coming closer.

Then close enough to be heard inside the Lost & Found between songs by server Clarisse whose sigh hoped for the most humane 911 outcome *out there* even as she hoped for a chance to meet a savvy cop and serve him her lasso smile.

In the parked car across the street, Jessie cried: 'Text him now!'

'Tapped!' cried Embry.

Sirens closer.

Maybe five blocks away.

Maybe four.

Light spilled out into the street from the Lost & Found's opening door.

A figure of a man steps out of the bar holding a glass in one hand.

Three royal strides and he's in the parking lot.

Staring toward where Jesse and Embry can't see from their parked car.

Bouncing flashes of light snap Jesse's eyes up to their rearview mirror.

He yells: *'Duck!'*

A man and a woman in a night-parked car sink out of view of the flood of headlights and spinning red lights as two police cruisers roar past, screech the left hand turn to slam to a halt bathing the bar parking lot with the law's glow.

The parked car's dark-haired man and platinum blonde rise together.

Catch the sight of police lights illuminating a man in a silver suit waving for them to what he can't quite see yet that someone has done to his car.

'Now his name is going to be in the police database,' said Jesse.

'Maybe with a note of what's been lipsticked for everyone to see.'

Jesse keyed the car he had to life.

Didn't' turn his headlights on.

Shifted into reverse.

'Won't they see our backup lights?' said Embry.

His strong shoulders shrugged: 'Life's full of chances.'

Her full ruby lips smiled: 'And what you do with them.'

They heard a pause in the faint music from inside the bar where just before the cops came, bartender Lorna played that one special sappy song of love and tomorrow. She breathed in. Breathed out. Blinked. Shrugged out of her FUCK OFF jacket. Hung it on a hook as she maybe – *maybe* – felt something more.

Jesse backed the car up the block out of sight of the Lost & Found ferment. Wheeled it into a turn the other way. Turned on the headlights. Drove forward.

Drove the streets of this now *new-to-them* city where they'd lived *before*.

'Sorry about your real date,' said Embry.

'I want to be with the blonde I got,' said Jesse.

They shared the look, those smiles, those twinkling eyes.

Turned back to face the windshield.

'Your blonde's lipstick is red,' she said. 'Not pink like on an asshole's windshield.'

'I lo –' Jessie swallowed those last two letters.

Instead said: 'Red is my favourite colour.'

'Or whatever you choose,' he told the image riding in his windshield.

Heard her reply: 'I'm not the only vote.'

The traffic light ahead flashed STOP.

He braked the car.

'We'll stop in the middle of the bridge,' he said. 'Toss in the Glock, your fake glasses, the burner phone.'

'And the pink lipstick tube,' she said. 'All gone down into the river.'

'Then I'll take you anywhere you want,' he said. 'Better than Uber.'

'Can we just drive around for a while?' she said. 'We've got a lot to see and find out and … and …'

'And go for,' he said.

The traffic light turned green.

They drove off into that starlit night.

for Richard Thompson, OBE.

About the Author

James Grady's first novel *Six Days Of The Condor* became the Robert Redford movie *Three Days Of The Condor* and the Max Irons TV series *Condor*. Born and raised in Montana, Grady has received Italy's Raymond Chandler Medal, France's Grand Prix Du Roman Noir and Japan's Baka-Misu literature award, two *Regardies* Magazine short story awards, and been a Mystery Writers of America Edgar finalist. He's published more than a dozen novels and three times that many short stories, poetry, been a muckraker journalist and a filmed scriptwriter for film and television. *Publishers Weekly* compared him to Larry McMurtry for Grady's 2024 novel *The Smoke In Our Eyes*. Grady's sequel novel to *Smoke – American Sky* – will be published July, 2025.In 2008, London's Daily Telegraph named Grady as one of '50 crime writers to read before you die.' In 2015, *The Washington Post* compared Grady's prose to George Orwell and Bob Dylan.

PARADIGM OF PAINS

Benjamin Kurt Unsworth

'Wonderful thing, pain. Without pain, no race could survive.'
~ *Doctor Who*, 'The Hand of Fear', Part One

'Mastermind' - not a word that Andrews hastily assigned to himself.

Until now.

He could finally say he'd calculated every odd, bribed each necessary official, and sent all the right miscreants out at the right time. He had even gained technical skills advanced enough to hack a video feed. Beside the day-to-day rigmarole of expanding his empire, his aim was to bring the world of drugs and criminals into the twenty-first century. Many a time, people had told him that his name didn't instil enough fear in rival gangs. Andrews disagreed, thinking instead that if maybe Pinkie from *Brighton Rock* had attempted being a little more under the radar, or if Moriarty had restrained his penchant for bravado and changed his name to something quieter, neither would have plummeted when they did. In fact, he had deliberately changed his surname to make himself far less attractive to the police force's watchful eye. Andrews was a name like any other: innocent. It behoved the man running the local newsagent or a business-owner's P.A. His first name was *his* though. It was bad enough that some of his underlings had managed to learn his full initials, let alone anything more. The day one of them did, it would be the day all hell broke loose.

His operations were all based out of his office above the barber shop. It was a room strewn with books and a colourful array of stereotypical posters, needlessly heterosexual in every detail, however they'd today all been shifted aside. Where they had clustered now sat the forty-four inch TV he'd wanted for so long. And, thanks to the unfortunate blaze at the technology store – open for barely more than three or four weeks – it had all been free of charge.

Andrews' pleasure came at a cost. His wife, Susanna. On both sides, it was more a union of crossed fingers during wedding vows and sleeping around with all and sundry than anything else – from the thinnest, wimpiest of boys like that Davies bloke who lived on the adjoining lane, to the spirited runner, Margot *something*, who used their front lawn as a shortcut home every Wednesday. Very little bliss wasn't equatable with very much anger though, and they enjoyed the odd moment of pleasantness. Susanna simply detested when her husband tried to push their matrimony's boundaries, when he needed *that* one sensation. She'd given him two children, Sally and Peter, and even that didn't sate his appetite. They were about as uplifting to him as unbound damnation, and he treated them as nothing greater than irritating side effects of his wild nights. His begging for more had become an unbroken exhortation for her to spit on him, degrade him, pummel his face during impending pleasure – that was when she finally grabbed her children and dragged them out of the house. It wasn't like Peter or Sally hinted at a murmur of protest. Andrews cared only that he was still yet to locate *that* sensation.

The man didn't know when it had commenced, let alone when he was first conscious of it. He supposed it didn't really matter. It was enough to know now that paper cuts and rope burns were not mere cuts and burns, they were something far more beatific. Ascending beyond the confines of simply cuts and burns, it was the kind of fire you could only stoke, never put out. And fire always demanded more fuel.

His beautiful family unit hadn't spoken in an age, but

wedding vows or not, they were still a part of his life. For tonight at least. An expertise his work in the world of lawless trades and intricate subterfuges had taught him was how to exact vengeance. Or more importantly when the right time to exact it was, and how to do it in the most luxuriant and fulfilling way possible.

The pinch of skin. A stab of satisfaction. An unrepressed lick of his lips. Lost in this reverie of the future, the final pad being attached shocked him back to the real world with a smile he couldn't control on his lips. He was sat like a spider in the middle of a web of wires and electrodes and sensor pads, the fruits of his labours one sensation away.

All he needed to do was sit back and enjoy the ride.

Tall Boy entered. Andrews deemed him the most useful of his employees – he seemed to read his mind, open the right door, upper cut the right nuisance, and best of all his handiwork left very little flesh to bruise. He was about to speak to his boss when Andrews in a single deft and polished move raised his hand. The man's other hand lifted a mug sloshing black fluid down his throat. Tall Boy's boss always claimed he liked his hot drinks like he liked his humour: dark and unsweetened. Coffee was the perfect complement to his raw tastes and the bitter, acidic backwash of life.

When he tried to speak again, Tall Boy was silenced by the waft of a hand. This time, the sip of coffee was more generous, the time spent swilling it around his mouth like a fine wine longer and more delicate, the dribble of excess down the side of the cup more prolonged and vulgar. In his previous life Tall Boy wouldn't have had to endure this sight. In his current one, he was being paid a better salary, and with that came as great an expectation for silence as the expectation for how carefully he slashed his knife.

After a final sip, which in the wrong context would've bordered on orgasmic, he placed the coffee mug back down on the table.

'Can I have a minute of your time?' Tall Boy asked.

'Of course,' came the reply.

Andrews was busy loosening his belt and ruffling sections of his clothing. Now wasn't the time to question why and Tall Boy imagined he'd resign himself to never knowing. It could be pushed to the back of an extraordinarily sordid cupboard and stay there. Thinking about some of his boss' previous antics, he feared that throwing himself from a bridge might be unavoidable if he understood the full network of events at play. When Little Hodbury's sole accountant died at Tall Boy's hand, it hadn't fluttered his stomach's butterflies in the slightest degree. His various other assignments, involving burned flesh, suicide videos posted online, and the careful removal of 'expendable' limbs one-by-one in a freezing meat locker, they were part of the course. But one tug at Andrews' web and that was enough for him to dive headlong into the Baltic currents.

'We've had a message from our friend.'

'Albatross?'

'No, he's too busy with that radio business he's, um, *investing in*,' Tall Boy replied. 'This is for our friend in the force. He's made sure two have been sent out. He assures me all will be ready before the hour.'

'Of course,' said Andrews, 'because he knows better than to make a mistake.' As the man grinned, Tall Boy allowed himself to reply with one of his own. He couldn't help noticing how different they both were. Where he made sure to keep his teeth covered during every scrape, his boss went in another direction. And as the swollen gaps amid the Andrews' ivory piano keys grew day by day, his smile appeared to do so too. 'Take him the envelope now and tell him we'll arrange something for next Friday as well. An extra two-fifty for his service if he's a good little nipper.'

'I understand.'

'We're in the end game now, Tall Boy!'

Tall Boy reiterated his previous reply.

Careful not to disturb the arrays of wires hooked onto Andrews, his employee lifted the small, heavy envelope off the desk,. Having fingered it between his two palms for a moment, he turned to leave and was just at the door when his boss called after him, determined to have the last word: 'He really better make sure I get some action.' Each of Andrews' words were dour and carefully considered, each of his syllables landing like pebbles dropped into a small pool of water. His was a voice you could never mistake.

Tall Boy shut the door and moved the envelope to his jacket pocket. He could feel a trusty shape beside it, *the* trusty shape. No matter what he wore he wedged the shape in such a way that he could flick it out at the slightest hint of risk. Careful that its serrated metal edge didn't slice into the envelope, he and his insurance policy set about their mission. If a blade could smile, he and it were baring their teeth alike.

Beneath the moon's discerning eye, a police car turned the corner. It was an hour when both police officers within wanted to be asleep in the cradling curve of a loved one. Instead, it wasn't dreams which met them, it was Sesame Street – bad name, everyone in the town thought so. The street lay on the furthest east patch of the town and year after year encrusted itself further into Little Hodbury's landscape. For anyone who expected fluffy puppets, the brutalism of glorified drug dens, disused garages, and marauding teenagers disavowed them of that notion. There once had been a proposed project to make it part of a slicker one-way system, but that went the way of all multiculturalism and friendliness in the town. As had the suggestions to renovate the road into flats. If it was true that nature abhorred a vacuum, it was just as true that the town, a dyed-in-the-wool town brimming with circular policies beyond belief, abhorred the slightest whisper of change. It just wasn't the done thing; here, out with the old meant out with joy.

Of the town's begrudged changes, the only one to affect Sesame Street was the police force's new initiative. And yet, if anything, it had bred a symbiotic relationship. Little Hodbury's policing was now handled by the nearest neighbouring town's force, whose sourness was essentially gospel, all the way to Police Chief John Harbottle and his recent insistence on a specific kind of police vest at the top of the tree.

'Christ, Tommy,' pleaded Aspinwall to her police partner, 'can't we take it off for five minutes?'. All her energy which wasn't going into being dismayed was going into tugging at parts of her clothing. Egg fragments continued to fall out of her hair. Some of the more congealed blobs were dribbling down into areas of her vest she didn't know existed, and even when she removed a fragment its claggy silhouette stayed budged against her neck. Her police partner, Tommy Martindale, tried to stifle his giggle underneath a rich layer of pity.

Night shift, nine in the evening, and the pair had been pulled away from paperwork and blueberry muffins in the direction of Denise Rosalie's home. Nowadays, it experienced the thunderous footsteps of patrol boots as commonly as it did the clipped clatter of home-care nurse pumps. Rosalie had taken a turn for the worst in recent months, bereaved herself of the floral clutter she'd adored so dearly, and taken up ringing 999 with tales more and more outlandish. It had to be tonight when one of her tales wasn't so tall. Aspinwall and Martindale were barely on the woman's driveway when the first splatter of yolk touched their face. The barrage of eggs had rained down from a sharp, towering hill which overlooked the house's gardens. The children had managed to deposit over four cartons onto them before the police officers had managed to tail the under-age idiots. They'd outpaced the pair just as quickly in the labyrinth of cul-de-sacs and alleys, leaving the shelly and sticky, yellow-white mass as the only evidence of the crime. As for Rosalie, the only consolation the pair could offer her was they had sated the teenagers' appetite enough that they wouldn't attempt the practical joke again this side of winter.

Then the command from dispatch came through. Police Chief Harbottle wanted them to do a routine check on Sesame

Street. Ever since the Perry kidnapping, he wanted the felony hotspots checked regularly – no, not just checked, their obnoxious head honcho wanted them patrolled thoroughly for a good quarter-of-an-hour. And when the head honcho gave orders, his stooges jumped to attention, stood upright, and clicked their heels – or else.

'No, no, pull over, please,' Aspinwall said while another blob of shell and yolk dribbled down the nape of her neck and began building its sticky home between her shoulder blades.

'We're here, anyway,' Martindale tittered back. She made sure to flick the gloopiest blob into his eye.

The headlights, in the gloom of Little Hodbury, picked out a row of storage units for the nearest flat complex. Where black paint used to coat nearly all of them, it now provided a patchwork covering for the uneven floor and the storage units provided new and exciting canvasses for people with too much brawn and spray paint. At this end of the street, there was hardly any difference between the road and pavement and the sinking paving slabs united with the weathered cobbles. The police car pulled in – if that's possible when one irregular bump of ground is as notched and uneven as any other – to one of the few areas without a carpet of shattered glass and discarded nitrous oxide canisters. Even when the car was still, PC Martindale kept the headlamps on; a year ago, he'd chased a suspect down here and had a shovel flung out of some darkened recess into the back of his head. The suspect had been arrested, and the shovel had had a good verbal assault from Martindale after he'd placed his attacker in the car, yet it had instilled a solid wariness within him. It was one of the few call-outs to leave him physically scarred, a slight swell etched behind right ear. While it wasn't a grandiose war wound of some sort, he did call it his 'spidey sense' since it did perennially stung whenever he went somewhere dangerous; tonight he couldn't deny a slight tingle was emanating from it.

Aspinwall was first out of the car. Before Martindale even had his hat on, she had launched herself into the street, regarding the car door as nothing more than a nuisance, and removed her protective vest. While he grabbed his torch to do what the many shattered streetlamps didn't, she was already dragging her hands down the vest's inside. The first few scrapes came away plastered in gooey mess, her hands stickier every time she removed them. In the time it took Aspinwall to put it back on with even a modicum of comfort, Martindale's canvas of the obvious hiding spots for druggy miscreants was over. He chose not to mention the smattering of egg fragments still clustered in her wilting blonde hair.

After she'd rearranged herself, the two of them started to walk up and down. Almost.

'What do you reckon happened to them?' she asked.

Martindale was a few steps ahead of her, his feet slackening to a halt when the question cut open the atmosphere and allowed emotion to start engorging itself. It was a conversation she had asked the day before. And the day before. And the day before that. In fact, every day from a fortnight ago – two weeks which might as well have been two aeons stretching out before them like immeasurable battlefields.

'I don't know, Heather.'

Martindale knew full well that Aspinwall was asking because she needed reassurance. You were taught in training never to make promises, and that applied to your fellow officers and constables as much as bereaved families. Even without the police officer's manual, it would've broken his own moral code too. As a man of facts, he knew survival wasn't one of those – death was though. It always was – in the end. The salient difference was the speed at which the miserable conclusion approached. The Perry family, taken in the middle of the night seemingly by the darkness itself, what could any rational man promise about their safe return? His time on the force was only a month or so longer than hers, yet Aspinwall used this gap as a crutch.

'Is that why we're patrolling here more often?' she pressed on. 'To find them? To find those two children?' For whatever reason she was less resigned to his answer than before.

Why did she continue like this? Why did she want reminding of the tragedy. *He* didn't want reminding.

'Maybe so. Maybe... so,' he muttered with a sigh, before moving forward. He felt he had to, because stopping was as good as quitting. If you allowed life's weariness to feed into the bleakness of the job, the two would feast off one another until neither had anything left to give. Put plainly, it was the ouroboros that had killed off a few of his colleagues, either to early graves or retirement houses.

Martindale took another step. His torch beam flitted over the storage units on the left of the street. Streetlamps unearthed over the various years by drunken drivers and allowed to topple still protruded from two of the units, but even those which looked intact were full of nothing more than echoes. The police constables knew only one was regularly used; a stubborn family of rodents refused to evict themselves, making more use of the space than any past tenant. Mother nature disowned them, never mind the rest of the town.

Heartbeat-like, their feet crunched the dislodged pebble-dashing. Aspinwall walked up and down and once or twice tried to pry a storage unit shutter open and jammed her beam of light underneath. Only two yielded. Martindale was faring little better, having diverted off to the remains of a bonfire at another section of the street, next to an abandoned caravan, (well half of one, and half an *upturned* one at that). The only thing even resembling a missing family there was the nest of insects sat atop a disarray of fly-tipped bin bags surging with food so mouldy it was now jelly. When he aimed the beam of light through one of the caravan's countless windows, he saw more dirt than anything. Kicking a single-use barbeque aside, his torch picked out only the remains of heroin needles.

But – these were the head honcho's orders.

A head honcho who was currently huddled in his office, surrounded by schemes of his own. Police Chief Harbottle was a short bespectacled man, his hair the shade of a used colostomy bag's insides. When he wasn't sporting a pair of pince-nez in an attempt to give himself a sense of style, the man wore a pair of thick-rimmed and oversized jam jars. Along with his rodent nose and scrunched-up cheeks, he would often give his subordinate the feeling they were on the end of a frotteur's rub. Nobody knew they were nearer to the truth than they might imagine.

From his office window the town was hidden behind a knot of hills, hugging the largest one like grieving families around a coffin funeral, but he knew the expanse of his empire. Every artery of the police force flowed through him to some degree. It was a beauty to behold.

However, his routine dictated that at half-past nine his realm of policing was swapped for another, one which if it was interrupted made him bare his teeth. A knock on the door fired around the room, just as the man's belt had loosened and his knees were feeling less enclosed by fabric. Having switched the lights off and piled sheafs of paper into immense stacks, he'd hoped to hide the blue glow of his laptop screen from anyone walking past his office. Harbottle's final telephone call through to dispatch, concerning Aspinwall and Martindale, was done, which meant to all intents and purposes he was home and hunkered down to enjoy the night's festivities.

'It's from Andrews, sir,' came the slick and unassuming voice.

The towers of paper couldn't stop the clipped monologue. It battered its way right into the police chief's ears. This explained it – it was that Andrews-fella's puppy-dog. Police chiefs crouched behind their desk, and bent double over a computer screen with their trousers around their ankles at that, were never a sight to be expected, he realised. Yet of all the people to walk away from the sight without a batted eyelid, one of that man's fellas was best prepared.

The unassuming voice battered the air in two again. From behind his desk, Harbottle only saw a silhouette. The light around the doorframe gave the man the air of something not quite there, something more prone to angelic visitations than errands. The voice spoke more – some congratulatory rhetoric, the sort of thing he'd usually lap up with self-centred relish. After a brief request for what Harbottle ought to do next, a flying square shape leapt over the piles of officialdom, landing with an undignified thud beside his feet. Picking up the firm, square package, Harbottle turned it over. Inserting his thumbnail beneath the flap on one side, the envelope sprang open and a stream of ten-pound notes slid onto his lap and exposed crown jewels.

Before the police chief even had time to say a thank you, light flooded into the room and then went away as soon as it arrived. It was just him and the blue light from the laptop between his legs. Never one for fancy technology, this laptop – this entire scheme – was possibly the one exception he made. All he needed to do with plug in one extra wire and his laptop revealed covert footage hijacked from two police constables' bodycams. He waited with bated breath for the signal to attune. It never occurred to him that he wasn't the sole viewer of the video feed, and that when Andrews' puppy-dog got the system working, he had given his own boss a secret back door to the feed.

Harbottle wasn't quite sure when this entire realm he'd unlocked had begun. He could just about place his criminal connections as being forged little over a year ago. It was a simple affair – he wanted a few people removing, and since they were the enemy of his enemy, an alliance forged itself. Ever since, Andrews would reel Harbottle back into his dungeon of deceit once more and give the man an instruction to implement or a sentence to be carried out to the letter of *his* law. As for his true love, the reason he allowed Andrews to reel him back in, the all-consuming that ravaged his every scintilla of being, he didn't know when that had begun. He imagined men cleverer than he would say it had been initiated when he first saw a paper cut on his mother's finger and wincing sensation flit across her face. Or maybe it was when he used to watch the other toddlers topple and scrape their knees on the floor.

With the monochrome image now appearing on screen, he was now too engrossed to notice that the money splattered across his lap was in reality ten-pound notes padded out with monopoly money. He didn't notice he'd only seen the door shut, not Andrews' puppy-dog pass through it. And he assumed the heavy breathing coming from the far side of the room was just an echo of his own.

On the screen was the bodycam view of the storage unit. *The* storage unit. Not that Aspinwall or Martindale knew that.

And, more crucially, they didn't know about Gruff within. It wasn't a name the man cared about either way: it simply did its purpose in the same manner that the muscly, bad-tempered brute did his.

On Monday a fortnight ago, his boss paid him. Handsomely. On Tuesday or Wednesday, he deposited the generous, illegitimate sum in his bank account. And on Thursday, he found the house and turned it into his private playground.

The van's plates were swapped the day before, and so all Gruff needed to do was pull the vehicle into the cul-de-sac, and then proceed to the house's patio door. It was late at night and so the oldest child – the girl, probably about fifteen – was still downstairs, standing next to the kitchen island while watching some stupid film. The girl, Sally, didn't notice the intruder until one of his shoes caught the entry rug's curved edge; he clamped his left hand around her mouth and extended his leg into the back of her knees before screaming or running away was even a vague notion. Sally tried to twist and face her attacker, they always did, but even sinking her teeth into his hand didn't register before he'd smacked her forehead twice with his other hand. One harder slap later and she crossed the divide from flailing to unconscious.

Extracting the boy, Peter, and mother was barely a problem either. The boy had been asleep and so he managed to cart him out of there in one fell swoop. Any fight the boy posed was more out of having his sleep and dreams of planes and weird marshmallow creatures curtailed. Not that it mattered: Peter shared the same fate as Sally, unconscious in the back of the van.

When Gruff took their mother, Susanna, he didn't even stop to indulge in the erotic smell of her bedsheets. During the entire operation, the only evidence he had been there was a lamp pushed off the bedside cabinet. There was one brief moment where it looked like the mother would get away, yet all it took was yanking the bedsheet from beneath her bare feet and keeping his phlegmatic gaze on her as her head and the bedpost connected. Down like a bowling pin. Once he'd paused to ensure her chest still rose and fell, he continued to obey his orders and carted the family to a storage unit on Sesame Street where they stayed tied up.

By now, it was the Monday two weeks after the bank transaction. Since then, he hadn't left the unit, his orders dictating he sate himself with foods prepared prior to his arrival. Once or twice, the hostages even partook. Not that they had the energy, but none tried to escape, and so his job was simply as overseer. If anything, the lack of chance to use his fists was the most disappointing part of events. He did everyday throw a punch, or maybe four, in the family's direction, but it was again on orders. His fists landed on target, in Sally's case bad enough to cause purple-ish welts around her chin. He'd repeat this at the same time each day, which robbed Gruff of violence and its onanistic pleasure, but it wasn't his show. The feed from the camera watching it all went somewhere Gruff wasted no concern over.

Today, however, was when the plan became the *master*plan. Once again acting under orders, Gruff carefully loosened the eldest child's bonds while she slept. The three were bound to a ramshackle bed frame screwed into the wall and by now an impression of it was chafed onto their spines like some red henna tattoo. During these last few seconds, Gruff enacted yet another of the orders – to nudge the eldest child awake when the police car pulled onto Sesame Street.

Caught in the No Man's Land between staying alert, greyhound-like and her desperate desire for sleep, Sally's jerk back to reality was a resistant but quick one. Her body outpaced her brain and curled into the foetal position. It took a few more seconds for her eyes to be so fast. On any other day, the sensation which greeted her morning, noon, and night was the metal bindings scraping another layer of skin from her hands. Today, they didn't, and she realised that possibly all those years of basketball might have a use. It gave her a nice group of friends, a social life, a few prospective girlfriends – and now it gave her the advantage of speed.

One dove-like tug broke apart the loosened cuffs. A few scrapes and scabs wouldn't stop her either, nor her arm which no longer bent in the right way. Burying her fist in Gruff's face, blessing him with his own remedy, would have to come another day. The teenager took to her bruised feet. She propelled herself under the two-foot gap beneath the unit door before either her mum or brother could flicker awake and see the miracle. They couldn't notice then Gruff's knowing smile watching the girl run.

Outside the storage unit, Sally had no clue where she was. Her feet were more purple than pink, every ounce of her energy going into keeping herself moving. She found herself bounding around a skip, tumbling over a patch of wire fencing, and briefly catching sight of a torch beam picking her out.

Then the hulking figure slammed into her. The wall of a skip smashed into her face. Over the last few days, she didn't realise her sense of pain could heighten any further. Now, from the tickle of Gruff's beard to the sharp jabbing sensation of his muscled elbow into her back, her body was alive with a new sensation. A sensation which summoned a scream from somewhere she never knew existed. With mainly his weight as the weapon he could fire, she felt his crushing blow knock her again into the wall of the skip. Not content just to slam into her, he now delivered half a dozen punches. Her neck broke no more onerously than the crackers from the monster's supper two nights ago. It took Sally a moment, her last moment in fact, to realise the screech of a pained dog filling the night sky wasn't in fact a dog at all.

Even in her very last moment, she couldn't keep the blood out of her eyes to see the figure of PC Aspinwall dart towards them.

The eternity of Sally's escape had taken no longer than a minute, and it was twenty seconds into it when the police constables spotted her. Aspinwall's torch beam highlighted the girl first, not that beneath her seared pink and mottled grey flesh she could tell the gender. Martindale's torch caught up a moment later, picking out the second shape haring along at a breakneck pace. The ruthless thing had watched, waited until the girl entered the police officers' line of vision, and then launched himself in the blithe assumption his legs would follow. By the time either torch beam made out the two figures properly, the scene was red above anything else.

Aspinwall was the first to give chase. Martindale heard his partner shout something, but with the rush of blood and adrenaline he hadn't time to decipher what. Like a monstrous slide of vomit, no sooner had the hulking figure delivered the final punch when he tore back towards the storage unit. His beard and its pungent aromas of ready meals left a slipstream which Aspinwall seemed to lock onto. Unsheathing her batons in space of a palpitated heartbeat, she knew the leviathan had it in himself to leave her only able to eat food through a straw. She continued after him anyway. A few seconds later, she was out of her partner's sight, her eyes and those watching via her bodycam trained on the killer.

She would never know the detonation building in between her boss' thighs; he watched on, lapping up every blood drop, flicking his hand back and forth with greater and greater speed.

At the storage container, she was moving beneath the door before sense prevailed. A carpet of glass shards greeted her. The crunch of it underneath her feet could be heard all over Sesame Street. A super-charge of adrenaline was lighting her body up. Yet even with it, the punch knocked her sideways, hard enough to send the pepper spray she'd been removing from her belt off into the darkness. Her face boomeranged across the unit. Like the girl she'd just watched die, her face had barely time to slam into the metal wall when Gruff's next assault arrived. As his knee reflexed outwards, so did her back. Seeds of pain sprouted all across her left side.

Why wasn't the protective vest doing its job? She might as well have run into the fray wearing woolly pyjamas. She registered a tiny tingle from the useless garment, nothing else. Little did she know it was actually doing its job perfectly. The second a connection forged between the vest and Gruff's latest attack, Andrews' body lit up with an electric charge.

Gruff struck again, this time with his elbow. As instructed, he was to aim for the chest, and he did so, delivering a blow with enough force to shatter four of Aspinwall's ribs. For all the Perry family were joining in the chorus of shrieks, Gruff and Aspinwall's world was penetrated by them and them alone. And it was a world in Gruff's favour. The heap before him was one big bruise. Despite this, she refused the floor as her death bed. Half on her feet, she gripped the baton with all her might and flung it at his head.

It missed by a mile, quiescently landing among the remains of one of Gruff's ready-meals. Enough was enough now. He could see the bodycam on Aspinwall's chest was still on, and so knew that Andrews' would have had his sadomasochistic fun. Savage and repugnant, or maybe rapturous and orgasmic, one final lance of pain skewered her body. Her chest, her shoulders, her back, her diaphragm. Each roared like a pride of lions.

Little did she know, both Harbottle and Andrews were screaming too.

For Andrews, the screen in front of him was nothing more than an eruption of white noise, flake after flake of TV snow raining down across where the footage was.

Martindale's muted feed continued blaring away to itself in the bottom corner, showing him still with the rent body of Sally as he tried to perform CPR and fail miserably, caught between duty to a corpse and to his partner. Adolf Andrews simply sat, alone with the glorious simulations of pain, his potent ecstasy drowning out any other thoughts until the beaming grin ceased being paralysed into his face.

Harbottle's screams were of a different calibre entirely.

They had begun as all the best screams do, the sight of blood and battered body parts detonating his lower region in ways he thought possible only in his dreams. A minute later, he was lying spreadeagled on the floor, trousers discarded across his chair; his newest struggle was regulating his breathing. It was a struggle he was destined never to win, his lower region demanding every iota of energy. The dizzying, speckled pattern sloshing beneath his closed eyelids swamped his vision. Warmth, blissful and undiluted. His muscles were spasming, endorphins and happiness replacing blood as the life force within his blood stream.

When a sensation spread from his leg, he assumed it was more of the same. Then he snapped his eyes open to see not euphoria but pain. Springing up in his right foot. Caressing his left knee. Bulldozing his hip. The glimpse of the man above him wasn't ecstasy. When the man's knife gambolled across his line of sight, it would find a new body part to open, darting to and fro until it found its final home. The heavy breath of the figure filled his ears, the waft of expensive cologne and unsavoury crisps reaching his nose. His eyes were shut before the blood reached the floor.

The figure's work continued over the next hour, his trusty knife doing things no-one else's could. The laptop beside the pair was frozen, showing Martindale's bodycam full screen. The twisted body of Heather Aspinwall and the slit throats of Peter and Susanna Perry in cinematic view.

It was five weeks since Heather Aspinwall died, three since her coffin walked its own road to the crematorium. When his dog, Truffle, had died, Tommy Martindale took a week's leave; when his mum had died, two weeks' leave; when he underwent heart surgery, four weeks' leave. Since Heather's slow descent behind the maroon curtain and into the crematorium's bowels, even a second's leave was the last thing on his mind. For every day that crawled by, Tommy was in work. He refused to accept that it could define him, grief. How he was the one helping to sort through her stuff either, he wasn't sure. He treated it as the honour it was though.

It was at her funeral that he learned of her two miscarriages. The battered notebook which he'd unearthed in her house the day before suddenly made sense: two little names inscribed in red pen on the first page, with dates next to them, all crossed out, the ink blotched from singular drops of water. Was it grief for them that had driven her on? Was it why she'd thrown protocol to the wind and given chase? Was it why she'd been beaten to a pulp?

He carried on. Because of her.

Today's patrol was near the riverside. This section flowed behind a row of small cottages lined up like soldiers at roll call at the uppermost part of the village. They were the kind of quintessential British Arcadia you assumed was for show and nothing more. Tommy half-reckoned the smoke billowed from their chimneys and their logs fires kept ablaze just to maintain the image. Ms. Rosalie, the woman outside whose home he and Heather were egged, now lived in one of these. Since moving a fortnight ago, she'd only made one phone call to the police. The woman's two widowed sisters were apparently back in touch with her too, having bought the houses either side and now spending their days watching their sister turn the garden into a paragon of beauty. Already, Ms. Rosalie had found a new reason to stop her knees atrophying, and so no matter the weather she spent every day either in the garden with some secateurs or in the kitchen making herself a cup of tea to accompany that day's pruning. She'd even found the time to turn some of the verdure into paradisical displays which might festoon the street's living rooms.

At least someone's life was going uphill.

Steep footpaths coursed below the cottages, a river below that, and a sparse huddle of reeds and mulchy grass below that. The last time anything of interest had happened along the riverbank, it'd been here as well, as an ejected kayaker struck a series of muddy rock formations – the rocks and frothing underflows hadn't released his submerged body for a considerable number of hours.

Those steep footpaths, hardly more than a metre wide, were where the homeless man currently led the policeman. As the two rounded onto the lowermost part of the path, he stopped. Crouching slightly under the creaking curve of his own spine, he directed PC Martindale's gaze downward towards a point in the river where the rapids slowed slightly. A sea of foam spilled around the clumps of reed, weed, and rock. There hung at their centre a mantle of misshapen lumps, held together by the tightest of threads.

Clutching his radio in one hand, he grabbed a long, thin log to use as a makeshift crook in the other. Martindale allowed himself to topple down the bank slightly, his feet gaining purchase on a tougher patch of silt at the very last moment. His arms flailed outward to steady himself – and the crook hit the murky water with a splash that coated his trousers and boots. Within seconds, a waggle of his feet announced the churned silt depositing around his socks. Stretching his hand over a particularly frothy patch of foam, the policeman attempted a grasp at the crook. His hand came away containing only the river's mucus. Wiping the disgusting mix of slime and forth off on his trousers, he didn't hazard another stab at the crook. Instead, crouching near the misshapen lump, he could only watch the tool commence its journey into the watery ever-after.

When at last he did grasp the lump, it was only by the very tip of his boot, the other half submerged in grassy quagmire. After he'd manoeuvred it out of the reeds and soaked his boot thrice over, he saw it wasn't what the homeless man had suggested; it was far too sticky and gelatinous to be ordinary fly-tipping. One marshy slap of the water later, Martindale had secured it on the bank, at least enough so it wouldn't drift back down stream. Every tremor rippled the pustules swelling along its surface, a few exploding with noises too similar to a man throwing up for the policeman's tastes.

He wondered why he wasn't calling people on his radio already – the way the mass acted, it might be radioactive, some poisonous chemical experiment. Perhaps he cared for his life a little less now.

His examination of the mass, having found another stick, was a quick one. It was bloated, purpling around every knot and craggy contusion. Obviously, some kind of saw had been taken to each of the distended sections, never totally though. Black and purple discolouration frequently flushed with raw, red-like scabbing. There was section around the middle not sanguinary like the rest of the heap – mostly swamped by an area where the substances had turned into nothing but jelly, a small triangle of white plastic poked out.

Gripping it carefully, leaves under each finger, he started to tug the object out from the mutilation. It was time to suppress another gag. In the few moments where it hadn't been coated in thick semi-liquid, Tommy had made out a few letters. He was on his radio a second after.

The station needed to be told he'd found the remains of Chief Harbottle.

About the Author

Because his obsessive love of *Doctor Who* and horror films wasn't nerdy enough, Ben is currently studying Latin, Ancient Greek, and Ancient Classical History at Newcastle University. When he isn't doing that, he's either confusing all and sundry or writing short stories and reviews for various outlets, drinking copious cups of tea, knitting, or buying far too many waistcoats, bow ties, and velvet jackets.

SCARS

Rhys Hughes

After they exhausted themselves with passion, he slumped beside her and she turned on her side. She ran her fingers over his body, tracing the scars that provided proof of his interesting life. For decades he had worked as a war correspondent and now he was resting, his powerful muscles relaxed, in this charming cottage on the outskirts of a quaint village. She spoke in a soft voice, her dark eyes wide.

'Tell me the stories of your scars. Each one must be associated with a memory. Your body is a book that the world has written. Recite to me this book, the tales of your adventures.'

'But I have already told you,' he answered.

'I want to hear them again.'

'There are many. Where shall I begin?'

She reached out and traced the jagged line on his left bicep. 'With this one. How did you acquire this mark?'

He glanced at his arm and smiled, then he gazed at the ceiling as if it was a cinema screen and the film showing there was one in which he was the star. He said, 'Cabo Delgado.'

She nodded but remained silent, waiting for him.

He licked his lips dreamily.

'That's in Mozambique, in the far north of the country. I was coming out of my hotel when a guy pounced. He was alone but he had a knife, a small one. He slashed at me and cut through my jacket but then he lost his balance. He wasn't a fighter, just an opportunist thief and he was nervous. Maybe this was the first time he tried to rob anyone. He fell and sprawled in the dust and began weeping.'

'Yes, I remember now. Who was the woman you had at the time? Her name was Carolina, wasn't it?'

'No, she was someone else. I think it was Gabriela or maybe Isabela, I don't exactly remember. They tend to merge in my mind. But the scar on my bicep, I know about that.'

'So many dusky beauties in your life!'

'A perk of the job. In wartime, a woman is a comfort. That's obvious, surely? I've already explained.'

'What about this one?'

She was touching a longer and deeper scar on his lower abdomen. His smile was bleak, his eyes glazed a little. He said, 'Bosnia, an hour before sunset. A rocket landed in the town square. I was sitting and drinking at a café table on a terrace. An attack wasn't expected at that time. There was an explosion. Shrapnel shredded the canopy of the umbrella above me. A piece of metal cut my stomach.'

'You finished your glass of wine before fleeing?'

He snorted with laughter.

'What do you expect? It's the job. You stop feeling panic. It's not the same as numbness, it's deader than that. But you still function. And then you recover. That's how it is.'

'Who was your woman during that conflict?'

'Nadija, I think. Ana too.'

'But which of the pair came first?'

'I probably had them at the same time. It's all a blur, too many years have passed. I know the scar.'

She stroked a puckered groove on his right thigh.

'And this one? Liberia?'

He shook his head and the sweat on his brow glistened as it caught the moonlight streaming through the window. He was like a demigod, supine, mahogany dark on the white sheets, and in his element now, recalling his exploits, downplaying them as he always did, his hyper masculine style a pretence no longer. It had become real, tempered in war zones all over the world, preserved in the resin of spectacular danger. She wondered with an almost audible pang what he would do if she rose and departed. Continue to tell his tales aloud, not to himself but to his scars, as if they had senses of their own, active intelligence.

'Sierra Leone,' he corrected her, 'and it happened when an insurgent high on a cocktail of drugs lunged at me with a bayonet. He didn't have a rifle to fix it on. He had converted it into a crude spear by lashing it to a broom handle. His balance was poor, his aim was bad. I must assume he was going for my throat. I stepped back. He lunged, muttering gibberish, but slipped as he did so. The point only gouged my leg but the blade was rusty and it gave me tetanus.'

'Your woman? Some name like Katie?'

'Almost. Kadie. I can hardly see her face in my mind. They come and go. There were others in Sierra Leone too, but their names elude me now. Who cares? It doesn't matter.'

'I'm sure you mentioned Liberia to me?'

'That's the scar on the *other* thigh.' He moved his legs apart and she saw high up, on his left leg, a zigzag. She leaned forward, kissed it, aware he would feel nothing. His scar tissue had no nerves. He was a hard mass of unfeeling flesh. But a beautiful man, too composed to be real. And his mind was scarred too. It must be!

'Barbed wire,' he said, and shifted his weight.

'It tore through your clothes?'

'Certainly, it tends to do that. We had to cross disputed territory. None of the militias really knew what they were doing. They put down wire and mines at random, never mapping them. They were insane or drunk. It was almost comical. They even mined their own ground, blew their own limbs off, fired bursts at their own men. I was caught on the wire but cut myself free with snips. It was nothing special. The wire was clean. No tetanus on that occasion. Just some blood loss.'

'What woman did you have then? Or women?'

'Beatrice. Theresa. Mary.'

Her lips descended to his kneecap. This kneecap was dented, it had an eroded crater in it that she could gently explore with her tongue, just as if she was licking the liquid centre out of a luxury chocolate. He was silent, passive, enduring her attentions without excitement or rancour. Inhuman, she thought to herself. Too manly, too nonchalant. Passivity could be the most virile of reactions. A paradox.

He said, 'Shot in Albania. A sniper in a bedroom window. I wasn't a designated target for him. He wasn't a regular soldier, just a *franc-tireur* taking a potshot. Everybody was shooting at everything back then. Later he apologised and bought me a glass of *rakia* in a local tavern. I couldn't walk without a crutch for six months. I was operated on by a specialist in Ireland. They have the best knee surgeons in the world. Plenty of practice, that's why, the IRA, kneecappings.'

'Dare I ask you the same question again?'

'Women? Dozens of them. Mirela, Rovena, Juliana, Mimoza. I never keep count. You should know that.'

She moved her gaze down his shins, both with multiple cuts across them. She touched these scars one by one, as if plucking the strings of a strange harp. It was a moment when the first tightening went through his body. Was she playing or tuning him? Without pausing, she asked, 'This one here. What caused it?' and before he could respond she began to tell him herself, her voice low, husky.

'You were harassed by a crowd in Algeria. Then a man in a burnoose ran out of the mob and swiped at you with a scimitar. But it was blunt, an old useless thing, an heirloom, and you dodged and it only nicked you. It meant nothing. The crowd fell silent and parted for you. But this scar next to it was the result of a knife fight in India. And the one next to that was from a stone thrown in Afghanistan.'

He shrugged and creased the sheets around his shoulders doing so. His legs twitched just a little. He sighed.

She said, 'With every wound, at least one woman.'

He ignored this comment.

'Too many scars, too many stories,' he said, 'and not all of them with a connection to war. Some were accidents. See that one down there on my ankle? I was nine years old, riding a bicycle without brakes down a slope, the steepest gradient in my town. I lost control halfway and came off, a dramatic lesson in physics. I tumbled through the air, over a spiked fence, and landed in a garden. I was lucky.'

'Yes,' she agreed, and there was a wistfulness in her tone. 'You are a lucky man, the luckiest I ever met.'

Before he could reply to this, she added, 'And this one? On the sole of your foot? Another misadventure?'

'I trod on a caltrop, a barbed one, in East Timor.'

'What is that exactly?'

He was extremely bland. 'An area denial weapon. Nothing special. It was hidden in the long grass.'

'I suppose she is just a blur as well?'

'Verónica was her name, but yes, she's hazy. They are all hazy. As the world turns, everything changes.'

He shifted again, perhaps waiting for her to suggest that he turn over, so she could begin on all the scars on his back. But there were still many on his front side she hadn't stroked or kissed. On his neck, his cheek, his forehead, along his jawline, one bisecting his lips, all down his forearms, over his wrists, his hands. Each one had a story connected with it. These anecdotes were short, brutal, dismissive, evoking nothing. She glanced at the clock and her voice changed.

'It's getting late. I am tired, so very tired.'

'Then sleep,' he responded.

'Tired, very tired. Let's not do all the scars tonight. Let's do just one more, the biggest, the worst.'

He was frowning. 'Which is that?'

'The scar directly over your heart, my love. That one. Deepest of all, deeper than I can ever reach.'

'What are you talking about? I have no scar there.'

He was clenching his fists.

She said, 'Over your heart, dear. My fingers can't probe it, my tongue won't touch the bottom. It's really remarkable. It's the most noticeable of all your wounds. It's astounding. And I am tired, so very tired. I am tired of what you do to me, the way you scar my life. You can't see those scars but they are real. And your heart-'

At last, he was agitated.

'There is no scar over my heart!'

'Yes there is, darling. Let me narrate now. That's only fair. I shall tell you the story associated with it.'

'You're playing games,' was his verdict.

'You once told me that everything is a game, both of chance and skill, but that it's a question of luck if we acquire the skill, and it's the skill that gets us the luck. It's all a game.'

'But this one is *stupid*. It's pointless.'

'Pointless? I don't believe it. The deepest scar must have been carved by a very sharp point indeed.'

'Please, you are giving me a headache.'

'No, that's not what I want. No pain in your head. The scar over your heart is the focus of the ache.'

'Damn you. What do you know about-'

She waited respectfully.

'Anything!' he spat, but he didn't sit up in bed. He was too valiant to protect himself, too trusting. He knew he was blessed by destiny, a special case, scarred but unscathed, a hero. He felt triumphant already. It wasn't a pathetic outburst but the plain truth. What did she know about anything? The control belonged to him, all of it.

She spoke softly, clearly:

'This is how you earned the scar over your heart. It's easy. You were sent to cover a war in Lebanon. You drove to the train station and parked there. But instead of catching the train to the airport, you boarded a train going in the opposite direction. You never left the country. The messages you sent me were full of lies. So where did you go? You went to see her. For three weeks. My own sister!'

He said nothing but shook with silent laughter.

Her voice was still mild.

'That's how you won the scar over your heart, and it's a miracle that you only learned about it now.'

She reached out to grope under the pillow.

His laughter turned into anger. He bellowed, 'For the last time, you little idiot, I have no scar there!'

She continued to grope. The kitchen knife was still in its position. The earlier passion hadn't dislodged it.

That was another surprise. He was speaking but not about the woman he had been with. He was saying words that were meaningless to her. He was boasting about the dangers he had to endure, about how he deserved every reward he had ever claimed.

'Nonetheless,' she said, 'You have a scar,' and while he continued to brag, she added, 'over your heart.'

He finally made a move, turning towards her. But it was already too late. By rotating his body, he succeeded only in pushing the blade deeper than it would otherwise have gone.

They both fell back, lying on the bed like unsheathed knives. But her real knife was sheathed, safely.

And later she conceded he was right.

Scars are proof of healing.

The wound that never heals will never leave a scar. The real scars had been in her, but none were stories.

Not stories worth risking the telling, anyway.

About the Author

Rhys Hughes is a short story writer slowly transitioning into a novelist. His recent novel *The Devil's Halo* is set in Hell's Waiting Room. Another recent novel, *Growl at the Moon*, is a weird Western about a man who is also a dog. He is currently working on a novel called *The Inside-Out Story*, set in an overgrown garden that turns out to be a pocket universe.

MAD MONEY

Paul Magrs

Mr and Mrs Braun were both almost thirty, with two small children and not very much money. They were saving for a deposit on a house of their own, but it was hard. Mr Braun worked in a shop and Mrs Braun was hoping to get back into the job market when their kids – two little girls under five – were both at school.

They hadn't had a holiday together for seven years. Their last had been a wild week in Benidorm, not long after they had met. This was their first time away from home since then, and it was quite a different story. A long weekend at the seaside much closer to home than Benidorm was as much as they could afford. They were staying at a budget hotel in a town that had seen better days.

'This was a mistake,' Kelly kept saying. 'I wish we'd stayed at home.'

'It's a change,' Terry said through gritted teeth. 'It'll do us good.'

Already they were at the point where they both wanted to scream. The hotel room had seemed comfortable at first, and large enough for them all. A family room, with a large bed for mummy and daddy and a set of bunk beds for the two little girls. The little girls spent the whole time much too excited about being away from home.

'This is a horrible holiday,' Kelly said, looking out of the window that was fixed so it couldn't even open to let in a breath of sea air. 'It's more like being in prison.'

That very morning the two of them had argued about a

news story on the TV in their hotel room. It seemed that a young boy with dreadful internal injuries was being kept on a life support machine, suspended between life and death. This was in a town in the south, and the whole nation had been watching with bated breath to see what would become of him. His tragic story and his weeping parents had caught the imagination of the whole nation.

'They should switch him off,' Kelly had said abruptly. 'It's the merciful thing to do.'

'*What?!*' cried Terry. He couldn't believe what he was hearing from his lovely wife. He wanted to cup his hands over his daughters' ears to prevent them from hearing this. 'That's so heartless of you.'

Kelly shook her head. 'No, it isn't. They have been told, those parents, by the best medical experts that there can be no good outcome. That little boy is brain dead and there is no hope. Don't you understand that? There is *no* hope. All they are doing is prolonging his misery, and their own.'

The news report was showing people gathering outside the hospital where the boy was hooked up to his machines. There were reporters and religious freaks and people who had been touched by the story on the news. They were singing songs and chanting loudly up at the hospital windows.

'But there are always more opinions to be got,' Terry said. 'There are different experts to consult, all over the world. There are experimental treatments they could save up for. Miracle cures! There's always hope, isn't there?'

Their two little girls were engrossed in some kind of game on the laptop. Thankfully, they weren't paying attention to mummy and daddy's serious conversation.

How could children understand matters of life and death like this? They would only be upset by such talk, Terry thought.

Kelly rolled her eyes at him. 'You have to take the experts' word for it. No amount of praying or singing or sentimental claptrap is going to bring that kid back. No way. It's sad, but there it is. Those ... parasites gathering outside the hospital are only giving the parents false hope. It's cruel. We're all cruel parasites, just watching and paying so much attention to his story. They should leave him in private. Allow the little mite to have some dignity.'

Terry was gobsmacked by his wife's attitude. 'I can't believe you. What if it was one of our two? Wouldn't you do anything, cling onto any faint hope that you could keep them alive?'

And so, the two of them had argued, awkwardly, furiously, in the cloistered confines of their overheated hotel room. They had come to no very settled conclusions and had riled each other up a lot. That's when they had decided to brave the rain and the cold outside.

'Let's get some air,' Terry had said, doing his best to sound bright and cheery.

They dressed up their two little girls – Mia and Ariel – in their anoraks and mittens. It was very chilly and windy out. It was still some weeks before the summer season began, which was how the holiday was cheap enough for them to afford it.

They walked along the sea front, wind and rain lashing at them, and Kelly was swearing under her breath all the way.

'Look at the waves coming over the railings!' Terry cried, getting their girls to scream with excitement every time the surf crashed onto the path before them.

'Where's the beach?' Kelly shouted over the noise. 'You promised us a beach!'

Terry smiled at her, with a bit of a warning in his eyes. She wasn't trying hard enough, she realised. She needed to look as if she was having a nice time, for the sake of the girls.

'We are making special memories for them,' their father said. 'That's the most important thing.'

'Oh, right,' said Kelly.

She was still thinking about their argument over the brain-dead boy on TV. It had surprised her, how differently she and Terry felt about that story. Did that mean they had very different views about everything? She realised that they rarely actually sat down and talked about their views on important subjects. Mostly they focused on day-to-day problems and things they urgently needed to do or get. Their discussion this morning had been heated and it had given her a headache, which the noise of the surf was doing nothing to ease. It irritated her still that Terry had been so thick-headed as to disagree with her. She wondered what other opinions he might be harbouring that she might find silly or obnoxious?

Perhaps it was best – for the sake of sanity – not to think about it too much.

'Shall we go in for a snack?' she called over the noise of the whipping wind.

'What?' he frowned.

She pointed at the café at the end of the row of shops across the road. Its painted sign was faded but you could see it was called 'All Night Long.' The windows were obscured by net curtains and signs cut out of fluorescent card in the shape of stars. Pink and orange hand-written signs were advertising 'Cheezy Chips' and 'Crisps and Pop!'

'We can't afford to be eating and drinking in cafes every day,' Terry frowned. 'We went to that burger place yesterday. I thought we'd just pick up some things at the supermarket and have a kind of picnic in our room …'

The thought of going back into that room made Kerry start to panic. She led the way over the road and peered at the prices on the menu pinned to the window. 'It looks really cheap, actually,' she told him.

Terry had a look for himself. The prices were weirdly cheap, and there was a strange kind of nostalgia about the things that were on offer. Roly-poly and custard. Spaghetti hoops on toast. Ice cream floats.

'Oh, come on,' Kelly told him. 'It looks all right, doesn't it?'

The little girls were tired now, after all their dashing about in the rain. They were pink-cheeked from the cold.

'All right,' said Terry. 'Just for a snack.'

The bell tinkled when they went inside and the first thing Kelly thought was that they had stepped back in time. It was hard to say what gave her that impression, or what time she thought she had been transported into, exactly. It might have been the glass cabinet on the counter displaying cream buns and chocolate biscuits and freshly-cut sandwiches. It could have been the juke box which was playing rock 'n' roll songs from the 1950s. It might even have been the lurid paintings on the walls – tropical ladies with flowers in their hair and peaceful mountain scenes – which reminded her of pictures from her grandparents' home a long time ago.

'Oh, it's lovely,' Terry said, leading the girls to a table in the middle. 'I wonder why it's empty?'

Just then the café's owner came through the beaded curtain from her own quarters at the back. She was called Precious and she was a large lady of an age no one could be quite sure about. She had lived and worked here for a long time, but her life before that was shrouded in mystery. All kinds of stories were in circulation about the past lives of Precious from All Night Long.

'Hello there,' she beamed at them all. She wore a very colourful, jazzy-patterned blouse and skirt combination, with a gingham apron over the top. 'Please take your time choosing from our menu.'

The girls started shouting at once about what they wanted and Kerry wondered if she had any headache pills in her bag. She could do with the loo, she realised. It would be a few seconds away from her noisy family, at least. Is this what her life had become, she wondered. Glad to go and have a pee, just to get some peace at last?

'Is there a bathroom?' she asked Precious.

'Oh yes,' the café owner told her. 'Downstairs, in the basement.' Then she fixed Kelly with a strange look. It was a look that made Kelly shiver. What was that about? It was like Precious was trying to tell her something.

Up she got, leaving the others to pore over the hand-written menu and she found the stairs to the basement in the back corner of the café.

Down two flights of wooden stairs there was a gloomy open space with two doors. One was labelled 'male' and the other was labelled 'female.' Kelly raised an eyebrow. Why couldn't they just be gender neutral? This place really was like stepping back in time.

She was just about to go into the ladies' toilet when she noticed the booth that occupied the space between the two lavatory doors. Properly speaking, she had already noticed it. A large cubicle like that, it would be hard to miss, but it was at this point that she really took note of it. What was it, a photo booth? Now, that really was a blast from the past. She could remember using them at railway stations, having a laugh with her friends when she was a teenager. Getting four daft photos in a strip that came shooting out of a little slot in the side. Silly pictures as a souvenir of a day out. Flash! Flash! She could remember how the bulbs would pop as the pictures were taken. Flash! Flash! And just the thought of that made her grin.

But, peering closer, she saw that this wasn't just any ordinary photo booth. Yes, there was a curtain and, by the looks of it, a stool inside. But the booth had a strange name – 'The Kindness Machine' – emblazoned on its side in green and pink lettering. In smaller painted letters underneath it said, 'Just fifty pence.'

Kerry blinked. Fifty pence? What could you get for fifty pence these days? Surely not four instant passport portraits. She wondered if this machine was even working still. And what was a 'Kindness Machine' anyway? What could it possibly dispense?

Perhaps it took photos and they were terribly flattering? Was that the sort of kindness involved? Well, she decided, she could do with a bit of that. What was more, she had a fifty pence piece in her purse, amongst her change. It wasn't really an extravagance, on even their limited budget. Before she knew it, Kelly Braun had pulled the nylon curtain aside and sat herself down on the stool inside the Kindness Machine.

Slowly the bright lights inside came on, as if they hadn't been used in years. She blinked in preparation, suddenly self-conscious at seeing her hazy reflection on the screen in front of her. 'Welcome!' came a message in large, friendly letters. 'Please insert your coin.'

She put her fifty pence piece in the slot below the screen.

At once the screen crackled and fizzed. Kelly frowned, adjusting her hair, though it was harder to make out her reflection in the busy screen. Why couldn't they put a mirror in here, so you could take a last proper look at yourself before you had your picture taken?

The machine inside the cabinet was groaning and growling. The faded fake teak of the walls was trembling, she realised. She couldn't remember photo booths in the past making all of this noise and palaver. They usually started flashing by now and snapping your pictures, one after the next. One, two, three, four. The experience wasn't really very long. In fact, that had been part of the whole fun of it – the fact that there wasn't quite enough time to be ready and compose yourself before the bloody thing started firing away. The funniest of the tiny photos from these things often caught their subjects looking unaware or distracted or surprised. Yet here Kelly was, still waiting and puzzled, as the so-called Kindness Machine made these whirring and clunking noises. It almost sounded like the whole thing was thinking to itself. It was grumbling and cogitating. The screen was buzzing with static and Kelly rolled her eyes at her own fancifulness. Of course, the machine wasn't thinking. It was just rusty and hadn't been used for ages. It probably didn't even work properly anymore, and she had wasted her fifty pence piece.

At that very moment a face appeared on the little screen in front of her. It was a pleasant, smiling face of a woman perhaps ten or twelve years older than Kelly. Her hair was cut short and dyed ash blonde. Her make-up was skilfully applied and there was a tightness to her expression, even through the smile. Her eyes were kind but there was a sadness in them. It felt as if the woman was looking straight at Kelly. She could actually stare back at her through the screen and what she saw in the younger woman made her wince with pity.

'She looks like my mum,' Kelly said, not realising she was speaking out loud. Her voice filled the small space and she was shocked to see the woman on the screen nodding in reply.

'Yes, I suppose I do,' the woman smiled. 'It took me years to realise that.'

Kelly was gobsmacked. 'You can hear me?'

The woman nodded. 'Now, you must listen to me, Kelly, because we haven't got long ...'

The tumbling thoughts in Kelly's head blotted out what the woman was saying. The voice and the features were so familiar, it was a bit like being in a waking nightmare. Who was she exactly? She couldn't actually be Kelly's mum, could she? Deedee had died ten years ago; from ovarian cancer they hadn't caught quickly enough. One of the great sadnesses of Kelly's life was being left without a mum to help guide her through the tumult of her twenties. Sometimes she found herself irrationally angry at her mum for leaving her like she had, though of course poor Deedee had had no choice in the matter.

But this couldn't be her mum. It was impossible and anyway this person was subtly different to her mum. She was similar but really she looked more like Kelly herself.

'I'm *you*,' the woman said. 'Are you listening? I'm you in ten years' time.'

'What?' Kelly couldn't compute. For a second she couldn't take it in. 'What are you talking about?' She half stood up off the stool to leave. 'This is sick. This isn't right.' She peered at the screen and thought: yes, that *is* me. A bit older. A few more lines. A bit more experience. I don't look half bad, actually, for forty. Then she thought: but it can't be real. What they've done is use some clever kind of camera trickery, to age me up slightly. Like when they have those apps that put beards on you or turn you into a drag queen or give you bunny ears or daft things to make you laugh. But there was nothing funny about this. She hadn't been made into something silly or laughable. She had been made to look slightly older and regretful. What was the point of that?

'Is this an app?' she asked.

'A what?' older Kelly frowned. 'No, no ... now look. Like I say, we don't have very long at all, and I must explain to you. I've got a message for you from the Kindness Machine.'

Kelly felt her legs going weak. All at once she knew that this was all for real. She realised that something extremely peculiar was going on. She had let herself in for an experience that there was no getting out of.

'G-go on …'

'Right. There's no easy way of telling you this, but I'm *you* in ten years and I'm living on borrowed time. I'm … dying. Same as our mum did. Of exactly the same thing.'

'What? But I'd have known, I'd have been up to date with my checks and …'

Her future self shook her head. 'Believe me. We're unlucky. It's got us, Kelly. I've been given less than a year.'

Kelly stared in horror at the screen and it was as if the woman's face was getting thinner and more drawn with each passing second. She could see quite clearly now – that smart haircut was a wig. The carefully-applied make-up was giving her colour. The truth was all in the hollow eyes. This was a woman whose life was ebbing away and there was nothing she could do about it.

'But I can't die at … at your age. I can't die then … What about my girls? What about … Terry? What …'

Her future self shushed her. 'Now, listen. Just calm down. There's something important I must explain. This is the Kindness Machine. There's only one of these amazing devices in the world, and you've stepped into it.'

Kelly found her mind fogging over again. She felt like she was sinking into panic and despair. 'What are you even talking about?'

'Kelly, listen!' shouted the face in front of her. 'You've never been very good at listening and taking advice from people. You've always shouted other people down. Now you need to button your lip and listen to your own self. You need to listen to me.'

'A-all right …' she whispered.

'The Kindness Machine can see the future and it can give you a choice.'

'What choice?'

'You can live your life, your next ten years, with the knowledge of what is coming next. You can make the best of those years and your eventual fate will come as no surprise to you. The pain and the loss will still be there, but the shock will have been taken away. You will know what is to come.'

Kelly's mind was racing. How could she live ten years with the weight of that knowledge? 'I could change it all ... I'd get myself down to the hospital every few months, I'd be vigilant and ... and ... I'd prevent myself getting sick ...'

Her older counterpart shook her head sadly. 'It doesn't work like that, sweetheart. You can't prevent any of this. When the Kindness Machine looks into the future, everything is set in stone. This isn't some science fiction story where you can mess around with outcomes and possible futures. The future is there as it was always meant to be, just as the past is.'

Kelly felt tears of frustration spring up in her eyes. 'Then what's the point? It's like torture. It's like having no escape ... no hope ...' She stopped abruptly as the horror of it all struck her. She went cold at the idea of living with no hope.

The older Kelly smiled sadly. 'This is where the choice comes in. You can do something rather than live those ten years waiting for the inevitable. You can trade in nine of those years. You can live instead one glorious year with your children and your husband.'

'What? Trade in? What does that mean? And why would I prefer one year rather than ten?'

'It would be one single year in which you enjoy perfect health and happiness. And a year in which you'll be given a million pounds to spend just as you wish.'

Kelly frowned. 'Health? Happiness? A million pounds?'

Future-Kelly nodded. 'All of those things. Instead of nine normal years and an inescapable fate, and the knowledge of when and how it's coming. You may have one truly fantastic year or ... nine rather more gloomy ones.'

'But ... but ...' Kelly just couldn't see how such a thing could be possible. 'What happens to the other nine years? What did you mean ... trade them in?'

'Ahh,' smiled the woman on the screen. 'They will go to a very good cause. The life essence you would release from giving up those nine years – they would be donated to a very needy cause.'

'A needy cause?'

'Someone who has a very great need of extra life and potential. Like this boy, for instance.' All at once future-Kelly's image was replaced by a picture of the brain-dead boy from the news. It was the same report that Kelly and Terry had watched on TV this morning. That seemed like a hundred years ago now. How long had she been down here, having this conversation inside this booth? What would Terry think she was getting up to down here? Kelly stared at the brain-dead boy and his weeping parents and the news reporter who was telling the nation that everyone was holding out hope for the boy who the experts wanted to simply switch off. 'I … I could give those years to him?'

'That's right,' said her older self. 'And you could use the million pounds to give your daughters a better start in life, if you invested some of it well. You could spend special quality time with them …'

'But I'd never see them grow any older than another year …' Kelly said, and gasped suddenly, as the enormity of it all hit her. She was going to die. This machine was telling her that she was going to die. It was some kind of cruel and hateful trick, surely. None of this could be real. It was crazy. It was impossible. It just couldn't be happening.

'Kelly?' asked the voice which, now she thought about it, was almost exactly like her own. 'What do you choose? YES or NO. Do you say yes to the offer from the Kindness Machine? Or do you refuse it? It's as simple as that.'

Two large plastic buttons had appeared next to the coin slot. Had they been there before? She couldn't be sure. One was green and was labelled YES, the other was red and it said NO.

'I can choose and just go, can I?' she asked. All at once she wanted to be out of this thing. She wanted to be away from its strange questions and suggestions. She wanted to be upstairs with her family. She longed to forget it all.

'Press a button and you can leave,' the voice told her. 'Nothing more will be said. The decision will be made. You can go.'

'Okay, okay …' Kelly said. She didn't want to think about it anymore. She wanted to get out of there. She couldn't even look at her older self in the face anymore. That drawn, pale face. It was as if, just by looking at it, she was becoming iller and sicker in herself. She felt her hand jab about spasmodically, almost of its own accord.

This was a Kindness Machine, wasn't it? Whatever it did would surely be kind and good. How could she refuse that? Surely there was more hope bound up in what the green button offered than the red? And hope was the most important thing. So she hit the large green button that said YES. She hit it as hard as she could.

'Our decision is made,' she heard her older voice say.

Then she got up without a backward glance and staggered through the curtain and back into the musty-smelling basement of All Night Long.

Upstairs in the vintage café her husband Terry gave her a funny look. She was relieved to sit down with her girls, both of whom were glugging away greedily at frothy ice cream floats.

'Hey, you were ages down there,' Terry smiled worriedly. 'Are you okay?'

'Bit of a tummy upset,' she smiled. But it wasn't true. Her mind was spinning with alarm and crazy questions but in herself – in her actual physical body – Kelly felt fantastic. Her awful headache was gone. She felt filled with new vitality. It was probably all in her mind, she told herself. She was just glad to be out of that creepy machine.

At that moment she locked eyes with the large lady behind the café counter. Precious was pouring out a fresh cup of tea for Kelly. She winked, just once, and gave Kelly a look as if to say she understood. Precious smiled at her and all at once Kelly felt her mind calming down. *Don't make a fuss,* she thought. *Don't make a scene. Don't upset everyone by demanding answers or quizzing the café owner. Just accept the choice you've been given and the decision you've made. Don't tell anyone else anything about it. Probably it was all just in your head anyway.*

Precious brought the tea over and it was exactly how Kelly liked it. Strong, milky and sweet. 'Everything okay, sweetheart?' she asked her, and Kelly nodded and smiled up at her.

'Yes, thank you. I think everything's going to be fine.'

The last couple of days of their holiday in that dreary town passed rather peacefully. There were no further arguments or hitches between mummy and daddy, and the two little girls even got to play on the damp beach on the final afternoon, when the rain let up slightly. Another afternoon was spent messing about in the amusement arcades, where they blew five pounds on silly one-armed bandits. 'Five pounds in two-pence pieces ... What a waste,' Terry said.

'It's "mad money",' Kelly told him. 'That's the word for it. That's what my mum used to call it, when you go on holiday and set aside some amount that you can use just for pure enjoyment.'

'It seems terrible to waste money, though,' Terry said.

Oh, he was such a worrier, Kelly thought. He was getting worse with each passing year. Fatherhood had turned him into an old woman. What had happened to the reckless dafty she had first hooked up with?

"Mad money". She liked the phrase and kept rolling it around in her head over the next few days. All the cash they had blown on their sojourn by the sea could be described by that phrase. The holiday hadn't really been much cop. They were just as stressed as they had been before leaving. In truth, their girls would be just as happy wherever they were. And then there had been that odd interlude in the photo booth under the café – but Kelly was deliberately not thinking about that. She stored the memory away like she would the lingering recollection of a disturbing dream that refused to melt away.

Then, several days after their return home, just as things were getting back to normal and their everyday routines sealed themselves back around them, two startling things happened.

On the Tuesday evening Terry came home from work and he was agitated, excited. 'Turn the news on,' he told her.

157

The girls were watching cartoons and complained loudly when Terry took the remote and found the news channel.

'What is it?' Kelly felt her heart hammering with dread. What was going on now? She hated the news. It was either posh people quibbling and maundering on about stuff she could hardly understand, or it was disasters that made her feel uneasy and disturbed: they seemed to be coming closer and closer to home, each time she watched the bulletins. Let's face it, the news never told you anything good.

Except for today, it seemed.

'Look at this!' Terry said, as the newsreader linked to a story in which people were cheering and celebrating outside of a hospital. Inside nurses and medical staff in blue gowns were weeping and grinning. Two parents talked to the camera and they looked jubilant, justified, triumphant.

'That boy,' Terry said. 'They say it's a miracle. That boy who they reckoned was brain dead – he's sat up and opened his eyes. He's perfectly fine now. He's completely recovered!'

Then the TV showed the little boy in question, sitting up in his hospital bed. He was pale and his hair was sticking up. His eyes were as big as saucers, blinking, looking puzzled by all the attention.

Everyone was delighted. No one could explain it. How lucky he was. How lucky they all were. How pleased everyone was that they had held out hope. Why, they might have switched him off. They might have just let him die. But somehow they had known that there would be this miracle.

'Isn't it wonderful?' Terry grinned at Kelly. 'It's amazing, isn't it?'

Somehow he was telling her, I was right and you were wrong. He was holding their disagreement over her. He had been right all along, hadn't he?

The other startling thing came on that Thursday.

By then so many days had gone by that it felt like they had never been away at all. Their lives had folded around them again so seamlessly and, at home, Kelly found herself feeling panicky now and then, for no very good reason. She kept thinking about that boy. Terry watched the news all the time, avid for any mention of the miracle. Kelly didn't like hearing too much about it. She felt oddly unsettled by the whole thing. Not guilty, exactly – but just unsettled and strange. She didn't like Terry going on almost gloatingly about it.

Thursday morning's post brought something that drowned out all her thoughts about anything else. In amongst the letters from the energy companies and the council there was a letter with a postmark she didn't recognise. The envelope was stiff, good quality paper. It was addressed to her and the dark, precise lettering gave her a shiver when she stared at it. She wasn't sure why.

Inside: a piece of card with embossed type. It said very little, but she understood at once what it meant.

'Congratulations, from the Kindness Machine. We hope you make good use of this.'

With the card there was a cheque. Just a normal cheque for a high street bank, signed with an unidentifiable squiggle on behalf of something called the Kindness Corporation. It was a cheque for exactly a million pounds.

It felt as though Kelly's heart had stopped. She wasn't sure if it was panic or joy or dismay that started it up again, thumping like a jackhammer in her chest.

Then, all she could think was: how the hell was she ever going to explain this to Terry? What on earth was she going to say?

'A *competition* …?'

He looked dumbfounded. He held the pale green cheque up to the light and stared at it as if the flimsy paper itself might give away more clues to its provenance.

'That's right.'

'But what competition? When did you do a competition?'

'In that café. There was a thing downstairs. Like a booth. I went in when I went to the loo. It was just like an easy competition thing ... easy answers. It was like putting your name into a draw. Anyway ... I thought I might as well. It only cost fifty pence to enter. And ... *I won* ...!'

He looked at her solemnly. His expression was so odd it made her feel hysterical. She wanted to laugh at him. He almost looked scared by the enormity of this moment.

'Kelly ... it's a million pounds. It's a *million* pounds.'

She nodded very slowly. 'I know.'

She knew more than she was ever going to tell him. She knew more than she herself really wanted to know.

It was all true, she thought. It was all for real.

But she put all other thoughts out of her head. Don't think about what it means. Don't even think about the future and all the ramifications.

'Let's get the cheque down to the bank first thing tomorrow,' she told him. 'They'll tell us if it's real or not.'

His eyes widened. 'Yes, yes ... it *looks* real. But it could be a cruel fake, couldn't it? It could just be a nasty joke of some kind ...'

Yes, the bank quibbled. A little bit, not much. The woman at the counter pursed her lips and went to fetch the manager. Kelly and Terry were called into his office, and they were offered coffee. Polite questions were asked by the manager who suddenly looked quite young and inexperienced. Kelly shrugged and talked about the competition she had entered. Someone from behind the scenes in the bank hurried in and gave a nod. The manager was very polite, and he talked about investments. Kelly said she was very interested in such things. She wanted to do something sensible with her windfall, for the sake of her daughters. 'I want to do right by them.'

Terry was quiet throughout most of these meetings that they attended in the following days. He was cowed by the whole thing. In shock, probably. He went to see his boss at work. 'I'm giving in my notice,' he told Nigel, who he'd never had any problem with, though some of the staff did.

Nigel was puzzled. 'Are you all right, fella?' To him, Terry looked pale and worried.

They settled on giving Terry a few months off. Terry could return any time he liked after he'd taken some time away. He was a good worker and Nigel wanted to give him the chance to return. There was clearly something going on with the poor guy's mental health and he needed time to get it sorted. Nigel was very alert to his staff members' mental health needs since his own boyfriend had suffered badly with such things and had taken his own life only two years previously.

At home, Kelly told Terry: 'You don't look as happy as I thought you would.'

He looked and felt shifty. 'I feel like we've done something wrong. I feel like we've stolen something. It's like someone is going to come knocking on the door to say there's been a huge mistake.'

Kelly laughed and returned to her laptop at the kitchen table. 'No way! It's all real. And we really have to get on. We have to hurry. We need to sort everything out.'

She was looking at fancy houses on estate agents' websites. Terry could hardly believe the things she was looking at. She had already booked flights for the four of them and next week they were going to Disney World. Terry's mind was boggling and, when they were told, Mia and Ariel went crackers with excitement.

'You're going to spend it all at once ...' He warned her. 'It's like spend spend spend with you. It'll all go in a flash and we'll have nothing left ...'

Boxes and parcels were arriving from her online shopping sprees in the middle of the night. Delivery trucks came every morning and she could hardly keep up with the unboxing. Fancy clothes and shoes for the kids, for her, for him. The rooms filled up with tissue paper and cellophane. The very air was scented with newness.

'I'm refusing to cook anything from now on,' Kelly declared, like the new queen of a country, making up laws.

'Hurray!' said the girls as delivery boys brought hot delicious food from restaurants each night: pizzas and noodles and spicy chicken. They even brought deliveries of sticky sweets and cold drinks.

'It's ridiculously extravagant,' Terry warned.

'It's wonderful!' Kelly laughed. 'But we'll need that bigger house very soon. Now, I'm ordering furniture. I'm ordering too much stuff to fit inside this old place!'

Their neighbours watched the vans arrive and all the boxes going in. They noticed all the fancy new clothes and the new car – a four-wheel drive type thing – standing in the drive. There was talk about where all this flash cash had come from, but the couple weren't talking. It was nobody's business but their own. No one had paid them very much attention in the past, and they were content to fly under the radar right now.

Off they went to Florida and had a marvellous time. They stayed an extra week, just because they felt like it. They returned via New York and felt like movie stars, staying at the swishest hotel they could find. They made themselves sick with rich food and the good life. The little kids became over-tired and a bit brattish. Kelly started researching posh boarding schools online. It turned out they weren't too young to be sent.

'You can't send them away …!' Terry gasped, appalled. 'They're our girls …'

To Kelly, though, it seemed like a good solution. For later on. It might be the best way. She kept researching, made a few inquiries. Yes, the girls were getting out of control. Grabby. Whingey. Things had suddenly become valueless to them. Too much, too quick. Well, never mind. She wanted them to have everything that she had never had, but they required discipline as well.

When the family returned to the UK they were bronzed and frazzled, not relaxed at all. They visited both Terry's parents and Kelly's dad and presented them with large cheques. 'We want to share our good fortune with you.'

'We knew it! We knew something wonderful had happened!' Terry's parents went dancing up and down their front room joyfully. Ten thousand pounds! They started gabbling at once about what they'd do with it. Terry's mum took her son aside. 'Are you sure you can afford it? We've never seen so much money. It's so good of you to share your good luck.'

'I wish it could be more,' he said.

'You … don't look as happy as I thought you would be …?'

He shrugged. He was feeling strange about the whole thing. Truth be told, he missed his friends in the shop. He found himself wandering there just to hang out with them in the daytime when normally he'd have been working. They took the piss out of his stiff new, trendy clothes. He too thought he looked a pillock in this designer gear. It all suited Kelly and the girls much better. He looked a fool in too-tight trousers and shirts, all of them with labels and writing on, and extra zips.

And the new house! That was a strange thing, too. It was clear across town, in a part of a suburb where they didn't know anyone.

'We don't need to know anyone,' Kelly said. 'We'll keep ourselves to ourselves. We don't need anyone else.'

Moving day came and none of them needed to lift a finger. The removals men did everything. Terry wandered around their new palatial abode and gasped at the pool and the jacuzzi and the sauna and the tiki bar. Did they really need all this stuff?

'Does a million pounds really go this far?' he asked Kelly.

'Of course it does!' she laughed at him. 'You look so worried! Stop it, Terry. You're spoiling the fun. If you worry it taints things. I don't want a minute of it spoiling. This has to be perfect.'

But it wasn't perfect, was it?

When they went to see Kelly's lonely, dirty, grumpy dad in his flat where he lived alone he flared up in anger when they gave him a cheque for five thousand pounds. 'Spend it on anything you like, Dad,' Kelly told him airily, fluttering the cheque under his purple nose. 'Just don't spend it all on Special

Brew, eh?'

Her dad exploded: 'I've heard that you two are minted now! They're saying it's the lottery or something you won. You're going round town like Lord and Lady Muck. A million pounds they say you won.'

'Nowhere near as much as that,' Terry said, alarmed by the force of the old man's anger. But at the same time, he was glad to see a genuine, heartfelt emotion. Lately everything had been so sugar-coated and sweet. Everything in their lives had been just lovely. Kelly had botoxed her face into plump, shiny submission and she could barely express anything at all. A touch of real anger was almost a relief to witness.

'You've got a million and you give me five grand?' her father yelled. 'It's an insult! You greedy, selfish buggers! Is this all I get? Is this really all you can spare your poor old dad?'

Kelly turned on her heel and called after Terry to follow her. Things between her dad and herself hadn't been right in years.

'It's harder than it should be, all this,' Terry said that night, as they floated in their underlit pool. Only that morning the girls had been shipped off to their boarding school and the new place was eerily quiet. Terry realised that, bobbing in her flamingo-shaped rubber ring, Kelly was sobbing. 'What's the matter, love?'

'I-I'm going to miss them,' she said. 'We shouldn't have sent them away. What was I thinking? I'm missing precious moments with them.'

'You're right,' he said. 'I miss them, too. Shall we bring them back?'

'Yes, yes, we'll hire private tutors. We'll have them taught at home. We won't waste another precious day ...'

Kelly started paddling to the side of the pool, anxious to get back to her laptop, to start making new arrangements.

Precious days, that's what it was all about.

The clock was ticking, and only she knew about it.

Their year of good fortune was speeding by. A life in which all problems and hitches could be solved with the application of cash turned out to go faster than a life in which each and every day was a struggle. Who knew? Terry had thought the luxurious days would be lazy and melt one into the next and time would cease to have meaning, but Kelly kept them all occupied and on the move. There were things to see! Amazing experiences to purchase!

He started looking at her strangely. He hardly recognised her these days, and it wasn't just because her face had been pulled and primped into a different shape.

'I wish you'd tell me,' he said one day.

They were in Morocco, at a souk, their arms laden down with goods they had haggled for. He had already forgotten what they had bought. The wool from a patterned carpet was tickling his sinuses and he felt too hot and tired all of a sudden.

'Tell you what?' she smiled.

'The secret,' he said. 'There's a secret, isn't there?'

There was a pause before she laughed him off. 'Of course not!'

But there was.

When they were back in the UK and travelling in their new car to a luxury apartment they had rented for a week by the sea, they passed through the town they had stayed in last summer.

'Remember?' Terry said, marvelling at how long ago it seemed. Already it was like a lifetime ago. 'Remember being crammed into that hotel room? And me getting annoyed because we spent five pounds on the amusement arcade machines …?'

She ruffled his hair fondly as he drove. 'You didn't get annoyed. You never did. You were just concerned, that's all.'

'Well, I needn't have worried. Our luck was just about to change, wasn't it?'

Something cold ran through Kelly's insides at these words.

'Hey, you know what we should do,' he said. 'We should stop here for a bit and go back to that café. What was it called? All Night Long?'

Kelly stared straight ahead through the windscreen as they swooshed down the motorway. 'Whatever for?'

'So we can tell that woman. The one who owned it. You can tell her you won the competition there. We could see the booth thing where you filled in the form.' Terry grinned at the thought. 'I'd like to see it. And I'd like to see that woman's face when she hears how much we won. Remember her?'

Kelly pulled a face. 'It's probably a bad idea.'

But Terry wouldn't be deterred. Before she knew it he had veered off the motorway and was storming into town, towards the sea front. It was another wet and windy day, just like on their meagre holiday … when had it been? How long ago?

Almost a year ago. Kelly knew only too well. It had been almost a year ago.

Terry parked his huge new flashy vehicle outside the café with the luminous stars on the window and everything looked just the same as it had back when they were poor. He couldn't stop grinning at Kelly when he thought about the last time they had been here. They had really come a long way since then. 'I wish we had the girls with us,' he said. But their daughters were in Spain with their Nanna and Grandad, and behaving quiet badly, according to the messages Terry had received.

The bell tinkled as they let themselves in, to find the café just as empty as before. The same cabinets had the same old sandwiches and cakes on display. The juke box was playing 1950s songs again. Slower, more sentimental songs than before, perhaps. Just then, Precious came out of her back room, in a similar outfit of brightly-patterned blouse and skirt with a pinny over the top.

'Remember us?' Terry beamed at her.

She frowned. 'Should I?'

All at once Kelly felt unnerved. She felt even more sure that they should never have returned. 'Let's go …' she whispered.

'No, let's tell her,' Terry said. 'She'll want to know.'

Precious smiled politely, patiently. 'She'll want to know what?'

'My wife won!' Terry burst out. 'Almost a year ago, we were here with our little girls, Mia and Ariel, and we were on holiday. Not a great holiday, to be honest. The weather was rubbish and we were pretty hard up. But we came here and my wife here, Kelly … well, she went down to use your loo and she entered a kind of competition, and … and she won it!' Terry realised he was gabbling under Precious's intense, questioning gaze. 'We won all this money and … well, our lives have changed out of all … um… recognition.'

Precious stared at them both. Her eyes were kind and understanding. Terry felt himself blinking fast, like all at once he wanted to cry. 'Is this true?' Precious asked at last. 'Well, well.' She looked at Kelly. 'You've been very lucky.'

'I have,' Kelly said stiffly. She jutted out her chin, almost defiantly, as if she thought Precious had suggested she hadn't deserved such good fortune.

'I'd love to see the … the … what was it called?' Terry said. 'The machine in your basement.'

Precious raised her eyebrows. 'It's called the Kindness Machine, but unfortunately – it's out of order right now. We are waiting for the repairman.'

'Oh,' said Terry. 'What a shame. I wanted to get a look at it. See what it looks like. What it does. Maybe take a selfie with it. Thank it somehow. For all our good luck.'

Precious shrugged. 'There's nothing much to see. Just an empty booth. While it's gone dark like that, it's not worth looking at, really.'

They settled on having frothy coffee at the café, which Precious was more than happy to fetch them. 'This is on the house,' she told them, ambling over stiffly on her old legs. 'To congratulate you. It's not every day we have such winners. And people never usually come back to visit.'

'Don't they?' asked Kelly, with a strange look on her face. Terry noticed it, but thought, rather sadly, that most of his wife's expressions were rather odd these days. He wished she had never altered anything about herself.

'Thank you, Precious,' he told their waitress, who he assumed was the owner of the café. 'The competition that my wife entered here changed her life. We have you to thank.'

Precious's face darkened for a second. 'It was nothing to do with me. The Kindness Machine isn't mine; it just occupies my cellar. And it isn't really a competition as such ...'

Terry glanced at his wife. 'That's what Kelly said it was. Or a kind of draw ...'

'No,' Precious said. 'It's not really that, either. But you'll see. You'll understand, I think, one day. Now, drink your coffee. Enjoy your day. Be happy that you returned here. And I will leave you in peace.'

When Precious was out of earshot Terry looked at Kelly.

'She's strange,' he said.

'Not as friendly as she was last time,' he added.

'Let's get back in the car and get away from here,' Kelly said.

So they did, and they never looked back at that dismal town.

Less than a month later the two girls were home and their house was noisy and full of life again.

'Let Mummy lie in today,' said Daddy, one morning after Mummy had drunk more wine than usual the night before. 'She's got a little headache.'

Mia and Ariel helped Daddy make cakes in the kitchen. The massive island in the middle of the room was soon covered in flour, smashed eggshells and melted butter. Terry didn't mind the mess in the least. Their fancy new kitchen had hardly been used at all and it was good to see a bit of disarray for once. They had music turned up loudly and the girls were squealing with happiness as they beat the sticky mixture and ate it from wooden spoons.

It was simpler stuff like this that Terry enjoyed the most. The things that reminded him of the best moments of his own growing up.

When the little cakes went into the oven, the oldest of the girls, Ariel, slipped off upstairs to use the loo.

'Give your mummy a shout too,' Terry told her. 'Tell her there'll be cakes soon.'

He felt like Kelly was missing out on the fun. But he also wondered what kind of a mood she'd be in this morning. Her excesses in the evenings were blotting out most of her mornings these days. She could be very snappy and bleary till mid-afternoon. Terry felt almost cross with her. He wanted to say: you're missing everything you ever dreamed about! The girls are still little and we're happy, aren't we? We've got everything we ever dreamed of having. Why can't you relax and enjoy it all now? Why are you still anguished like this? Yes, that was just the word. Kelly was anguished. She was eaten up with some kind of upset and she wouldn't let Terry in on the secret of it.

Ariel came out of the loo and realised that her mummy was already out of her bed and downstairs. She was in the large entrance hall to their new house, and she was answering the door to strangers.

Ariel was just about to go running down the stairs when some strange instinct stopped her in her tracks. Her bare feet prickled on the plush new carpet. She clung to the shiny banister and stared down at the men who were standing in the doorway, talking to Mummy in low, reasonable, professional voices.

'*Today?*' Mummy asked. It was the only word in the murmured conversation that Ariel could pick out at first.

The men were dressed in drab, old fashioned business suits. They wore hats with wide brims that shaded half their faces. They were stiff and polite, filling up the doorway.

'Mummy...?' Ariel said, taking one step and then another down the staircase. All at once she was gripped with terror and she didn't even know why.

The two men were taking hold of Mummy. They both took hold of one arm each. Mummy was still in her crumpled nightgown with her hair hanging down unwashed. She resisted and twisted in their arms, but she couldn't resist their strength. Ariel cried out again but no one could hear her. No one took any notice. There was music coming from the kitchen and Daddy didn't hear anything either.

The men were dragging Mummy out of the new house. They were taking her out to their waiting car, which was an old fashioned grey one with dark windows. It was waiting right outside the front of the house.

Mummy's voice came again. It was loud and panicky-sounding this time. 'I don't want to go!' And then, as they got her out to the waiting car Ariel heard her shout: 'But I've changed my mind!'

Ariel found strength in her legs and went pounding down the staircase. 'Daddy! *Daddy!*' she screamed.

Outside the car doors slammed. Mummy was in the back; the suited men were in the front. The engines roared and then they were off. The front door was still standing way open.

Daddy came out of the kitchen with music blaring and the smell of baking cakes wafting round him. Now he could hear Ariel screaming in the hall. 'What is it, love? What is it?'

But Ariel was so upset she could hardly get her words out. She kept pointing at the open, empty doorway.

ABOUT THE AUTHOR

Paul Magrs was born in Jarrow in 1969 and grew up in Newton Aycliffe, County Durham, where he went to Woodham Comprehensive School. He got a First in English

Literature at Lancaster University, and then a Distinction for their MA in Creative Writing, and then did a PhD on Angela Carter. He brought out his first novel in 1995 when he was 26. He was a Senior Lecturer in Creative Writing at UEA and then at MMU. Over the years he has published over fifty books for adults and children and has written many audio dramas for radio and download.

In 2019 he published his book on writing, *The Novel Inside You*. In 2020 Snow Books republished his Brenda and Effie Mystery series of novels. In 2022 he won the Crime Writers' Association Silver Dagger for best short story of the year. In 2023 Harper Collins published his book of cat portraits, *Puss-in-Books*. Under the name 'Elsie Mason' he has written six historical sagas for Orion. He has written many *Doctor Who* stories over the past twenty-five years for BBC Books, BBC audio, Big Finish Productions and Puffin Books. His latest novel for the series is, *Doctor Who in Wonderland*.

This year he began a bookish channel on Youtube where he talks about all the books on his shelves and in his life.

He lives and writes in Manchester with Jeremy and Bernard Socks.

PIOTR FALLS TO PIECES

Benjamin Adams

Piotr Mytiukov liked to think he'd never hurt a fly.

But now, as he sat in a dingy motel room in Enumclaw, his head in his hands, all he could think about was the old man he had killed.

Piotr had watched the little family-run Chinese grocery on Seattle's Pike Street for weeks. Studied their every move. It should have gone like clockwork, dammit.

Like clockwork.

The middle-aged couple behind the counter hadn't clocked him as a threat when he first entered, clad in his white tracksuit with blue piping. The tense scene was then set as Piotr aimed his smuggled Grach pistol, its matte-dark metal like a black hole in his hand, at them. His demand for them to hand over the cash in the till – 'the dead presidents' – was met with terrified compliance.

But then, unexpectedly, an old man burst through the rear door of the store, his voice filled with rage and speaking in a language that Piotr couldn't understand – some kind of weird tonal Asian gibberish that didn't sound like Chinese to his ears.

'Koo noh! Koo noh!'

Piotr's mind raced as he tried to assess this new threat. He hadn't planned for this unknown element. Had the old man been kept locked up somewhere by these strange people? The uncertainty added a new layer of tension to the already volatile situation.

The elderly man appeared to be on the brink of death,

his weathered skin etched with deep lines that spoke of a lifetime of experiences. A thin, wispy goatee clung to his wizened chin, swaying slightly in the wind. One of his eyes was concealed by an intricately embroidered patch, while the other glimmered milky and clouded with cataract. Despite his frail appearance, the old man showed no signs of slowing down as he approached Piotr.

In fact, the old man ran – ran *fast* – holding his hands out in some kind of strange chop-socky move, like in the martial arts flicks Piotr liked watching on cable. And all the while he kept yelling and yelling, *'koo noh! Koo noh!'*

Piotr turned his Grach toward the old man and fired. Just to scare him. Just a warning shot.

The concussion of the shot was like a cannon in the grocery and continued echoing in his ears. The weird old man's forward momentum carried him a little bit further forward as blood spray exited his back, and he collapsed at Piotr's feet. More blood sprayed from the man's mouth as he gurgled 'KOO NOH' one last time; it spattered on Piotr's Nike Shox sneakers, his treasured White Obsidians.

That was the moment things turned to crap for Piotr Mytiukov.

A keening wail went up from the middle-aged Chinese woman behind the counter, who raised her hands to the side of her face in horror. Her husband had ducked down on hearing the shot, but he rose again in a flash with his own pistol, a Saturday Night Special, in hand. Piotr turned to run as the first shot whizzed past his head, and he somehow made it to the open front door and outside into the early morning Seattle rain. He expected to feel the next bullet at any moment, but the middle-aged Chinese man didn't follow him.

Piotr ran for his life anyway.

This area of the city was like a warren, with alleys and small side streets he was able to duck down. With his tracksuit and sneakers, he looked like any other jogger out for a morning run, and the light rain helped blur the blood that had spattered his Nikes. After a few minutes, he slowed his pace and began thinking about where to go next.

Piotr found himself confined to the cramped, dimly lit Room 105 at the Motel 8 in Enumclaw, Washington. Seattle had become too dangerous for him to stay, the streets boiling with tension and danger. His local contacts had discreetly arranged for him to flee here, but not without strict instructions to lay low until they gave word otherwise. The Chinese community was in an uproar over the death of someone they considered to be a revered monk or priest.

Country and Western music drifted in lazily from the room next door. Some kind of sad song by Patsy Cline. Rain drizzled down outside in the neon dark. The air carried the damp earthiness of surrounding farmland mixed with the metallic scent of approaching mountain storms. Faintly he heard the constant hum of trucks passing on the highway. At least they had some kind of freedom.

Now he was paying the price for his impulsive action.

Piotr Mytiukov, who in his fifteen years of small heists in America had never hurt a goddamn fly.

Piotr Mytiukov, the killer.

He couldn't bear to turn on the television and see yet another report about the old man's death ... although from what he had seen, police had no idea of his identity. The market had no CCTV cameras, which was one of the reasons Piotr had chosen it. That was the only bright spot in this whole mess. So he sat alone in his shabby motel room, listening to the country music drifting in from next door. The sadness in Patsy Cline's voice seemed to mirror his own.

I fall to pieces ...

He put his head in his hands and wept again, so lost in his misery that he didn't hear the softest click made by Room 105's door latch.

As he lifted his eyes, Piotr's heart dropped with a thud. Seven men of Asian descent, draped in all black, moved towards him with silent steps – their expressions stoic and unyielding like hunters closing in on their prey. Their faces were chiselled and angular, giving off an aura of discipline and danger.

Piotr felt the weight of dread settle in his stomach. He knew this was the end for him; from his upbringing in Khabarovsk along the Sino-Russian border, to his attempts at assimilating into American life in Los Angeles, to his final move to Seattle, these men had always lingered on the outskirts of his criminal world. The Triad, the notorious Chinese syndicate, had finally caught up to him. He no longer had to worry about evading the police; the Triad would exact their own form of justice here and now.

With a resigned sigh, Piotr raised his hands in surrender. 'Seven against one is more than enough. Just get it over with,' he muttered bitterly.

But instead of carrying out their deadly intentions right then and there, the Triad enforcers dragged Piotr outside and shoved him into the back of a plain white Ford Econoline van. They wasted no time blindfolding him and securing his hands with handcuffs to a metal brace in the cargo area. And then, without warning, he felt a sharp pinch in his arm as a needle pierced through his skin – the last sensation he registered before slipping into unconsciousness.

He plummeted into an endless, dizzying vortex of violent green light that thrashed and pulsated to a deafening rhythm. The sheer speed of his descent was like being caught in a maelstrom, reminiscent of Dorothy's journey to the fabled land of oz. Ahead loomed a towering wall of coarse brown material with jagged pits and crevices, close enough to touch but he knew any attempt would shred his skin from his bones.

As he looked down at his body, naked as the day he was born, a sudden sense of dread washed over him. The source of the blinding green light was revealed to be massive, star-shaped symbols emblazoned on the wall. He hurtled towards one of them, feeling minuscule in comparison to its colossal size. Finally, he came to rest on the scalding sienna surface within the confines of the star.

But there was no respite from the intense light as it formed an impenetrable barrier around him. Desperate to escape, he stumbled towards the edge only to encounter a solid wall of darkness beyond. Tentatively, he extended his hand outside the perimeter and was met with a texture resembling thick elephant hide–rough and rubbery. Recoiling in horror, he hesitated before venturing further into this strange realm where only the eerie glow provided any illumination.

After a long while the scent of incense, sweet and delirious, reached him, and there was a calm genderless voice at his back.

– you must make it right.

'What do you mean?' he asked.

– the balance must be restored.

'I don't understand.'

– all must be as it was.

He turned, but no one was there. 'where are you?' he cried.

'Right behind you.' this new voice was different; male, with meat and gravel and age behind it.

Unwillingly, he forced himself to look.

Into the elderly man's vacant, grinning face. 'Meet the new boss,' said the old man, and slugged him in the stomach. 'Same as the old boss.' the old man's knee caught him in the face. 'Won't get fooled again – and that goes for your little dog, too!'

He staggered under the old man's assault and lost his footing, falling into the darkness outside the glowing green perimeter. Instantly the wind picked him up and swept him, like a child's kite, into the yawning void beyond, screaming uselessly. Impotently.

Piotr's mind was a blur of sea and sky, a disjointed feeling of speed and disorientation. Each time he tried to come back to his senses, the drugs would drag him under again. But eventually he surfaced to find himself in a different van, the bright sunlight seeping through the cracks around the rear door. He felt parched and desperate for liquid. 'W-water,' he managed to croak out.

In response, a cool plastic bottle of mineral water was pressed against his cracked lips, offering relief to his dry throat as he eagerly swallowed it down.

The Triad remained eerily silent as they drove on for what seemed like endless hours. Finally, the van came to a stop and Piotr was freed from his restraints and roughly pulled out. His blindfold was ripped off, causing him to squint against the harsh daylight as the panel doors were flung open from outside.

He blinked, his eyes taking a painful moment to adjust to the bright late afternoon light, and found himself facing sand-weathered ruins emerging from rolling dunes, their wooden structures remarkably preserved by this unknown desert's arid climate. Ancient dwellings stood as silent sentinels, their walls still bearing traces of elaborate carvings and faded pigments. The air carried the perpetual whisper of wind-blown sand, and the ruins cast long shadows that seemed to dance with ancient memories.

The Triad members pushed and prodded him forward, their rough hands grasping at his arms as they marched through the deserted, ancient streets. The buildings around them were crumbling, their once-grand facades now nothing but decaying remnants of a forgotten time. But amidst the ruin, there stood a structure that seemed untouched by time. It was not just a monument, but a temple on a raised platform, its red walls shining in the dim light with gleaming golden accents adorning its arched entrance and sloping roof. Its presence seemed to radiate power and importance, like a beacon in the desolate landscape.

'Where *am* I?' he croaked, his throat dry with fear.

A small Chinese man, adorned in bright saffron-yellow robes, emerged from the temple and after fifteen steps forward down a set of carved stone steps, bowed before Piotr.

'Welcome to our temple,' he greeted in a melodic sing-song voice. 'It is good to finally meet you. You have been brought here to restore balance. You have taken, so now you must give. The balance will be restored.'

The distant, haunting toll of a deep gong echoed

through the air, sending shivers down Piotr's spine. He could feel beads of sweat forming on his back as he tried to comprehend the situation before him. The monk standing before him wore an enigmatic smile, his teeth glimmering in the light that was quickly fading to dusk.

'What do you mean?' Piotr stammered, his voice shaking with fear and confusion. He couldn't believe what was happening.

'Come,' said the monk, smiling with perfect teeth. 'Dine with me. All will be explained.'

Without warning, the group of men dressed in all black began to chant in deep guttural tones that sent shivers down Piotr's spine. The sound was reminiscent of Tibetan monks he had once stumbled upon in a park near the Space Needle in Seattle, but he knew they were far from that familiar city now. With grace and precision, they glided to places along the short path to the temple, three of them on one side, four on the other. Like an honour guard.

The monk wore a kind smile, nodding in encouragement as he motioned for Piotr to come closer.

Seeing no other option, Piotr reluctantly followed the monk into the building.

Stepping into the temple, Piotr was struck with a sense of overwhelming awe. The grandeur of the interior took his breath away. A central path, polished to a mirror-like shine, led through its expanse to a raised golden dais at the rear. Towering above it all were six immense carmine pillars, each two feet in diameter and reaching up to the ceiling that stood thirty feet above. As he walked, Piotr couldn't help but notice the intricate golden inlay work that adorned each pillar in swirling patterns and strange angles. This same decoration continued onto the green walls on either side, fifteen feet high and seemingly endless. But something about the designs made him feel uneasy – they seemed to warp and twist before his eyes, causing a sense of vertigo to wash over him. Despite his unease, Piotr couldn't tear his gaze away from the mesmerizing display.

Near the dais, a low table stood, adorned with vibrant silk pillows scattered haphazardly on the floor. The intricate designs on the pillows gleamed in the dim light of the room, adding a touch of elegance to the simple setup. The monk gracefully made his way to the end of the table nearest the dais and motioned for Piotr to take a seat beside him at his right hand. As Piotr followed suit, he noticed the faint earthy scent of incense lingering in the air, adding to the atmosphere of tranquillity and reverence. The wooden table was smooth under his fingertips, worn from years of use by devoted monks. A small candle flickered gently in the centre, casting dancing shadows on their faces

Piotr nervously lowered himself to the pillow and knelt.

'No,' said the monk, smiling widely. 'Sit. We will share a meal now.'

As he clapped his hands, the heavy wooden doors on either side of the dais swung open, revealing more Triad members carrying an array of dishes. The tantalizing scent of hot, steaming meats wafted through the air, followed by the fragrant aroma of fresh bread and ripe fruits and vegetables. Piotr's stomach growled in anticipation; it had been days since he had last eaten.

The dishes were presented on gleaming golden plates and in ornate bowls made of the same precious metal. Piotr couldn't help but wonder at the value of such lavish tableware. Surely, this must be pure gold, worth a small fortune.

'Who are you?' he managed.

The monk filled a bowl with rice and meat in a savoury brown curry. 'I am your host, merely your host. You are our honoured guest.'

'I don't understand. Where are we? Why have you brought me here?'

'Do you know of the Silk Road, my friend?'

'The ancient trade route from China to the West.'

'Yes. You are near its start, in China. You are in Xinjiang Province, in what you may know as the city of Niya. My people call it *Jingjue*.'

Piotr's eyes widened in disbelief. This was insanity. They had taken him on a journey across the world to CHINA, of all places. And as he processed this information, a familiar name began to nag at the corners of his memory – Niya. It held a certain weight and significance, something that even the most powerful crime syndicates and black-market dealers feared and avoided at all costs. A place of mystery and danger, shrouded in secrets and darkness. Piotr's heart raced as he tried to piece together the puzzle before him.

'You could have just killed me back in America and saved a lot of time and effort,' he finally said.

'Kill you?' The friendly monk seemed disturbed by the idea, his smile dropping slightly for a moment. 'Why would we want to do that? We wish to thank you. You have helped us immensely. Won't you have some milk tea?'

After a server placed a chilled glass of tea in front of him, Piotr finally took a sip. He could taste the subtle flavour of taro root in the drink.

'I still don't understand.'

'Ah. The old man you killed in Seattle was one of ours, a monk like me. But he lost his mind. He stole something of great value to us and fled to America, hiding with relatives. Your actions brought him back to our attention and allowed us to locate him. And, after some ... *persuading*, your friends underground there allowed us to locate you as well.'

'My friends aren't exactly the type who take well to persuasion,' Piotr said slowly.

'Yet they were indeed persuaded.'

'I don't like the way that sounds.'

'It is of no matter. We simply wish to thank you.'

Piotr's gaze swept across the grand temple hall, taking in the ornate decorations and the imposing figures of the Triad members. His eyes lingered on their stern expressions before returning to the serene monk sitting at the head of the table.

'So – tell me. What did your insane droogy steal?'

'Some ancient wooden tablets from this very location. These specimens are unique for their exceptional preservation and unusual linguistic features that differ from standard religious texts. VERY old. VERY ancient. VERY rare and important to us.'

'Religious texts. This is all about religious texts?'

'The language used in the tablets represents an obscure dialectical variant that only a handful of scholars worldwide can interpret. The script exhibits peculiar characteristics, including previously unknown ideograms and syntactical structures that suggest it may have been used for specialized or ceremonial purposes. The wood itself is of an unidentified species, remarkably resistant to decay despite its age.'

Piotr blinked again. 'I – uh, this is beyond me.'

'You must forgive me,' smiled the monk. 'I am a linguist by trade, and this is very exciting to me. You must think I like to hear myself talk, but no – I merely want you to understand why this is of paramount importance to us. You see, most striking are the tablets' references to geographical locations and historical events that don't align with conventional historical records, including detailed descriptions of a location identified as the Plateau of Leng. The text contains numerous astronomical observations and mathematical formulae that seem advanced for their era, along with recurring symbolic patterns that have defied traditional analysis.

'We were very, very close to translating them and finally … opening the gate.'

'Excuse me? "Gate"? What gate?'

'The tablets describe ancient entities of immense power. These beings are believed to have descended from the stars in Earth's distant past, with strong connections to this very area. Their true nature remains largely unknown, as translations regarding them are often contradictory or unclear, suggesting their very existence defies conventional human understanding.

'They are described as beings capable of manipulating the fundamental forces of reality, though the exact extent of their powers remains unclear. Historical records suggest they departed Earth eons ago, returning to the stars from whence they came, though certain texts hint at their eventual return. Their departure left behind artifacts and knowledge that various secret societies have sought throughout history. Of course, modern scholars debate whether these beings were literal entities or metaphorical representations of natural forces in ancient mythologies. However, the stolen tablets proved they were real, and showed how the gate can be opened that allows them to return.

'This knowledge drove my associate … insane.'

'Drove HIM insane?' Piotr burst, losing caution. 'It doesn't sound like he's the only one. In fact, he may have been the only sane one of your whole bunch.'

The monk kept smiling. 'Oh, my friend, you will soon see that I am not mad. Every word of this is true.'

Piotr felt the truth of it in his marrow, and his blood ran cold. He'd heard of Niya before, and this Plateau of Leng, in dark whispers shared by the criminal underworld. They warned against seeking its location, claiming that those who find it risk terrible transformations of body and soul. Multiple ancient societies appear to have had strict taboos against discussing certain aspects of the plateau, particularly regarding its residents and their supposed abilities to alter the fundamental nature of reality. But other secret societies still existed, maintaining a network of operatives in academic and cultural institutions worldwide to identify and acquire artifacts of interest.

And he was in the hands of such a terrifying group. This was not the familiar Triad he had encountered before; this was a menacing force, cloaked in shadows and driven by twisted desires.

'Our work will usher in a new age of enlightenment,

though others might view our goals as potentially ... catastrophic,' the monk admitted, seeing understanding dawn across Piotr's horrified face.

'I still don't know why I'm here,' Piotr said. 'What do you want with me?'

'We still seek the tablets, of course,' smiled the monk.

'How would I know where they are? Ask the people who were hiding him from you.'

'We tried. Regrettably, they did not know.'

'You killed them,' Piotr said flatly.

'Regretfully.'

'Then the only person who could help you is dead.'

'This is true. He is dead. But this can be rectified.'

Suddenly, something emerged from the temple doors on the side of the dais. Something that didn't belong in daylight.

It was a grotesque form, resembling a decaying human with greenish-pink skin and oozing blisters covering its face. It glowed with an unearthly and diseased green light that seemed strangely familiar. But despite the thing's revolting appearance, Piotr could still recognize the wispy goatee and embroidered patch covering one eye - it was the old man from the grocery store. It stumbled towards Piotr, emitting an overwhelming stench of decay.

Piotr tried to bolt from the table, but the nearest cultists grabbed his shoulders tightly, immobilizing him, and resumed the same deep chanting as earlier.

'The issue,' said the smiling monk, 'is that he can no longer talk. But you can.'

The creature reached out and carefully grasped Piotr's head in its swollen hands before leaning in to kiss him on the lips with its putrid, decaying mouth.

Piotr felt a surge of dizziness, quickly followed by a feeling worse than death - as if he were already dead.

He raised one rotting hand to his face, attempting to wipe away tears that refused to come. In a last desperate attempt to save himself, he clawed at his cataract-blinded eye only to rupture it, releasing a thick, viscous fluid down his ravaged cheek.

'Why?' Piotr managed to choke out, his tongue twisted and bloated with decay.

But deep down, he knew the answer.

The balance had been restored. Soon the old man would be telling the smiling monk where the ancient tablets were hidden. Using Piotr's mouth. Using Piotr's body.

And as his consciousness faded, leaving behind only rotten flesh and bones, the small-time thug Piotr Mytiukov finally realized true despair and damnation.

Poor Piotr Mytiukov, who'd never hurt a fly.

About the Author

Benjamin Adams was a 2002 Bram Stoker Award nominee for the anthology *The Children of Cthulhu*, co-edited with John Pelan. His short fiction has appeared in the 1998 Bram Stoker Award-winning anthology *Horrors! 365 Scary Stories*, and in anthologies such as *100 Wicked Little Witch Stories*; *100 Vicious Little Vampire Stories*; Miskatonic University; *Blood Muse*; and *Delta Green: Dark Theatres.* He has also written professionally for *Doctor Who*, in the Big Finish anthologies *Short Trips: Snapshots and Short Trips: The Centenarian*. He has recently returned to writing after a ten-year hiatus.

THE GIRL WITH THE CREEPY HOUSE

Raven Dane

1

The house was a nightmare from decades of neglect. Nature had done its best to reclaim it with rank black and green mould smothering the internal walls and tendrils of ruthless ivy growing into and smothering the once mellow yellow brick exterior.

Cate Malvyn's plummeting disappointment in her inheritance, deepened at she gazed across the tangled wilderness that purported to be a formal garden.

Not even a wild life refuge, she sighed.

Any wild flowers that may have self-seeded would have lost out to the rampant brambles and nettles. An overhanging canopy of large, unkempt yew trees blocked out the sunlight from east to west. Larger, looming yew trees lined the long driveway stretching to the back of the house and to a coach house and brick stables converted to garaging.

'Who the hell thought that was a good idea? Such dark, depressing trees.'

She spoke out aloud, not expecting her friend Dominic Aston to answer, he was twitting about pretending to be an explorer using a stick as a machete to clear his way through the tangled growth. Cate would have laughed but for the crushing disappointment at what a cousin had bequeathed her. A six bedroomed Georgian country house with ten acres of garden and paddocks. Born and raised a townie in Manchester, the idyll of a country life had never appealed. There was everything she needed back home, a good job in advertising, a modern flat close enough to walk to the city centre where there was lively café culture by day. At night the city came alive with all the theatres, clubs and party venues that kept the city vibrant and desirable. And friends. Good, supportive ones that shared her lifestyle of hard-earned hedonism.

Dom paused his attack on the malign undergrowth and turned to her with a shrug and a smile.

'Does it matter? This is a bloody goldmine, sell it straight away to a developer and let them sort it out. The prices for homes in the Cotswolds are already sky high. It will get snapped up straight away.'

Sighing, Cate glanced back at the house, hidden by its baleful ivy guardian and tormentor.

'If only, my Weird Cousin Richard left it to me with a strict covenant that it must not be sold or given away and had to remain in the Malvyn family in perpetuity. I can't even walk away and leave it to rot; I am now responsible for all the council rates and upkeep.'

'Weird Cousin Richard was a wanker.'

'You don't know the half of it, Dom. He was the over indulged, precocious only child of my father's great Aunt Joan and Uncle Derek. I was only four when I discovered that my parents were worried about them visiting us and I didn't understand the unease when any family adults spoke of him.'

Dom clearly found the idea of this malignant child hilarious.

'What did he do? Pull the wings of insects and put on your mother's underwear?'

'To start with.'

Her friend stopped slashing at the nettles, studying Cate's face for signs of joking, by now she should have had a fit of the giggles but her expression remained weirdly impassive.

'As he grew older and out of control, he became fascinated by taxidermy … only he didn't wait until his subjects were dead before proceeding.'

Again, Dom paused, still expecting Cate to give in and laugh. She did not, her already porcelain pale face blanching, clearly recalling past awful stories within the family.

'Can you rent it? That would give you a tasty monthly income.'

'I think so, nothing in the will says I can't. But I haven't the money to put this place right. He also put in some devious clauses in his legacy to prevent 'accidental' arson or runaway bulldozers.'

Cate turned away from the impenetrable tangle and looked back at the house. The windows were as hidden as the house and garden, heavy old curtains covered with decades of dust and cobwebs shut out the outside world. With Dom's help she had already managed to open the front door but had not ventured beyond the entrance hall and first reception rooms. The air was stiflingly still, a musty mixture of dust, mould, rodent faeces, and urine. Who knew how long it had been since a human had breathed in the stale air. Cate could not bear it and had rushed back out into the garden. A wave of anguish tightened her throat and chest. Tears threatened to brim in her eyes. Damn Weird Cousin Richard, his fascination with cruelty had reached out from beyond the grave. Dom saw her distress and steered her away from the building.

'Let's get far away from Hell House. I spotted a great looking pub with a restaurant a few miles away from the other side of the village. We could sit in the garden, breath in fresh air.'

Cate nodded, briskly leaving the house and heading for her car, not wanting to look back at the house or garden again. Never would not be long enough.

'Throw me the house keys,' called Dom, 'you have enough problems without squatters moving in.'

'They're welcome to it, they can't make the place more

horrible than it is.'

She sat in her little lilac Corsa with the engine running, impatient to get away. She glanced back at the garden wondering what was keeping Dom. Her gaze stopped at the tall nettles at the edge of the drive. Wasn't that where her friend had beaten them down? There was no break in the plants, all as tall and soundlessly threatening as before. Cate decided she had mistaken the extent of his destruction until she noticed his stick lying beside them on the weed infested gravel. One broken nettle stem lay trapped beneath the makeshift blunt machete. Creeped out, she leaned on the horn, where the bloody hell was Dom? Seconds that felt like minutes later he appeared around the corner, nursing his right hand.

'Pass me some tissues, hon. As I locked the front door, I must have caught my hand on something sharp.'

Cate helped him clean up the wound, small but deep and in a serrated half circle. Like a bite.

'Looks nasty, I think we should skip the pub and head off to the nearest A&E.'

'Nah, just a flesh wound, I'll live.'

She shivered, that house was making her edgy. Why did Dom's flippant remark make her feel such dread, so much fear for him over a scratch from a rusty nail, Watching too many films on Horror Channel, too many books by her favourite authors, Adam Nevill, Joe Hill and Phil Rickman. It had to be that.

'I'm right up to date with my tetanus shots,' Dom said, noting Cate's anxiety. 'Look, it's stopped bleeding now.'

He held up his hand to show her. With the blood flow stemmed, the wound looked no less strange. Against her determination not to be spooked, she could imagine a row of teeth making it. Too big to come from a rat, the blunt shapes of the grooves were unlike any creature she could imagine. It couldn't have been from anything living, a broken piece of metalware on the door perhaps. The house was making her have irrational, fearful thoughts, no doubt part of Cousin Richard's cruel legacy. Cate refused to give into his mind games, she had been tortured enough as a child of four and he was twelve. Memories she had try to stay locked down and forgotten now re-emerged in a dam burst of past horrors. God's teeth, he was an evil little shit behind his angelic looks. The clear blue eyes, gentle smile and golden curls that never reflected anything but the sweetness of a Renaissance cherub, even when he had drowned her pet rabbit in a garden pond. Richard's parents believed his story that Bunny had fallen in and his soaked clothes were from trying in vain to rescue it. They always accepted his word, at least made a show of believing their son. Her own parents were struck dumb in shock, her mother gathering the sobbing, hysterical Cate in her arms. Bunny was the last pet Cate dared to own as a child.

Tying back her dark red hair, Cate opened-up all the car windows and drove swiftly down the neglected, yew-lined drive, over nettles and dock leaves breaking through the concrete. Once on the main road, she pushed the Corsa into a speed-limit-breaking rush, eager to put as much distance as possible away from the house. She shivered as if memories of its ghastliness were reaching out like tendrils of a tainted miasma. Cate sped past the pub Dom had suggested and continued until far away from the Cotswolds and heading back north. Only sheer luck had saved her from being pulled over from the traffic police. Finding another pleasant looking pub with a garden, she pulled in and paused, hands gripping the steering wheel. Dom had travelled in silence, not pleading with her to slow down. His partner Sean was a speed demon on his BMW motorbike. He wasn't frightened by Cate's driving or of the old wreck of a house she had been burdened with, Dom had a plan.

They found an empty table comfortably partially shaded by the early afternoon sun and ordered a light lunch and two glasses of Prosecco. Not to celebrate the legacy but being off the grounds and miles away from it.

'While you were doing your Louis Hamilton impersonation terrorising the well-heeled dwellers of middle England, I was putting together a plan.'

Cate took another sip of her wine and though sceptical, inclined her head, ready to listen.

'You know that new girlfriend of Robin's.'

'Someone not just beautiful but intelligent and lovely for a change, nothing like the hard-faced bitches he usually favours. I love Robin but he is such a glutton for humiliation and heartbreak.'

'I agree, never understood his attraction to those users and gold diggers. Well, Chandice is head of programming for Best TV's reality shows. Including *Make Or Break*

Noticing his friend's grimace, Dom laughed, 'I know, appalling title but people don't forget it even when taking the piss.'

'That's the show where they send in a big team of decorators, builders and landscape gardeners to transform awful houses. But they always choose people who have hard luck stories and no money. It is supposed to be heart-warming. A single yuppie from Manchester's Northern Quarter district hardly fits the brief.'

'Nothing that cannot be tweaked in your favour, it won't be the first time. I can see it now, lonely, single young orphan stuck with a terrible white elephant legacy.'

'True-ish. But for the fact I am not lonely and I am a bit too old an orphan to tug on the public's heart strings. Also maybe not single for much longer.''

'Gareth? The Welsh Adonis?'

'Hands off! You've got Sean.'

Relaxing, Dom was pleased to see his best friend smiling again, her green eyes recovering their sparkle. It was as if the house had drained her lively spirit, even on that briefest of visits but had released its grip with every runaway mile.

'I'll speak to Chandice, she may find another angle to get the team on board. It would make a great one off special. 'Exorcising Hell House. A *Make Or Break* special.' Does it have a name by the way?'

'Alastor House.'

'Odd, I wonder what's the story behind it?'

Dom pulled out his smartphone from his discarded jacket. The temperature had a benign warmth in the pub gardens in contrast with the unseasonal chill at Cate's baleful inheritance. He brought up Google Search, typed in a few words, then shut down the phone in a brisk gesture, put it back in his jacket.

'Nothing there, not a single mention. Probably a made-up name like 'Dunroaming.'

A young man bringing their lunch on a tray interrupted any further conversation on the name of the house. Dom hoped he had done enough to stop her looking it up. In some mythologies, Alastor was a sadistic demon who took pleasure in torturing damned souls in Hell. In others he was a demon who took pleasure in fomenting feuds and rifts in within families. He had clearly researched among lists of demonic entities and chosen this one with deliberate purpose. It was another cruel mind game from Cate's Weird Cousin Richard.

The weight of unwanted responsibility for Alastor House pulled Cate into a state of anxiety and melancholy for the first time since she lost both parents to the pandemic. Letters began to arrive at her address transferring to her liability for rates and water bills. None for heating and light though, had Richard ever even lived there? The last time she had seen him in person was for a family funeral three years earlier. She had been surprised to see him there as he had further scandalised the Malvyn family by not attending the funerals of either of his parents. He had grown into a tall, slim, good-looking man, the cherub curls replaced by well-cut short and darker hair. His eyes retained their ice blue shade but were as cold and spiteful as ever. He had become a top scientist, a precocious young prodigy. One highly respected in his field of genetics, enough so to have received many awards and generous funds to further his research. Cate had avoided him throughout the service and wake. She had wondered then how many more 'Bunnies' had suffered from his sadistic experimenting. Unsettling her, Cate had seen him watching her intently many times that day as if scrutinising an interesting specimen. Cate had fled the gathering early to avoid having to talk with her cousin.

She had read about his premature demise on internet news channels. 'A great and grievous loss to science' apparently. He had been knocked down and killed instantly by a hit and run driver in Berlin, a drunken one from the statements from shocked witnesses. She had not felt sad, not even though he was the last male in her branch of the Malvyn family. Deep down she had felt the drunken driver had done the world a favour. Nothing beneficial to mankind would have come from Richard's experiments, altruism was not in his nature. An inherent malice that had reached out to her beyond the grave.

Cate roughly shoved the unwanted letters to one side; she had nothing in her bank account to pay the bills beyond a miracle lottery win. The occasional £2.60 on the Euromillions was not going to fill the coffers. She had already blown her savings on the new Corsa and a trip to New York, going first class all the way. She was young, unfettered beyond the mortgage on her flat, savings and pensions belonged in the future ... distant concept to her now 23 year old mind. She tried to force aside her stress by a long, hot shower and preparations for her date with the divine Gareth Ellis.

At the latest heir's rapid departure, the house breathed out with the faintest whisper. A sigh too slight to disturb the veils of dust encrusted cobwebs. Yet there was nothing static or quiet within its rancid walls or dwelling in the tangled grounds. There had never been total stillness and silence even in its most distant past, before anyone considered building a dwelling on the malign site. Many 'owners' came and departed over the centuries, their bones long forgotten dust. It could wait, as long as it needed, the new one would return, of that it was certain. Best of all, the female would not come alone.

2

No doubt to impress her, the Welsh Adonis took Cate to supper at *Les Fourmis Affamés*, an achingly pretentious restaurant just opened in Manchester's trendy Northern Quarter. Cate wished she had eaten before Gareth had turned up at her flat. The prospect of neo nouveau cuisine meant ridiculously overpriced, minimal food, something that had never appealed to her. If he got the chance to know her better, Gareth would have realised a nearby curry house or even a Macky D would have been welcomed. The most important part of a date for her, was the company, the adventure of getting to know someone new both in and out of bed.

They were ushered to their table by a maître d', deliberately haughty to the point of rudeness. Cate was aware of other diners looking up from their meagre meals to watch the new arrivals. They must be staring at Gareth, she decided. He was ridiculously good looking with long, tousled black hair and eyes a startling shade of violet blue that they just had to be coloured contact lenses. Gareth looked like he must be someone famous. Not tall enough to be a model but maybe an actor or rock star. In fact, he was a press photographer with the weekly Manchester Vanguard newspaper, snapping fetes and the aftermath of car crashes with none of the cachet and glamour of a fashion shoot or foreign photojournalist.

If Cate had been a mind reader, she would have discovered the diners were also intrigued by her beauty too. Again, she was too small to be a model but was a trim, gamine waif with a short pixie cut, naturally dark red hair and big, doe like dark brown eyes. She wore a daringly short little black dress that emphasised her slender form and pale skin. For adornment she just wore a simple silver chain with a tiny, sparkling Swarovski crystal cube and matching earrings that caught and twinkled with any light in the room. Of which there was little.

Gorgeous to look at, Cate found her date to be hard work at first, she suspected he was intimidated by the restaurant and didn't blame him. After they finished the first course of two small, thin asparagus spears, drizzled with a peppery, runny jus of lime ash and juniper berries, or more likely just one berry, Cate decided to take the initiative and called over the nearest server.

'Can we have the bill please? We are already stuffed full with that amazing starter. Don't have room for anything more.'

Gareth didn't bother supressing a wide grin and grabbed the hardly touched bottle of Grand Bateau Blanc Bordeaux and tucking the wine under his arm, paid with his credit card.

'Oh, and give our compliments to the chef,' he added, 'and to the warm welcome from your maître d'.'

The couple made their way through the gloom and the ant nest inspired décor and out onto a warm, dry summer evening.

'I wonder how many other diners were wishing they had the balls to do that.'

Gareth said with a relaxed broad smile from discovering something new about his date, something he liked … lot.

Cate returned his smile, 'maybe the lack of balls had something to do with it, I have nothing down there to lose.'

A warm, dry night and a full moon competed against the street lights. The night was too lovely to endure sitting in another restaurant, so they bought bags of chips and sat on a bench, washing their meal down with the white wine straight from the bottle. Their conversation was easier away from the stiflingly disdainful *Fourmis* allowing Cate to remember why she had found her date attractive apart from his obvious good looks. Gareth was open, honest and depreciative of his work, in his own words he was 'just a snapper, I'm no David Bailey.'

With the wine going to her head, Cate told him about the misfortune of her unexpected legacy, trying to make her account light-hearted but failing miserably, wiping away unwanted tears. She felt his comforting arms enclose her shoulders.

'What a total shit, if he was still alive, I'd tell him that to his face after I'd flattened him.'

'If he was still alive, you wouldn't need to I'd have done it first.'

The mood lightened as they laughed at the absurdity of their jokey bravado. They sauntered arm in arm back to Cate's nearby flat and paused by the gated entrance.

'This is the point we have a goodnight kiss and I invite you in for coffee …'

Gareth interrupted her by kissing her, not a polite, brief farewell on her cheek, but with a deep, passionate, full on smooch.

Once inside Cate's flat, they bypassed the coffee and headed straight for her bedroom.

Getting back to ordinary life was difficult now for Cate, with the millstone of Alastor House weighing her down. The executors of Cousin Richard's estate were adamant the wretch had not put aside any money for the upkeep of the house. He'd left his considerable remaining financial assets to further his research into whatever unnamed project he had been working on. Something highly secretive apparently for all attempts at finding out had drawn blank. In desperation, she had called her old school friend David Briggs, a fellow Mancunian, now a reporter for one of London's evening papers. He had sent her copies of all his research on the elusive Professor Richard Malvyn which had been disappointing, no more than the facts already available on Google and Wikipedia. Cate did her best concentrating on her work and the welcome distraction of being among people whose lives were full of everyday issues. Office life had never been more welcome. It was the time alone back in her apartment where her baleful inheritance overtook her thoughts.

Two weeks after that visit to the Cotswolds, Cate decided to call Dom, he had a way of making her see through difficulties and cheering her up. With no answer from his mobile, she rang the land line. His partner, Sean answered and was unusually terse at hearing her voice.

'Can you talk any sense into him? He needs to go to A&E straight away.'

'Oh no … what's wrong?'

Sean gave a long, deep sigh, his voice becoming emotional. Something was very wrong.

'Silly idiot came home from his jaunt with you nursing a cut hand. Waved away all help as usual. 'Just a little scratch,' you know what he's like.'

Cate knew too well.

'I had insisted we went straight to the local hospital when Dom hurt himself at the house but once his mind is made up …'

There was a long silence in reply, she had never heard Sean so lost for words, so deeply anxious.

'Will it help if I came over?'

'Maybe … but bring a face mask.'

He hung up the phone.

Again, so unlike him, though not as ebullient as his partner, Sean was always happy to talk to Cate. Indeed, any long, meaningful conversation she would have was always with Sean. Dom was too flighty, too quickly bored. She couldn't bear to ignore this situation which would make her a rubbish friend. The lads didn't deserve that. She stuffed a face mask in her bag and rushed down to the underground car park. The journey across the city to Salford Quays was normally not long but that afternoon the roads were clogged up with traffic, the delays making her stress deepen with every red traffic light, every road works, every broken-down car.

The guys lived in a spectacular, ultra-modern flat overlooking the Ship Canal sparkling at night with the bright lights of this vibrant part of Manchester. As she parked her car, a thought flickered through her mind, if only she could sell that awful dump, she could have her pick of flats in this desirable area. If only … Maybe renting would give her enough. A frisson of hope buoyed up her mood, that only lasted the seconds it took to press the button in the apartment block lobby. Instead of a cheery welcome from either of her friends, she was let into the building without a word. What the hell was going on?

The door to the flat was left open and as she gently pushed it wider and walked in, the reason for Sean' instruction to bring a face mask became horribly clear. The reek of infection made her gag, so out of place in the pristine property. Both Dom and Sean were house proud and enthusiastic minimalists, seeking a calm and restful living space. Where was that awful stench coming from? A blocked drain? Something had died under the flooring? Sean stepped out of their bedroom, his stressed-out demeanour clearly showed he was at the end of his tether.

'I need you to talk sense into that bloody idiot, God knows I have tried. He still refuses help, I am calling an ambulance, with you here as well, he will be outnumbered.'

Now worried sick, Cate approached the main bedroom door, the stench was hard to bear now, had Dom contracted an especially aggressive flesh-eating bug? A form of deadly necrotising fasciitis? She was no expert in medicine, but she remembered an outbreak in a hospital in Leeds four years earlier, a new strain, one that resisted antibiotics and had caused many casualties. It ended when the hospital was given some experimental treatment from Russia using phages to attack the bacteria. That gave her a welcome sense of hope for Dom.

She took in a deep breath and entered the bedroom. Dom was sitting fully clothed at the side of the bed, whimpering, rocking back and forward in agony as he held onto his right hand. It was bound with a bandage, sodden through with some foul-smelling substance that was staining it a peculiar, sickly shade of purple. What in hell was happening to him? She spun around to confront Sean.

'Why isn't he in hospital already? How long as he been like this?'

'This awful purple seeping began two hours ago.'

Cate gasped, such a short time, it had to be an extreme case of flesh-eating bacteria.

'Call an ambulance, now! There's too much traffic to risk me taking him and the sooner he sees a medic the better.'

'I am still here, you know.'

Dom's voice was weak and shaky, all his natural exuberance lost to the infection.

'We are going to make sure you stay with us,' Sean answered, 'an ambulance is on the way. And no, you longer have any say in the matter.'

It was only minutes away, but time seemed to freeze and stand still during the awkward, anxious wait for the ambulance crew. Cate left the couple for some alone time and walked out onto the wide balcony that stretched the width of the flat. It wasn't just to give them time to themselves, she needed fresh air, as much as she could before facing the appalling reek from Dom's 'just a flesh wound.' The balcony was a disorderly riot of colour in comparison to the flat's stark white minimalism. One of Dom's hobbies was growing vivid coloured, strongly scented flowers, Cate breathed in their perfume deeply to fill her senses with their beauty but still the festering odour remained as a fetid undercurrent.

The doorbell rang, as help arrived downstairs. Fortunately for them, the paramedics wore masks but could see the seriousness of Dom's condition. They showed their disbelief that the infection was only hours old, even behind the face coverings. Cate hated their quick glances at Sean, clearly believing this was a case of domestic abuse and neglect. She had to speak out in his defence.

'Look around you, look at how pristine and orderly this

place is. Not exactly a rat infested, squalid drug den in a squat is it.'

Embarrassed, the paramedics mumbled something and got on with getting Dom ready to be taken down to the ambulance. Sean was allowed to go with him. Cate followed them down to the ground floor but didn't want to intrude. She gave Sean a quick, tight hug and braving the stench, kissed Dom on the forehead. The ambulance crew got on with getting their patient into the lift. Cate walked beside her distraught friend.

'Let me know how he is as soon as you can, please, Sean.'

Nodding assent, he squeezed into the lift leaving Cate to descend in another. There was nothing more she could do to help Dom. She sat in her car, wiping away tears, the stench of the infection seeming to pursue her from the flat as if it had a malign life of its own. Should she follow the ambulance, be there for her friends, or would it be an intrusion? She felt guilty too, Dom would not have been injured had she not taken him to that dreadful house. Cate struggled to stop her hands from shaking as she tried to start the car and stalling it. She was in too much of a state to be any use to Sean and Dom. No fit state to be driving either. She locked up the car and walked to a nearby still open café. A stiff brandy would be ideal but she settled for a large latte, giving herself time to calm down and behave rationally. Only then would she consider her options over a visit to the hospital.

Cate took her time finishing her coffee and decided to go home before she made any more journeys. She had not been imagining things over the reek following her down from the flat. Other customers and staff were obviously becoming aware of it, embarrassing her when they looked in her direction for the source of the noxious odour. She scurried out of the café, marking it as one she could never visit again and drove home with all the car windows open. Once inside her apartment, she tore off all her clothes including her shoes and bundled them into three large black plastic bags put into one. She then showered, drenching her body and hair with the most powerful smelling body wash she possessed, an unwanted secret Santa Christmas gift from someone in her office. Someone who didn't like her, most likely. She had just finished drying herself when her phone rang. It was Sean, his voice barely audible.

'Dom's been taken to the intensive care unit. It's not looking good, Cate. They have no idea what it is.'

'He said it was just a scratch from some metal on the door,' Cate murmured through her distress, 'but to me it looked like some sort of bite. He made so little of it at the time.'

'Typical of Dom, he likes to think he is Mr Immortal, a 21st century Dorian Gray.'

'I am going back there, Sean. To see if there is any clue to what is poisoning him. I can't think of anything else practical to do but I can't just sit here, wringing my hands.'

'Hope you find something, and quickly.'

Sean hung up, leaving Cate holding her phone left in abrupt silence. She had sworn to herself she would never set foot again on Weird Cousin Richard's ghastly property.

With Dom's life under serious threat, she had no choice.

3

If she didn't love her friend so much, Cate would never have made the long drive back to the Cotswolds, not alone and in darkness. She never wanted to see it again. But she was certain Dom's life was in danger, what else could she do but pull up her big girl's pants and face her toxic inheritance again. So armed with a high-power torch, a fully charged phone, a pen knife, and some sealable little plastic bags from a short-lived craft phase. Cate headed across country to Alastor House, once again cursing her overactive imagination. She was sure Gareth would have come with her if asked, but with one friend in danger, she couldn't risk her new lover too.

As she reached the tall, rusty iron gates that guarded the driveway to the house, once again they creaked and groaned as they slowly opened for her. Something electrical was still working, the gates must have a sensor triggered by her car's approach. Not the best system for security purposes but Cate didn't care. Let anyone up to no good do their best to vandalise the place. It wouldn't be her fault and therefore not trigger financial repercussions from the terms of Cousin Richard's malign will. In theory.

In the darkness, the wall of yew trees seemed to loom inwards when lit by the Corsa's headlights. They seemed to act as silent, forbidding sentinels signalling a warning to turn and leave this dire place. Cate shuddered at what she knew was just an illusion, no more than a trick of the light. They were just overgrown, old trees. Time to focus on her task, she still had the house to deal with. Driving as close as possible to the main door, she parked right up to the stone steps. She kept the Corsa's engine running, hoping the headlights at full beam would keep away whatever lurked in the darkness beyond the twin beams. Common sense told her there was nothing in the neglected, tangled grounds other than England's unthreatening wild life, shy creatures of the night, the foxes, badgers and deer that would never dare to approach. Again, she cursed her love of horror films and novels, stoking up her overactive imagination.

With the unwelcome thought that the only dangerous predators were all too human, Cate grabbed a handful of the plastic bags and a sharp penknife and scurried out of the car and up crumbling steps in the process of being overtaken by determined nettles forcing their way through the cracks. With the bags under her arm, she shone a torch around the double front doors, old oak with rusted iron fittings. Nothing seemed the obvious culprit behind Dom's injury, no broken spars of wood or projecting metal. Nothing that could resemble a bite mark. Relying on the headlights, she put down the torch and began to scrap samples of the painted wood and rust into the bags.

So focused on getting the samples and making a quick retreat, she hadn't noticed the silence from the surrounding grounds. As she finished gathering her evidence, Cate paused and became aware of the lack of night sounds. A city girl, born and raised, as a child she had spent time in the country on holidays with her parents. There should be the sounds of owls, foxes and the flutter of bats above her. There was nothing. Not even the gentle soughing of the wind through the yews. The silence triggered a strong fear response in Cate, why was nature this still? Was the wildlife afraid, and of what? She ran down the entrance steps and pulled the car door open wide. As she threw in the bags, knife and torch, she heard a fast-approaching grating, skittering sound, like metal nails clawing for purchase on concrete. Cate leapt into the driver's seat, slammed the door shut and drove away, the Corsa's wheels spinning, throwing up stones and shards of broken concrete. She did not dare look in the rear mirror, the sight of whatever was making that weird noise could weaken her from terror and panic.

Speeding too fast for the rough track, her fingers blanching from her tight grip on the steering wheel, Cate prayed to any listening deity that the sensor on the entrance gates would open them wide at her approach. She was helpless if not, at the mercy of a barely used electric system. If they remained closed, could she batter them open with the Corsa? A small, compact car, it was an unlikely candidate for such an action film manoeuvre. Cate had no idea what had made the sound that had spooked her, or whether it was following her, she just knew she didn't want to find out. Ever.

Where were the gates? The drive was lengthy but not this long. Had she made a turn somewhere, unnoticed in her panic? She became disorientated, surrounded still by the overbearing living wall of dark yew. She rounded a bend too fast and in too high a gear momentarily losing full control of the Corsa. As she straightened the little car, Cate whimpered in shock and despair. Ahead of her lit by the car's headlights was Alastor House. No longer still, the overgrown tangle surrounding the house was bristling with agitation, a wave of movement. Once again the chittering, scurrying metallic sounds warned of approaching unknown menace. Cate had no choice but to push the car into high speed in a spatter of gravel and protesting engine. She dared not look in the rearview mirror, the sight of whatever was following behind her could sap her resolve from terror. This time the gates came into view and allowed her to escape.

She drove away as fast as the winding country road would allow until reaching well-lit main roads and the semblance of normality around her. Cate pulled into a large, busy service station and parked under a bright overhead lamp close to the main doors. It was 2.30am on the Corsa's dashboard clock. Even that late at night, the complex was an ant's nest of lorry drivers and delivery vans. The mundane normality around her was both a relief and a dissonance. How could this safe, unthreatening world exist at the same time as Alastor House? She sat in the car and with plenty of fuel in the Corsa's tank, resisted the lure of going into the station and getting a strong coffee among normal human beings. Getting the samples to the hospital was too much of a priority to stop now.

4

Cate delivered the samples, stumbling into the hospital in the early hours of the morning. Dom's medical team rushed them off to the labs, leaving her to collapse onto an uncomfortable, upright chair outside the ward, unable to face the short drive to her home. Terror had drained her, the rush of adrenaline that saw her through the ordeal had gone, leaving her physically exhausted and shivering but not from cold. One of the ICU nurses put a blanket around her shoulders and offered to make her a cup of tea, 'a proper one not that bitter liquid in a flimsy paper cup from a machine.' Cate looked up at the concerned face of the nurse and nodded a grateful assent, even talking was an effort.

At some point, she must have drunk the tea, for there was no sign of broken China or spilled liquid. She awoke to the bustle and bright lights of the early changeover of medical staff on the ward. A nearby clock on the wall told her it was 5am. Stiff and aching from sleeping across two plastic chairs, Cate found a doctor checking the overnight stats for the department's seriously ill patients. She started to explain who she was but the doctor held up her hand and smiled.

'We have met before Miss Malvyn. I am Doctor Torres. I know you are close to Mr Aston and went to a great effort to rush those samples to our labs. I am off duty now, how about having breakfast in the hospital canteen with me. I can talk about his progress and you look dreadful, if you don't mind me saying.'

Cate found her voice and with a weary smile, agreed. The eerie, threatening experience felt increasingly like a bad dream in such everyday surroundings. The canteen was brightly lit and busy with hospital staff. A freshly cooked English breakfast and a round of hot toast and marmalade washed down with freshly brewed tea helped ground her. She was surprised just how hungry she was now, when was the last time she had eaten? Had anything to drink? Dr Torres was speaking to her, shaking Cate out of her confused jumble of thoughts.

'Go home, call in sick and straight to bed. Doctor's orders. You will be of no use to Dominick if you get unwell.'

'How is he?'

'Hanging on, he's a fighter. Hopefully the samples will give us an idea what we are dealing with. The infection has slowed down, which is some good news. But he isn't out of the woods yet.'

Cate shivered at the mention of woods, the memory of those godawful dark sentinels flashing into her mind with sudden, unwelcome clarity. Thoughts that broke through the comforting reality of her surroundings. Thanking the doctor for care of Dom, she left the hospital, relieved to find the car where she had left it in her panic. It had not been towed away and no zealous parking warden had pasted a ticket on windscreen. It was still very early in the morning, most of Manchester's inhabitants were still asleep. She drove back home through empty streets and remembered how those metal gates had let her escape the baleful spell of her inheritance, thwarting whatever nightmare had pursued her. A twisted game of cat and mouse? But what was the cat?

Once home, she had a quick, hot shower then left a message at her office, calling in sick for the first time in four years working there. She had always worked long hours and many weekends over that time. She had no guilt taking the day off. Once in bed, Cate succumbed to a deep sleep, one curiously free from nightmares. Maybe her 'dream director' had decided they couldn't compete with her bizarre reality.

Cate woke up late afternoon. After checking her answerphone and mobile for any messages, she took a mug of coffee out to the balcony and sat taking in the familiar surroundings. The sunlight sparkled on the steel and glass windows of surrounding buildings and on the huge mural art installations painted on brick walls that helped make this area of the city so memorable. Such welcome normality but it jarred with her memories of the night before. How could this peaceful scene exist at the same time as the nameless horror of Alastor House? There had been nothing left for her but a 'hope all is ok' message from Jeanie, her office assistant. Nothing from Sean. Maybe no news was good news when it came to Dom's battle against the mystery infection. She felt so helpless, guilty too. If he hadn't gone with her to the Cotswolds, he would be well now.

The hard-won samples from Alastor House came up negative for any toxic contaminants. The dedicated medical team fighting to save Dom's life concluded the wound that had triggered his deterioration was from a bite. A virulent and totally unknown infection that defied known medical science.

5

Life for Cate slipped into a more familiar pattern of work. The focus on real life challenges in familiar surroundings helped during office hours. So much so that she took every opportunity to take on taxing assignments that required longer hours and long trips to meet up with clients in person. It earned praise from her bosses, feigned protests from the creative teams that had an increased workload but it left her emotionally uncommitted Cate had become a workaholic to block out having to think about her legacy.

Her friends had gone away on an indefinite trip to the USA to seek help for Dom's drastic amputation. They were wealthy enough to pay for the latest state of the art prosthetics and a prolonged stay. They had left without letting her know. A sign that she was no longer part of their life? A living reminder of what led to Dom's life changing maiming from a still unknown assailant? She only found out from their mutual friend, Robin. They had even arranged for someone else to care for Dom's balcony garden while they were away, something Cate had always done.

After a week of full-on work, Cate's Friday evening plans were for an early night in bed with a good book- definitely not a horror. Gareth was away all weekend, dealing with an urgent family problem back in Wales. She was disappointed he hadn't suggested taking her with him. Even being cooped up in a hotel while he was sorting his elderly parents' problems would have been preferable to being alone with her thoughts. She had a long, hot shower, zapped a ready meal in the microwave and turned on the TV for some mindless distraction. It was times like these Cate wished she was not so highly allergic to cats, an affectionate, purring companion would have been so welcome. She was halfway through an amusing episode of Judge Judy when the phone rang. Maybe Gareth had changed his mind. It was not too long a journey from Manchester to Flint in North Wales, just under an hour in good driving conditions.

'Hi lovely, are you free tonight?'

She hid her disappointment; it was not Gareth but her friend Robin. She could hear Chandice in the background calling 'Hi, Cate,' in friendly greeting.

'I am in my pjs with my hair in a towel enjoying a quiet night in. Work has been insane recently.'

'With Gareth?'

'No, he's away with family problems. His dad's dementia is sadly worsening and his mum can't cope.'

Robin paused, possible muting his phone and talking to his girlfriend.

'Can we pop over? We won't outstay our welcome, promise. We have an exciting proposal for you that can't wait.'

Intrigued, Cate agreed.

'And don't change out of those jimjams.' Robin replied, laughing, 'we will be sporting our favourite onesies.

Within the hour, her friends were as good as their word, Robin in a plush lion onesie, Chandice in a sparkly unicorn. Wearing her fleece Wonder Woman pyjamas, Cate's laughter came from a welcome, recently hidden place. The gathering was so light-hearted and frivolous and so unlike the Robin she knew before Chandice came into his life. If she didn't already love the woman, she did for this. He looked ten years younger, a sparkle in his eyes that no other female in his love life could create. Cate's thoughts about missing Gareth and the other, forbidden, dark thoughts were chased away by laughter and a bottle of a good, old Merlot and a large platter of cheeses, olives and cold meat cuts.

'Maybe I should have brought ice cream, fizzy drinks and jelly babies too.'

'We must do this another time, with all the gang. Never grow up, it's a trap!'

At Cate's mention of the others, a shadow seemed to

cross Robin's eyes. He took a deep swig of the red wine and murmured.

'Can you imagine 'Mr Oh So Serious and Effortlessly Cool' Sean doing this? Especially now … what with Dom …'

Before the mood could darken further, Chandice interrupted, 'Who knows? His loss. But I bet I could persuade Sean.'

She launched into a lilting Louisiana creole accent. 'Remember I have that good ol' New Orleans voudoun power. He would be helpless and unable to resist.'

Her friend's attempt at levity fell flat with Cate, the unwelcome reminder of the horrific assault on Dom and her own flight from … from what? She belonged in the rational world as did Chandice born and raised in Britain as were her parents. It was her grandparents who originally came from New Orleans.

'I can't supply jelly babies but I have an unopened tub of crushed chocolate cookie ice cream in the freezer.'

She hurried into the kitchen as if the pleasure in sharing the luxury treat could dispel the dark cloud in her mind.

By the time the get-together had reached the coffee and brandy stage, Cate's tearful state had mellowed. Her laughter had become natural and unforced, as it had always been in happier days. It did not last. Robin reached over the table to refill everyone's brandy glass.

'By the way, Cate, before he got so unwell, Dom mentioned your old house and thought it would make a great candidate for *Make Or Break* …'

He paused, surprised by Cate's reaction. All colour had drained from her face, tears brimmed in her eyes and she dropped her thankfully still empty glass onto the thick wool rug.

Grant Dalston once presenter of the *Beyond The Veil* TV show, was firm but as polite as he could muster at yet another request to get him back in front of the camera. He had turned down many highly lucrative offers from American and Canadian producers to front their paranormal shows. He despised them, despite the generous fee always offered. He called them 'Loud Americans bellowing at "spirits" or UK teams screaming at any noise' productions. Tacky and phoney though highly popular with worldwide viewers. UK based *Beyond the Veil* had strived to be unsensational, respectful and used leading edge paranormal science and an incredibly genuine medium. Dalston had abruptly quit the show during an investigation into a notorious derelict shop in Lincoln's old Bailgate area. One that led to stories of many strange deaths over the centuries and had tragically cost the lives of two colleagues during the show's investigation. He had tried to have the Veil's footage destroyed but it was considered ratings dynamite, the most terrifying haunting ever broadcast. Perhaps the only genuine one. Network bigwigs had made it clear, he was only the handsome, charismatic presenter. Easily replaced.

Shaken to the core of his being by the events at Bailgate and mourning the loss of two members of the team, both good friends, Dalston had found a remote retreat in the Scottish Highlands. There he stayed well clear of all social media and only a few, well trusted friends had access to his mobile phone number. Clearly one of them had broken under pressure. How else did The Veil's producer have his number and was on the line now. A new voice, so unlike producer Amanda Selec's brittle tones. This was a soft-spoken young woman, perhaps bait to keep his interest? That would not work on him. He had seen and experienced horrors in Bailgate, he had no intention to witness more proof that the supernatural was all too real. As were the nightmares that woke Dalston with his own screaming. Some things were best left alone. The saying 'don't poke the alien', worked just as well with vengeful spectres.

'A one-off special, Grant. Maybe with a substantial donation to charity? The situation needs the very best team. No one can replace you in front of the camera.'

'Oh, I think that you can,' he answered with a cynical

sigh, 'there is no shortage of good looking young men and women who would kill their own grannies to get a shot of headlining a successful show.'

'But none with your experience and massive world-wide fan base.'

Ah, his fan base … another reason to stay well clear of the show … any show. From agreeable letters and cards from the genuine, sensible fans, to wild, incoherent, and often deluded, missives scrawled in green or purple ink from the worryingly deranged. There was also a regular deluge of death threats from hardline religious fanatics promising an eternity in Hell unless he found Jesus. He suspected their saviour had also gone into hiding with unhinged followers like that. He was grateful when the production company hired someone to deal with all the mail. He had no such filter now. Hopefully the more obsessive of his fan base has moved on to someone else as the centre of their fantasies.

How could he express to this young woman how ardent he was about staying away from ghost hunting on worldwide media? Working on *Beyond the Veil* had convinced him right from filming the earliest episodes that the supernatural was all too real. Lost, confused and sad earthbound spirits did exist. A far rarer occurrence than the plethora of ghost hunting shows would suggest. It was not just the evidence gathered from the expensive state of the art used by the techies on the team, it was the medium Rosa's calm, authoritative manner and overwhelming compassion towards the trapped earthbound. Her cooperation with the series was gained only by agreeing on her insistence that she released the spirits at the end of the investigation. This made her unpopular with those wanting to experience the unknown for themselves or owners of the property being investigated wanting to cash in on having a haunted house to exploit financially. Dreams of coachloads of tourists seeking a spooky thrill evaporating along with the residential spooks.

Only once was Dalston made painfully aware that malign and deadly forces also existed.

That was at an abandoned, derelict building in Lincoln's Bailgate area. The heavily burnt shop was demolished after the discovery of its final victim, the charred debris removed. Such was the unease and unspoken fear of the site, it was never developed again, it was purchased by the City's council and an ornamental garden planted in its place. A public one, that sadly did not remove any of its negative ambience and that all the local and most visitors shunned. It appeared that even those who did not know of its notorious past instinctively sensed something unknown, something deeply malevolent lurked there.

Uncomfortable with the silence, the woman persisted, a shrillness underlying her previous, upbeat smooth tones.

'Grant? Grant, are you still there? I hope you are thinking seriously about our proposal; it will make wonderful television.'

Sighing, he replied, 'I have made myself perfectly clear. I have no intention of working on any supernatural themed series or one offs. Even if it was a programme about interior design or the secret lives of naked mole rats, I would still refuse. My "demotion" would be all over the social media and press again, all focusing on my past on *Beyond the Veil*'

He paused before continuing in an unfamiliar harsh tone.

'Also, we have never met, you do not know me. I do not even know your name. Addressing me as Mr Dalston would have been far more appropriate. I am hanging up now. Do not attempt to contact me again. I will consider it harassment and invasion of privacy. Make no mistake, my lawyers would be involved.'

Dalston threw his phone onto a nearby sofa. In his unease, he had behaved like a jerk to the young production assistant. He had never behaved like this before, never been a diva and had treated all the Veil's production team as equal to him. No one had ever had a bad word to say about him on the show. That he was highly unpopular with other supernatural 'reality' shows was a matter of pride. They hated that no edition of the Veil was faked or exaggerated whether viewers believed what was shown or not. He had also upset some people eager to have the team investigate their property. A haunted hotel or pub was good for business, or claiming a council house was haunted might be useful to get an upgrade. The Veil team never wasted time on these properties. Producer Amanda Selec would arrange a meeting at the suspected haunting, bringing the show's medium Rosa Smith. The Romani woman only needed one sweep of the building to ascertain it was spook free. The disappointed applicants hadn't even managed to meet the star, Dalston Grant. The insistence on integrity had made him proud to work on the series. But enough was enough in face of that evil force in Lincoln.

6

A curious impasse had fallen over Cate's life. Her work and social life continued as before. The relationship with Gareth had grown into a comfortable and pleasurable rhythm and he got on well with her family and close friends. The only exception was the 'boys' who he had never met. They were still in America as Dom continued to adjust to the prosthetic arm. Her experiences with the wretched inheritance had now faded into an uneasy background fear, never far enough from her mind for comfort. Her hope was that this situation would continue. A hope soon dashed when woken up by unexpected loud knocks on the door of her flat. Groggy and disorientated, her sleep blurred eyes looked across to her alarm clock on a bedside table. The green digital numbers danced as she tried to focus … 2.46am. Again, the brusque knocking. Whoever was behind the door was not bringing her good news.

Pulling on an oversized wool cardigan, her bleary gaze through her security cam revealed her visitors were a formally attired middle-aged woman and a uniformed male police constable. The woman held her warrant card up to the camera and a deeply concerned Cate let them in, a world of bad news whirling in her mind. Had something dreadful happened to Gareth? She opened the door and gestured to them to enter her home.

'Please, take a seat in my living room, can I get you anything. A cup of tea or coffee?'

The woman gave a polite smile.

'Tea would be lovely, no sugar for me and three for Sergeant Brook. My name is DI Margaret Farrell.'

Busying herself in her narrow galley kitchen, Cate was grateful for the opportunity to compose her conduct. Having the police at her door was a new and unsettling situation.

Once brewed, she brought in the refreshments on a tray, adding a plate of custard cream biscuits.

'You must be psychic, Miss Malvyn,' murmured the detective, 'Those are my favourites and a total undoing of my diet.'

'Call me Cate, please,' she answered unable to suppress the tremble in her voice, 'and they are also my less than secret vice. As well as fig rolls.'

The officers settled down on the chairs opposite Cate. She could not read their expressions but didn't seem to be the manner of someone bringing dreadful news about a loved one.

'Miss Malvyn … Sorry … Cate, I wish to confirm you are the owner of a property in the Cotswolds, Alastor House?'

Now her mind raced into a Formula One overdrive. Had the ghastly house burnt down? She wasn't guilty of any insurance scam and silently thanked the unknown arsonist. She nodded a wary assent. Nothing involving that house was ever going to be good news.

'You had a break in late last night. A passing motorist spotted a gang of men prying open the front gates.'

'If they took anything, I wouldn't know. I'm sorry. I have only visited the property twice and only glanced briefly inside the house. It was unfurnished as far as I can remember. There were no heirlooms or anything of value listed in my late cousin's will. He was the last owner.'

She took a few sips of tea; it was still far too hot but she needed a moment to gather her thoughts.

'We were never close; in fact, my only memories are from rare visits to my parents' home when Richard and I were children. He was a few years older than me. I have no idea why he left me the house. I have never been in need of any financial assistance from my family.'

Cate wanted to add that she wished he hadn't burdened her with this toxic inheritance, and that she had never heard of Alastor House. That might have triggered more curiosity from DI Farrell and her near silent accompanying officer beyond 'May I? and 'Thanks' when he helped himself to three more custard creams. Clearly a fellow 'sugar monster'.

'There is more to the incident than the break in. There was a nearby patrol car in the area and the officers arrived in time to block the entrance. But the officers were unable to make entry to the property. Our motorist witness clearly saw the raiders enter the grounds easily through the main gates. Yet the officers found the gates were securely locked.'

Her expression set as neutral as she could manage, Cate just nodded as the DI's report of the strange event unfolded. How could she talk about the unknown aggressor that had cost a man his arm from just one bite or the vicious swarm that had chased her out of the tangled grounds of Alastor House. She had no idea what those unseen predators were beyond something murderous. Something unnatural ... how could they not be? Cousin Richard did nothing benign in his twisted life, no matter what the media accolades said after his early demise. The DI continued as her uniformed officer helped himself to two more custard creams. Yep, he was definitely a confirmed sugar monster or maybe just hungry from a long, busy night without a break. Maybe she should offer her visitors something more substantial, a sandwich maybe? Odd thoughts to have now, Cate admitted to herself but mundane was better than the unfolding horror story.

'The officers arranged to send a police helicopter with search lights and an infra-red camera to sweep over the house and grounds but there was no sign of the intruders. No heat source, no movements. The team in the helicopter made it hover as low as they could safely and shone the lights over the house itself. None of the windows or doors had been tampered with. It was as if the ground had opened-up and swallowed the intruders.'

Cate could not prevent her face blanching, her hand holding her mug of tea trembling enough to spill some on her lap. The spreading hot dampness went unnoticed but not by the two police officers.

'Cate,' the DI said, her tone less reassuring, 'I think you should tell us all you know about your house. Your friend Mr

Aston, was seriously maimed when you two went there. Shortly after you went back there seeking an answer to what bit and poisoned him.'

Hands still trembling, Cate put down her mug and sat back into her chair. These officers had done their homework. The officer said 'bit' instead of injured, in some ways they knew more than she did. Yet that did not give her confidence to describe the horrific headlong flight being pursued by unknown assailants.

'I wish I could tell you more. I want to know what had hurt Dom so badly. I do not want this inheritance; it is more than an unwanted white elephant. It is a whole herd of them.'

She sighed as she gathered her thoughts.

'I was never close to my cousin Richard. He was a sadistic brute as a child. Crazy as it seems, he left me the house with so many rules. A last act of mean mindedness. I cannot sell it or demolish it or set it alight but I have to pay for its upkeep. I have a good job but I financially stretched myself to get this flat. Alastor House will bankrupt me in no time.'

The uniform policemen paused his raid on Cate's biscuits.

'Could you live in it?'

'I would lose a job I love and end up rattling in a house too costly to maintain,' she replied, putting down her mug on the nearby low table.'

'I would rather sleep on Manchester's streets than ever set foot on that property again.'

She realised she had made a mistake with that admission, as DI Farrell lent forward, her face taut with a grim intensity.

'You know something, Cate. I can sense you are holding something back. We need to know what that is. Using cutting equipment, ten officers on foot went into the grounds. Two with tracker canines. None have come back out.'

Cate could not control her shudders yet anything she said now would be treated as a sign of delusion or insanity. She stayed silent as the DI continued.

'Naturally we suspect a hostage situation. The intruders have somehow found a place to hide that shielded them from the search lights and from infrared heat sourcing. We urgently need to send in a rescue squad. Every second counts. So, if you have any information about this house, we need it now.'

She could not tell the truth, because she did not know what that was. The malevolence that defined the house and grounds was beyond her comprehension.

'I wish I could. The thought of anyone in danger let alone police officers and their dogs distresses me greatly. I feel so helpless. All I know is my cousin was a strange and twisted child. A horrible, sadistic child, he loved doing cruel things to animals and played mind games with people, even from an early age. He became a famous, brilliant scientist, but I suspect much of his work was kept secret. His covert work could be the answer behind this awful situation.'

'In what possible way, Miss Malvyn?'

'He had always enjoyed being cruel, maybe the government or some wealthy corporation sponsored him to do secret and nasty experiments … for the secret services perhaps. I don't know what he could have been up to. We have not spoken since my parents' funeral.'

Cate did not add that he had most likely attended that just to savour and gloat over the sorrow of the bereaved, especially her as a newly orphaned little girl. She did not want to add another layer of strangeness to the interview. She could see the uniformed officer Sergeant Brook surreptitiously glancing across at her book case, at the novels by horror authors such as Dean Koontz, Stephen King and Adam Nevill. That he might conclude her imagination was stoked up by tales of evil scientists or malign supernatural beings. Would she have been taken more seriously if she had shelves of Mills and Boon romances and historical bodice rippers?

'Would approaching the staff at his research headquarters be of any use?'

Looking directly into DI Farrell's piercing and steady gaze, Cate's answer was born of an uneasy but growing certainty.

'You could try, but my cousin was a wily, cunning child. I don't believe he was a reformed character as an adult. If he was working on something strange and sinister, it would not be at his above reproach and philanthropic research headquarters. You do not win awards for humanitarian endeavours and yet openly dabble in anything dangerous and malign.' Cate shrugged, 'At least, I don't think so. Maybe I am just a naïve person working in the superficial field of marketing. Nothing in Richard's world had any connection to mine. Until he died and lumbered me with bloody Alastor House.'

The two police officers exchanged glances. Cate knew what those unimpressed looks implied, that there was much more to this strange story and they were right. Cate could not avoid being involved, however remotely though. She owned the bloody house, an insane white elephant with blood dripping from its tusks. Farrell and the sergeant stood up to leave with the uniformed officer murmuring thanks for the refreshments. The detective gave her a card.

'If you think of anything, however trivial, let us know immediately.'

Taking it and nodding, Cate showed them to the front door. Only once it was firmly closed and the sound of their retreating footsteps fading did she drop her guard and sink to the floor, her throat choking with sobs.

Cate had no idea what was going to happen next, the surreal nightmare of her life had taken a deeper, more sinister turn.

'If Hell exists, Richard, I hope you are in it.'

Cate did not know, nor did anyone else in the outside world, but a shocked and bewildered Sergeant Brook and DI Margaret Farrell did discover that the well-armed specialist police squad had found the front gates unlocked in the early hours of the morning and their progress to Alastor House had been unhindered. When all contact with the squad was suddenly lost, and many squad cars sent to find out why. On arrival, the astonished team of officers were speechless in shock. What they did not find were any of the raiders or the police who gained entry to arrest them. There were no vehicles left either. Not a single clue they had ever entered the property remained.

Badly shaken by the visit from the police, Cate felt a sense of unavoidable menace growing around her, like an invisible, stealthily woven spider web. She would have preferred that, a web can be seen and broken with nothing lost but an instinctual shudder and the loss of the spider's pride, hard work and supper. Trying to carry on with her normal life was becoming increasingly difficult, especially after a late-night visit from the police. What could she do? She felt just as trapped as that imaginary fly.

Cate sat down on her sofa with a big mug of coffee and switched on her TV, hoping for something to take her mind of her dilemma. Inevitably, she did check through all the news channels first, a report of the police squad arresting the intruders in her horrible house, there was nothing. Instead, she found one of her favourite diversions, the American tattoo competition *Ink Masters* what she and Gareth called 'Bitch Masters'. The hilarious, barbed rivalry and skilful, intricate artwork was not enough. Her mind then turned to Gareth. She needed his company but how could she bear to allow him into the turmoil and danger of her world?

Inevitably, Cate was drawn deeper into the nightmare. After her morning before work routine, spoiled by the sight of her face in the bathroom mirror while putting on her makeup. Her usual pale face was marred by deep, grey shadows under her eyes. She used up stick of concealer to hide them but the shadows kept showing through the make-up. Her favourite shade of red lipstick only added to her grotesque appearance. She wiped it all off, going into work looking sickly was preferable to being a zombie clown.

Somehow she made it through a long day's work, catching up on her time away. Eventually all the staff had expressed their concerns about her appearance and eventually they gave up and let Cate get on with the welcome distraction of work.

Once back home, Cate wanted to spend time with Gareth, but not looking so dreadful. It was still early days in their relationship and he only knew her as a lively, attractive young woman. One that still went to bed with her makeup on, the stuff that boasts lasting for thirty-five hours though she hadn't needed that much time. Her past insecurities about her appearance were never far away, that or she had only dated good looking or shallow men in the past. Gareth was different, a potential keeper, she just didn't want to take any chances this early in their relationship. While fretting about the dilemma, her phone range. She waited close by until the answer phone clicked in and snatched the phone up when it was DI Farrell. The detective wanted to come over to the flat, her manner measured and ambivalent. Cate agreed and put the kettle on, hoping the constable was not with his boss, she had run out of biscuits,

DI Farrell arrived alone this time, her appearance so pristine on her first visit was replace by shadowed, puffy eyes, a weary expression and the same clothes she had worn then. Cate doubted the woman had any sleep since the incident at Alastor House. Had the police captured the thieves? Cate hoped that was the reason for the unexpected visit, unaccompanied by another officer. It would be such a relief if nothing weird or deadly had happened to either the raiders or those who pursued them. A hope swiftly dashed.

'None of what I am about to tell you must be repeated to anyone, not loved ones and most definitely not the Press. If you do, there will be unfortunate consequences for you. We are keeping as low a profile as possible in this situation.'

Cate collapsed into the nearest chair, her body shaking, tears ready to flow uncontrollably. DI pulled a chair up in front of the distraught young woman and waited for her to gain some semblance of composure.

'We think we know what happened. The squad car was hijacked by a five strong, heavily armed and notorious gang, our officers were kidnapped and all the vehicles left the property. We have no idea if our people are still alive and there has been no sign of a ransom demand or an abandoned squad car.'

Her mind spinning, Cate instinctively knew this was a cover up story, a preposterous one, but that just may be believed. No wonder the officer wanted no mention of the story, especially to the ever-hungry Press who would have a field day with something this sensational. Why was a heavily armed gang of thieves at the house in the first place? It was an empty derelict, a dilapidated, decaying shell. Not one thing of value was left in the property. It made no sense, but neither did the dark secrets of Alastor House.

7

Gareth's return to Manchester later that night was a mixed blessing for Cate. She wanted to see him; she needed him but didn't want to scare him away from her shipwreck looks and mental anguish over that damned house. It deserved to be burnt to the ground, fuck the consequences. She left work early and devoted the rest of the afternoon in getting a beauty makeover in a salon. Not something she had ever done before but anything that made her less of a wreck might help her relax and enjoy Gareth's company again. He had never seemed a superficial man when it came to women but Cate was not taking any chances.

He had phoned her while at the salon and asked if she would like to catch something at a cine multiplex, then have a meal at a nearby restaurant. She readily agreed. Cinemas were always welcomingly dark and a later meal would be candlelit … always flattering. She wasn't vain but didn't want to risk Gareth being turned off by her appearance. She was relieved the beauticians and hairdressers had worked their magic at the end of the session, it had cost her an arm and a leg but Cate was relieved as she looked in the mirror. Totally worth it.

Once home, she had a scented bath, careful not to muss up her makeup or hair and put on a figure hugging but not too short dress he had not seen yet. With hours to go before Gareth's arrival, she decided to lose herself in a book. Not one of her favourite authors' horror novels but a sappy romance her friend Elsie had bought her for a Secret Santa Christmas gift. The young woman didn't know her well enough to choose Cate's favourite genre. Luckily, it was well written and kept her attention long enough to help her relax a little.

The date went well, an exciting, noisy, action film in the *Mad Max* franchise followed by a lovely meal in a Lebanese restaurant. They returned to Cate's apartment for making love and for the first time, Cate had put all thoughts of Alastor House to the back of her mind.

It would not last for long.

A few days after their cinema date, Gareth was busy photographing a big charity fashion show in Manchester's most trendy district that night. Cate expressed her disinterest and planned a night in. She had zero time for increasingly desperate, aging Z list 'celebs' from past TV reality shows seeking free food and drink and a chance of a photo opportunity. A harsh judgement and part of her felt guilty for her cynicism but another part thought if the charity benefited, who was she to judge? Wanting a total chill out evening, she removed the days makeup, showered and washed her hair and slipped into another pair of pyjamas this time one covered with *Deadpool* images ... she was such a geek.

She ordered a takeaway Indian meal planning to have half that night, the rest tomorrow evening and turned on the TV. She had become addicted to American cop procedure shows and was working her way through all the *Law and Order* series. Playing 'spot the famous actors' before they were successful was part of the fun.

The phone rang just as a very young Sam Rockwell was taking the stand as a witness at a murder trial. Pausing the TV, she answered the call. It was Chandice Ailhaud. again, brimming with energy and enthusiasm. After the usual to and fro of catching up their news, Chandice took a deep breath and announced her idea of another plan for Alastor House.

'Forget *Make Or Break*. I have a much better idea. What about getting the heavenly Grant Dalston back out of his self-imposed exile from TV? Just for a one-off special with him investigating your creepy encumbrance.'

Without a second's pause for consideration, Cate gave an emphatic, 'No, never, ever!'

Her mellow mood switched to rising terror in a heartbeat. Frustrated that she could not tell her friend why, even if Chandice believed her. Cate had never watched the man's successful haunted house investigation show. It was lauded for being level headed and with zero screams and special effects but even with the tall, dark and handsome Dalston at the helm, it had never interested her. Even if she did consider an investigation, Cate was sure that the police would not allow it. She also would not allow it; it could only cause more victims of whatever dwelled behind those high gates. More than enough blood had been shed, her chest tightened with tension, all hopes that the missing police officers would be found dead or alive had long gone in her opinion. More innocent sacrifices to Cousin Richard's bloodthirsty insanity. No one else must ever set foot in the grounds and house ever again.

Chandice took her silence as a good sign, that her friend was considering her proposal.

'You know I used to work on the team, we were like a family. Grant treated everyone with the same kindness and consideration from the network's executives to the cleaning staff. That nightmare in old Lincoln cost the lives of two of the team, we were all like family members. Grant escaped with his life but was badly injured and traumatised. But his curiosity must be still there somewhere, maybe it is time for him to come out of exile.'

'You are not convincing me,' Cate replied. 'That poor man has suffered enough, why put him into another bizarre, dangerous situation?'

Cate stopped talking, she had said far too much and only sharpened her friend's determination. Being part of a team making great TV was still in Chandice's ambitious mind and Cate sided with Grant Dalston who had the courage to walk away after the tragedy. Chandice took her silence as a signal to continue her pitch.

'With cameras set up automatically to record anything weird, they could find out why this house is so creepy. No one need be put in any danger. It might be a way to stop the house being dangerous … you could rent it out and stop it being such a burden to you.'

Cate was close to slamming the phone down on her friend, Chandice had not seen the horrific maiming of poor Dom, she must never know about the disappearance of a police squad and the crooks they had been tracking. Cate had never felt so trapped, so desperate. The idea of an act of arson, one so huge, so thorough that not a cinder of the house remained., returned. A jail sentence seemed increasingly preferable to this ongoing nightmare. It was her house to burn down anyway and not for insurance purposes. She didn't want a penny from the house, it would probably be cursed money.

'I have to say no, Chandice, for many reasons I cannot talk about. I am stuck with this horrible situation and can't see a way out. Getting Grant Dalston involved can only make it so much worse.'

'How, Honey?'

'I wish I could tell you,' Cate was sobbing now, her whole being wracked with misery and hopelessness, 'but I can't.'

She switched off her phone.

Not sharing her despair with Gareth or with anyone for that matter was eating Cate up, like a clenching grip on her heart and a weight pressing down on her chest. She experienced panic attacks, dizziness and nausea too whenever the phone rang at home and now also in the office. She had done nothing to Cousin Richard to warrant this torture and had no way of finding out why. Her sorry state had not gone unnoticed.

Gareth had held off pressing her for an explanation for

her haunted appearance no makeup could disguise, her nervous behaviour whenever any phone rang. He had waited for the right moment to bring up the reason for her obvious distress. A cosy night in at his flat with a delicious Lebanese takeaway and a mellow red wine later and still on his sofa, Gareth bit the bullet and asked her what was wrong.

'I hate seeing you struggle with some awful secret, whatever it is, you can share it with me in complete confidence. Even if you are some sort of psycho killer in a bunny onesie.'

He expected her to laugh, or even just give a wry smile but Cate curled up into a defensive position, knees drawn up to her chin, arms wrapped tightly around herself. Unwanted but determined tears rolled down her face, Cate let them fall unhindered. Gareth's concern was confirmed by her distress. He held her tight, not speaking, waiting until she felt ready to share her fears. Hoping with all his heart that she would. Cate went into the awkward snuffling phase, forcing her distress to abate by an act of willpower but failing miserably. She needed to share her ordeal. It was time to let Gareth into her insane but all too real world but leaving out the mystery of the missing policemen. He was her boyfriend but also a professional member of the press. Even though the horror of the latest and most likely fatal contact with whatever cursed her house was in the Cotswolds, a newsman's nose for a big story was no barrier to selling it elsewhere beyond Manchester. It was in their genes.

Gareth fetched her a box of tissues and rejoined her on sofa as she gathered her wits and tried to remain calm. She then told him the whole story, from her cousin's toxic childhood behaviour to the cruel legacy of Alastor House. Carefully as she could, she related how Dom got scratched, poisoned and maimed by the house, her nightmare, narrow escape from it later that night. To his credit, Gareth did not interrupt her or find any amusement in such an outlandish story and was silent until she had finished.

'I don't expect you to believe me …'

Her voice trailed off, why should he? She wouldn't have believed it.

'This cannot go on, *Cariad*,' he murmured, holding her tightly, 'that damned house is killing you even from a distance.'

'What can I do, I am caught in a trap with no escape.'

'Not anymore, we are going to get to the bottom of this nightmare and end it even if it does involve arson. Totally justifiable in my mind, it is not even a listed building, so it is up to you what you do with it.'

To Grant Dalston's displeasure, Chandice Ailhaud proved to be a woman hard to shake off. There was a time such a weird, disturbing story would have intrigued him and created a memorable episode of the programme. The horrors of his encounter with real, supernatural evil in Lincoln had purged him of all curiosity about the unknown. He would never stop mourning the two, much loved friends killed by the fiend that haunted an old clock menders' premises in Bailgate, Old Lincoln. His memories of the times before the horror returned. Chandice had worked on his show in the post shoot department and he remembered her as an intelligent and hard working member of the team. She must have pulled hard on some strings to get his unlisted phone number and a confidence bordering on arrogance to call him at home. With a weary sigh and with no other useful thing to do as an excuse, he listened to the woman's outrageous story. To his astonishment, the existing atoms of his past instinct to make great TV fired into life again, maybe just one more story but could he break his self-inflicted embargo on something this strange?

'I really don't think it is anything supernatural, Mr Dalston, but it is bizarre and defeated all known medical knowledge.'

Without a reply, she tried one more time to trigger his interest, it was so sad he had lost the instinct for a good story and this one was a corker.

'Grant, please, we worked together for long enough to share an instinct of a great story … I think our lost friends Jed and Emery would have been intrigued.'

A low blow, he was on the verge of cutting off the call but the tributes to his friends and workmates had long faded from public view. If he dedicated the documentary to them, with photos and tributes, it would be a good thing. A small salve to his troubled conscience.

'I'll give it some thought, Chandice and let you know as soon as possible.'

She smiled as she thanked him and ended the call. Now she had to overcome another obstacle, persuading Cate to allow this investigation.

8

Even with Gareth's comforting arm around her shoulders, Cate felt trapped in her own home, overwhelmed by Chandice's enthusiasm for her proposed project at Alastor House.

'Just imagine it, lovely, the reunited team from *Beyond The Veil* with the divine Grant Dalston at the helm investigating that bloody millstone of yours once and for all. '

'Bloody is the word,' Cate managed to reply not hiding the bitterness in her voice, 'Wasn't enough blood shed at his last investigation? Two members of the team died, horribly.'

Cate ended the phone call and went back to sit beside Gareth on the sofa.

Conflicted more than ever, she couldn't bring herself to spill out her secret knowledge. Cate had no doubt that whatever infected the house had killed both the police officers and the intruders. Somehow also making their vehicles disappear beneath the choking mass of the malevolent foliage of Alastor House's extensive grounds. A mad theory but what other could there be? She dreamt of a phone call from the police officers investigating the disappearances telling her the vehicles had been found, the thieves arrested and the missing officers safe and rescued from being held captive in some remote farmhouse. A dream that faded with each day without news. How could her friend be dissuaded from her plans to make a startling documentary without revealing what Cate already knew about the house.

It was all too much for her to bear alone now. For right or wrong she needed to unburden herself of the weight of hidden knowledge. She drank all her glass of neat brandy and related the call from Chandice to Gareth, testing his willingness to know more about the house. She would still not mention the missing police and thieves, but did tell him about the real reason for Dom's maiming and the horrific attack on her by what seemed to be malign, sentient foliage. Crazy of course, but it wasn't a bad dream or the ravings of a hysteric. At least not for her or Dom. It was a gamble though; she wouldn't blame Gareth from walking straight out of the door and out of her life as certifiably unhinged and try to sell it as a sensational story to some national rag.

She poured them both another measure with shaking hands triggering great concern from Gareth, whatever was up with Cate, it was serious. After she had a big swig of the brandy, aware that Gareth was ready to hear whatever she was about to tell him, she told him exactly what happened to Dom and in as much detail as she could remember of the terrifying flight from the house. There was a long, unnerving but understandable silence. Then he held her in a tight embrace … a farewell or a comfort of understanding and compassion. Agonising seeming endless seconds passed. Then Gareth stepped back, eyes watering with tears.

'Too much for one person to carry on their own, Cariad, far, far too much.'

'So, you believe me?'

'Yes. I do believe there is something very horribly wrong going on at that property, maybe not supernatural, something connected to that madman cousin of yours, something perhaps concerning his research. Probably a project his own people knew nothing about.'

Relief flooded through her in a wave of emotion, she looked up at Gareth's face for any sign of ridicule but only saw his deep concern.

'That makes sense.'

It was the first thing that did make some sort of logic since the nightmare had begun. Something the police would consider too outlandish to investigate but maybe Chandice was right. Could Grant Dalston's team that always contained scientists expert in their field actually discover the truth?

9

Alastor House

It took several weeks to gather the right team for Grant Dalston's investigation. No one from the police had interfered with the investigation, officially sticking to their story about what happened to their missing in action officers. From the start, caution was key … no unwanted advance publicity , no risk of nosey bystanders or gate crashers. No filming at night that could have alerted the inquisitive beyond the gates. Gareth had done the most interaction between the owner of Alastor House and Dalston's team, sparing Cate from added anxiety.

The house and grounds were quiet, poised as if luring the investigation team into a false sense of security, into complacence while it waited to strike. The lack of interaction was both a blessing and a curse. Cate knew the team would only stay as long as the investigation was likely to unearth some dark secret or even a newsworthy hoax. A blessing if Dalston and his team left the property unharmed. A curse if it meant she was still trapped with this most malign of white elephants.

Cate stayed away most of the early days of the investigation with Chandice on site phoning her with progress reports. Samples had been taken from plants surrounding the house and along the driveway up to and around the grounds. None of the outbuildings contained anything suspicious on any of the photos or on samples. The inaction from the exterior of the house and its grounds was partly a relief, Cate wished for no one to be harmed. The lack of an answer was however frustrating.

A week after the investigation began, Cate got a call directly from Grant Dalston. After a few moments of small talk about the investigation and the good work done by Chandice in charge of the operation, his voice became serious.

'My wonderful medium Rosa Smith has made a very short visit into the house and found it totally free of any remnants of human souls. She called it a total void, not even a single fading residue of past unhappiness. Unusual in a house that has stood for nye on four hundred years.'

He paused before continuing, the next thing he had to say to Cate was going to be difficult.

'I believe there is nothing going on because whatever is behind the strangeness is waiting. The house was bequeathed to you by the late Professor Richard Malvyn. You mentioned his cruelty as a child. Targeting you as a little child was part of his malignancy. As is lumbering you with the house. It wants you.'

'I can't go back in there, especially as it might trigger whatever is attacking people. Call the investigation off –straight away, if you cannot find any information from the grounds.'

There was a long pause, an impasse that hung heavy with unspoken needs. Dalston broke the silence.

'This will go on for as long as you are alive, maybe even longer. In theory at least, fire erased the murderous malignancy at the clock mender's house in Old Lincoln. Maybe that is what is needed to happen here and to hell with the consequences?'

Cate's voice sounded defeated; Cousin Richard had set a trap for her. Maybe she should stop being so afraid and stand up to the bastard, show his ghost that she was no longer afraid, that she was defying his cruelty and bullying once and for all. He was dead and could no longer touch her. Except she was afraid, for herself and for all that entered the grounds of Alastor House.

'I'll do it.'

She was startled by her own words but didn't back track.

Grant Dalston paused before replying.

'Are you sure, Cate? I hope I haven't pushed or guilt tripped you into doing this.'

'It will never end until I have faced the bastard's machinations. If me dying stops his campaign, then so be it.'

Dalston sighed. She was so young but already a brave soul but so were his companions lost to the fiend haunting Bailgate.

Breaking the awkward silence, Cate continued, 'One

condition, one not up for debate. Absolutely no one must breathe a word of this to Gareth. He will do everything in his power to stop me, stop the investigation. He has had to return last night to Wales to be with his dying mother. I hate to take advantage of a family's grief but there won't be a better time for us to face whatever is infecting Alastor House.'

The team organised a car to take Cate up to the Cotswolds; its mellow beauty was lost to her as she battled growing anxiety about what she may face. As it turned down the drive, she focused on the road ahead to avoid looking at the surrounding greenery. She had not spoken to the driver during the journey, too wrapped up in her own thoughts but now she had arrived, she wanted the driver to leave as soon as she got out of the car. It would be one less person to worry about. His glance at her pale, anguished face was enough to convince him and he would be early enough to pick up his kids from primary school. A well-paid job and an early knock off, a win win situation.

Cate watched him drive away unharmed then turned to meet the team in person for the first time. Dalston was as good-looking as Chandice had described but he was a few years older than the last broadcast and had dark shadows beneath his eyes and the start of grey at his temples. He strode over, shook her hand, and introduced her to the rest of the gathering.

Chandice magicked up some coffee which she took with a grateful smile despite her hands shaking uncontrollably. She had never smoked, but for some reason having a cigarette seemed a good idea.

The surrounding dark wall of trees began a sinister susurration as if they were whispering to each other. Maybe they were, thought Cate shivering with dread. The banks of overgrown brambles that were once ornamental flowerbeds also seemed to come to life, stretching their barbed, fat tendrils towards the gathering of humans.

'Just what I was expecting,' Dalston murmured to himself but his words cut through the dawning awareness of wrongness from the others. The investigation had hit a critical phase. With no need for orders, the technicians ran to their vans to monitor the outside activity with a variety of scientific instruments. The camera crew were already focused on filming the bizarre movement and unnatural, swift growth of the brambles. Alastor House was preparing to show its teeth, no doubt fangs dripping with poison.

'Stay back from the undergrowth, don't let any of it touch you!'

Dalston shouted to the team, tempting as it was to collect samples of this malign foliage, they had to hold back. The inert samples they had already taken had to be enough. Cate felt a pulling sensation engulf her body and when she heard sibilant whispers, her mind was overwhelmed too. It had to be the house calling her, dragging her to an unknown fate from her dead torturer. She looked toward Dalston, noted how his features were fearful, all colour drained from his face. She didn't want to be brave but she wanted this nightmare to end … one way or another.

'Give me one of those little camera things, like the police wear on duty,' she called. 'No need for anyone else to be in harm's way. I will go into the house alone and you can record all that happens.'

'Not a chance,' Dalston insisted, snapping out of his fear frozen state. 'We go in together or not at all.'

With shaking hands, the techies on the team fitted Cate and Dalston with an array of lightweight recording equipment, one of the team asking if the pair were 'absolutely sure' about entering the house. Both gave a terse nod, looked at each other to confirm their mutual commitment and walked together into the house.

The same lack of anything wrong existed in the house. It was exactly how she and Dom had first found it. How Rosa Smith had found it. The desiccated corpses of insects lay on window sills ready to collapse into fine dust if touched and on the windows and ceiling corners were dust coated spider webs with no living prey to sustain their weavers. It smelled of stale nothing, no remnants of any past human inhabitants, not even the echo of their fading shades.

Dalston walked around the entrance hall, the sound of his footsteps curiously muted on the flagstone floor. Cate remained just a few steps from the entrance, the ornate oak and filigree iron work doors left wide open to make any escape easier.

The house had other ideas.

Cate shrieked as the doors slammed shut, too heavy for any wind to affect them. Dalston hurriedly returned to her side, the house was waking up.

With a cacophony of screeling, whining and guttural groans, particles of the fabric of the house's interior peeled off the walls to whirl then coalesce into a central mass. Still making its eerie howling, the growing mass squirmed as if in pain as more and more matter joined it. Dalston grabbed Cate and pulled her towards the closed entrance as they attempted an escape but more matter peeled off and became a seething, malodorous wall blocking any hope of swift exit. Transfixed with horror, they watched as more particles joined the mass. No longer featureless and amoeba like, it took shape with every new addition of particles.

Cate whimpered; it was becoming human in form though not in nature.

'Richard …'

Even above the hellish noise, they could hear sounds of pandemonium outside, as Dalston's transceiver buzzed. Without taking his eyes off the still evolving figure, he answered with a terse, 'Yes?'

Chandice, her voice shaking in terror shouted, 'We are under attack, the plant life is moving, surrounding us, getting closer and closer.'

Dalston shouted back, 'Get out, everyone of you! Now! Forget the equipment, get everyone in the stretch Hummer and leave, break through the main gates if needed, the Hummer can take it. GO NOW!!'

'How about you and Cate?' whimpered a shocked Chandice, her voice joined by the shouts and screams of the crew.

'Go now! We are finishing this nightmare now. You have no more time. LEAVE!'

He switched off the transceiver; his crew were on their own outside and with at least a hope of survival. The cause of the horror was immerging with increasing speed before him and Cate. They had the only chance to stop the monstrous entity, end the terror right now like he hoped he had done in Bailgate, but only hope … an evil that ancient had very deep roots. This was a twenty-first century monster with no centuries of past lore to help them.

Cate was terrified of the manifestation but its predation had to stop, if it wanted her as a sacrifice, she would accept her fate. She took in a deep breath and steeled herself to approach the apparition, praying it had the ability to communicate, to reason. Dalston took hold of her arm to prevent her nearing the coalescing mass but she pushed his hand away with a firm shove. Without taking her focus on the apparition, she spoke to Dalston.

'It wants me, it always has. We are the last of our family.'

'So, you know of your family's past?'

Cate nodded, 'not as a child though, I sensed there was something different about us without knowing why. When I saw the house was called Alastor, I did some digging. I came from a dynasty of long past alchemists, astrologers and of all crazy things, demon worshipers. A past kept well-hidden for so many years but of course, Richard was the perfect candidate to research and believe in their hidden interests.'

'How long have you known this?' Dalston asked.

'Would you believe just a few days, thanks to the wonder of the internet and the chance discovery of a keen and talkative professor of folk horror and British arcane history.'

The writhing mass had become more solid, Richard Malvyn's features were forming made up from the colours of the surrounding walls, mould green, dust grey, shades of black and stained, yellow-white like some monstrous pixelated image. A ragged maw opened and closed, an orifice struggling to communicate.

Cate remained within easy reach of Dalston, she was not

that brave, she was still the young woman who had to ask a neighbour to remove big spiders from the bath. One too frightened to notice the cold rivulets of sweat running from her temple down her face and a fear produced river soaking her back. She glanced up at Dalston, a man who had faced a different deadly eldritch enemy, had lost friends, nearly lost his own life. Beyond a pallor and clenched jaw, he also seemed resolute. This encounter had only two results, their death or victory. Victory had never felt like such an empty word.

'Why me, you bastard? Why did you focus your cruelty upon a little girl?'

The entity gave up trying to speak, instead spider web thin tendrils splayed out from its body and connected to Cate's head. A voice made from many, all shrill and bordering on hysterical filled her mind.

'You are a Malvyn, you were born to be visionary, a pioneer but raised to as a feeble nobody. A tedious drone like all that pollute this pathetic planet. You disgrace your proud lineage.'

Seeing Cate frozen by the grip of the tendrils, Dalston was conflicted, unable to risk pulling them free of her skull but terrified they may be harming her, doing something vile to her mind. Still held tightly by Malvyn, the being continued to speak.

'I used my brilliance and mastery of both science and old arcane magickes to blend atoms of matter and paranormal ethers to bring the seemingly inert to life and what a life! Created with no interfering human consciences, no arbitrary scientific rules of matter and anti-matter. I control it all, every living thing on my domain and soon in all domains. This world and all others will be mine.'

In an act of cruelty, it forced the tendrils even further into Cate's head, sharp dagger like protuberances began to drill into her skull. Dalston could not bear his own inaction a moment longer … this thing infected the living with deadly consequences.

'Not on my watch, you bastard!'

He began to rip out the tendrils from Cate's head, ignoring the pulses of pain as the threads fought back both stinging with venom and pain from minuscule jaws ripping at his hands. All the anger from Dalston's past close brush with the uncanny rose to strengthen his resolve. Blood from all the cuts streamed down his hands and arms only making his attack on the entity stronger.

The assault triggered Cate's long lost ancient memories from her Malvyn genes, messages coded in her DNA that may never have been discovered were on her side, pushing back at the aberration in powerful pulses of energy, the mysterious, universal dark matter that holds all of creation safe. Even with her eyes open, Cate could see strong and distinct images of faces, one after the other they appeared before her, with each image she was given a strength of resolve and courage. Enough to push back at her attacker, pull out the invading tendrils from her skull, oblivious to the pain. The creature shrunk back, puzzled then angry at being challenged by a force it intended to control for itself. A weakness from being once a human, a fatal flaw it had not considered problematic.

'Why!'

Its eardrum wrecking screech pulsed through Alastor House and in sonic waves rippled through the grounds causing all the infected foliage to shrink back and wither. The platelets that formed Malvyn's corporal form struggled to hold cohesion but failed as they began to fall away becoming no more than stained plaster and grimy cobwebs again. The screech became a whimper, became a sigh, became silence. The interior of Alastor House was just a sorely neglected Georgian country mansion. The grounds just overgrown and neglected.

'Is it over?' Cate whispered, too exhausted and bloodied to say more.'

Equally battle wounded, Dalston gave a weary shrug of maybe.

Epilogue

The plant samples had remained in their Petri dish, inert and unremarkable. Just scraps of ragwort, ferns, brambles, thistles and shreds from one rose bush. The scientific investigation was going nowhere and would soon be shut down and mothballed. One ambitious young man, eager for promotion, waited until he was alone, made a cut in his thumb with a scalpel and let a drop of blood land on each sample. He sighed in disappointment at the lack of reaction and turned away. It was his worst ever decision and last move as a living being.

About The Author

Raven Dane is a UK based author of dark fantasy, steampunk novels and horror short stories. Her first books were the dark fantasy Legacy of the *Dark Kind* trilogy, *Blood Tears*, *Blood Lament* and *Blood Alliance*. These were followed by a High Fantasy spoof, *The Unwise Woman of Fuggis Mire*.

Her steampunk novels so far are the award-winning *Cyrus Darian and the Technomicron*, and sequels *Cyrus Darian and the Ghastly Horde* and *Cyrus Darian and the Wicked Wraith*. She has had many short stories published, including one in a celebration of forty years of the British Fantasy Society and in international horror anthologies. These have included Tales of the Lake 2, alongside Richard Chizmar, Ramsey Campbell, Tim Lebbon and the late Jack Ketchum. She also had a story in the late Billie Sue Mosiman's Frightmare –Women Write Horror which was shortlisted for a prestigious Bram Stoker award in 2016. 2019 saw her appear in the anthology Shallow Waters Vol II, and in 2021 she contributed to the charity anthology Criminal Pursuits.

She has appeared in two international lists of best female

horror writers. In 2013, she was signed up by Telos Publishing for her collection of Victorian ghost stories, *Absinthe and Arsenic* and in 2015, the alternative history/ supernatural novel, *Death's Dark Wings.*

A lifelong *Doctor Who* fan, Raven was delighted and honoured to be part of the script team on a spin off film, *White Witch of Devil's End* by Reeltime Pictures in 2017. She also contributed to the novelisation of the film.

Raven has written two horror novellas so far: *The Bane of Bailgate* in 2018 and *House of Wrax* in 2019.

Grant Dalston and his team's encounter with evil is one of the stories in a novella by Raven entitled *The Bane of Bailgate*, available from Amazon and to order from all good bookstores.

THE ISLE OF MA'AN DU

Samantha Lee Howe

'So why isn't this place on any map, Mom?' Keira asked as the helicopter travelled over the ocean towards the small island of Ma'an Du.

'It's privately owned, dimwit,' said Jake. 'Thought it was obvious.'

'Jake, don't call your sister a dimwit, she's just got into Harvard!' Ella Martina said.

Jake shrugged. Keira was smart, but had so little common sense when it came to everyday things. Just because she was going to Harvard didn't change that. So to him, she *was* a dimwit.

'Anyway,' said Ella. 'It's a good question. Why isn't it on any map? It exists – doesn't matter who owns it, surely?'

Perry Martina glanced over his shoulder at his wife even as the helicopter pilot began his descent down to the beach.

'It's owned by the CEO of a *very* big corporation and I suspect he paid to keep this place a secret,' Perry said.

'Really? I wouldn't have thought that could happen in this day and age,' Keira said.

'See. I told you she was a dimwit,' Jake said.

Keira hit him hard in the leg with a clenched fist.

'Ow!' Jake yelled.

'Stop it you two!' Perry said.

The helicopter touched down on the sand of a large beach and the occupants fell silent. They waited until the blades slowed and the sand around them settled once more.

'Okay folks,' said the pilot. 'It's time to hop out. Keep your head low until you're clear of the blades.'

'Where do we go?' yelled Ella above the declining din of the rotors.

'Just wait over there by the trees. The house staff will have seen us arriving and will be heading down to guide you through the woods.'

They followed the pilot's advice, each grabbing their rucksack of personal items before leaving the helicopter, crouching low until they were clear of any risk from the rotors.

Ella had fought a little over leaving their suitcases with a total stranger to bring across a few days earlier on a boat, but now they were here, she hoped this experience would be all it was supposed to be.

Ma'an Du beach was beautiful, with fine white sand, and the bluest water. The pilot gave them a wave and lifted off again turning the helicopter back towards the main land. The rotors whipped up the sand once more and the Martina family all covered their eyes.

'Mr and Mrs Martina?' a male voice said behind them.

As Ella turned, she caught her first peripheral sight of the man and her first impression was confused. She'd thought him overly tall, with long arms and extra-long fingers. But when she saw him clearly, there was nothing unusual about him at all.

'I'm Hal, the caretaker of the house. Can you follow me please and I'll show you the easiest way up?'

Without waiting for their response, Hal turned and walked back into the trees. Ella glanced at Perry then shrugged and followed even as she saw a small frown appear on her husband's brow.

'C'mon kids,' Perry said, and the family plunged into the woodland without further hesitation.

Hal remained just a few feet ahead at all times, even when the family slowed and tired. The route up to the house wasn't easy, and Keira found herself wondering why anyone would build a holiday home on an island without also creating easy access to the beach. But as they reached the summit of the hill all became clear. Ma'an Du was a resort in itself. A huge manor house with a pool dominating the island. It reminded Kiera of Masada: an old ancient fortification that had been built on a rock plateau in Israel. She'd learnt about it in religious studies at school and this place was designed very much the same.

'If you like the sea and beach there is a small bay that way. The owners built a staircase down to the water. Just beyond the glass barrier,' Hal said.

Keira and Jake walked over to the barrier and looked down. Below was the perfect beach, a sheltered cove with sun loungers and a wooden structure, much like a tiki bar area, built on the sand.

'This is so cool!' Jake said.

'I prefer the pool area,' Ella said after eyeing the steep steps. 'That and a good book. Rest and relax is all I want to do.'

'I'll show you your rooms,' Hal said.

The family followed Hal inside the house and Ella 'Ohh'd' and 'Ahh'd' with pleasure when she saw the interior. The house was so fresh and clean and had all the modern conveniences of a five-star hotel. In an instant, all of her concerns about the trip to an isolated island disappeared.

Jake and Keira were happy to find a games room and a cinema room with a huge screen.

'Wow! Wish we'd brought some movies to watch on that!' Jake said.

'There's an extensive library of films,' Hal said. 'You'll find the list there.'

He pointed to a thick ring-bound booklet, placed on a console table by the door.

'There are full instructions on how to use the system, so please enjoy,' Hal continued.

'This place is just ….,' Keira said and then stopped. She turned her head and looked hard at Hal as though she had completely forgotten what she was about to say.

'Dimwit,' Jake muttered

Keira thumped Jake in the arm and then turned full circle in the cinema room.

'I'm in heaven. I want to get out of these travel clothes and into my swimsuit,' Ella said.

'Then I need to show you the rest of the house, and your personal rooms,' Hal said.

They left the games room, and turned right, away from the huge bi-fold doors that stood wide open in the games room overlooking the pool and the incredible view of the ocean.

They came out of the games room in the hallway where Ella gasped at the sight of the impressive staircase that ran up the center and veered off on both sides. There was a white wooden balustrade that was almost out of keeping with the rest of the house in its slightly old-fashioned style but it worked with the staircase nonetheless.

'Is this ... was this part of the house built at a different time to the rest?' Ella asked. 'Only everywhere else is sleek and contemporary. I would almost have expected a glass panelled staircase with a chrome balustrade based on the rest of the design.'

'Well observed,' said Hal. 'The house was originally built as a plantation. At the other side of the island, sugar cane still grows wild. Although the days of slaves harvesting it are now long gone. But the house and island have been in the hands of the owner's family for generations. The games room, pool, the cinema room, were all added to the property in the last few years.'

'But it's been modernized elsewhere too?' Perry asked.

'Of course. We have every comfort for our guests,' Hal said.

He gave a crooked smile that Keira thought was supposed to be reassuring but in reality, made him appear stranger. She couldn't figure him out. There was something so *off* about him. Perhaps it was the overly formal way he spoke, the lack of any genuine personality or friendliness. A thing she was quite unused to on holiday resorts, where the staff were usually approachable. He was odd to look at too, though Keira couldn't quite understand why because there was nothing that unusual in his appearance. Unless you caught him in a certain light or at a specific angle.

At the top of the stairs Hal led them into the first bedroom.

'This one is for the young lady of the household,' Hal said.

It was a pleasant room with a large double bed that had the obligatory mosquito canopy draped over it.

'For your comfort,' Hal continued. 'I'd keep the windows closed at night and always sleep with this over you. The air-conditioning is in full working order. Ensuite bathroom is there.'

Keira spotted her suitcase at the foot of the bed.

'I can't wait to try out that pool,' she said.

'Come and see the rest of the rooms first,' Ella said. 'That way you'll know your way around.'

Keira shrugged and followed her parents and Jake back out onto the landing. The house wasn't so big that she would get lost in it but she conceded this to her mother, who sometimes spent her days just watching real estate programmes, dreaming, no doubt, of a day when she might own a house like this one.

On the opposite side of the staircase was Jake's room, a clone of Keira's, with almost identical furniture, bedding, and bathroom.

From Jake's room they walked around the balustrade to the next room.

'And here is your parents' room,' Hal said.

This bedroom was bigger and grander than the two teenagers' rooms and Ella and Perry's cases had been placed on the bed ready to be unpacked.

'As you might expect,' Hal said. 'The other bedrooms are locked. Our owner's own private rooms therefore are off limits.'

Ella's face fell, and Keira noted how disappointed her mother was to not see the whole house. Even so, she was too polite to beg.

'That's understandable,' said Perry to smooth out the sudden silence from his wife. 'And these rooms are fantastic and comfortable. Thank you.'

Hal nodded his head once, in a way that Keira thought was more a bow. 'Downstairs to the left of the staircase is the drawing room and kitchen. The fridge is fully stocked with all kinds of foods. Feel free to help yourselves. The housekeeper comes over once a day and will make the beds and tidy up. I'll have breakfast ready for you, perhaps to eat on the pool terrace, if you like?'

'That would be very nice,' Ella said.

'What time do you wish to eat?' Hall asked.

'We are early risers …' Perry said.

'Well, not too early,' Jake butted in. 'We are on holiday after all.'

Ella sighed. 'Of course. How about 8.30 am?'

Hal nodded again.

'I'll let you settle in,' he said. 'I'll be here until 4pm today if you need anything else. Otherwise, I'm only here in the mornings.'

Hal left them upstairs.

'It looks like I'm left prepping meals for the rest of the day other than breakfast … I thought this was a holiday,' Ella said.

'We'll all pitch in,' Perry said. 'We won't want much, just salads and stuff anyway. Right guys?'

'Sure dad,' said Keira.

'I'm going to get changed,' Jake said. 'The sea is calling me.'

Ella went to explore the rest of the house alone while Perry, Keira and Jake went down to the private beach. The kitchen was immaculate, hotel standard, with stainless steel worksurfaces, polished to a high sheen. She looked in the fridge and found fresh meat, fish, chicken and vegetables and salads. Lunchtime was nearing and she knew that the family would be ravenous once they had finished swimming in the sea and climbed back up those rickety looking steps and so she decided on making a Caesar salad with smoked salmon as an easy option.

She opened cupboards and drawers until she found everything she needed for lunch, while working out what they might like that evening for dinner.

Halfway through Ella realized that she hadn't really taken in where the table and chairs were on the pool terrace. By then she'd chopped and assembled the salad and placed the salmon on a plate that they could serve themselves from.

She covered the salad bowl with a plate and tipped a bowl upside down over the salmon. The house was cool, and although it appeared insect free, she wanted to make sure that no tropical flies or bugs landed on the food. Then she picked up the plates and walked back out of the kitchen, into the hallway.

As she passed the staircase, Ella had the distinct impression that someone was watching her from above. It was as if she sensed a shadow falling over the balustrades onto the stairs. She looked up and saw a blur of movement, but there was no-one there.

She remained still, plate and bowl in hand as she studied the landing above. The hairs were ever so slightly up on the back of her neck. The house was silent. Too silent. And then the air-conditioning kicked in and a blast of cold air hit Ella from above. The AC was obviously on some form of sensor. Working only when there was movement, or perhaps body heat, to set it in motion.

Ella walked away from the hallway and back into the games room.

Outside there was the same vacuum of sound, punctured by occasional laughter floating up from the bay. Ella found the patioed area with the table and chairs and also discovered a bar area, with fully stocked drinks fridge and a gas barbeque. There was also a sink and a dishwasher behind the bar.

After placing the food down on the table, she walked to the glass barrier and looked down. Jake was still in the sea, but Keira was now out and wrapped in a plush robe.

Ella cupped her mouth with her hands and yelled 'Lunch!'. Keira looked up. She waved and shouted to Jake and Perry, conveying the message that they were being called for food.

Ella returned to the patio and opened the fridge. Inside were several bottles of expensive white wine, beers and sodas. Everything a family on holiday needed. The bar was impressive too with gin, tequila, rum, bourbon and whisky vying for space.

She pulled out some sodas for Jake and Keira and a bottle of the wine and poured some into glasses which she set down on the table.

'This holiday starts now!' she said taking a big glug from her glass.

Then she went back to the house kitchen to get plates and cutlery so that they could enjoy their light lunch.

When she returned, Keira, Jake and Perry had reached the top of the beach stairs. Ella waved and they joined her on the patio.

'Wine? During the day?' Perry said.

'We are on holiday,' Ella snapped. 'And I'm the one who needs the rest.'

Perry sat down and held his hands up. 'You're right.'

'You and Jake are cooking tonight,' she said nodding her head towards the barbeque.

'Sounds good to me,' Keira laughed. 'As long as Jake washes his hands first.'

Breakfast was served every morning as promised by Hal, and the family had fleeting contact with an aged housekeeper who made their beds and tidied the house while they ate and then sunbathed by the pool.

Keira noticed how her normally uptight mother was starting to relax. But by the third day the teenagers became bored by of the lack of contact with anyone other than Hal or their parents.

'Where do you think he goes when he leaves?' Jake said as Hal waved his goodbyes and disappeared back through the house.

'I suppose we could follow him and find out,' Keira said.

Jake nodded and they both stood up, slipping on their sandals as they hurried away from the pool and back towards the house.

'Where are you two going?' asked Perry as he poured himself another glass of white wine.

'Just to explore a little,' Keira said.

'Don't go far. You might get lost,' Ella said as she picked up her glass and took a sip.

Jake waved his agreement and he and Keira picked up speed and hurried through the hallway.

They saw the front door closing behind Hal as they came out into the hallway.

'Give it a minute,' Keira suggested. 'He might not like us tagging along.'

Through the hallway window, Jake watched as Hal strode down the path the way he'd originally brought them to the house from the beach.

'He must have a cottage somewhere close,' Jake said. 'Okay he's out of sight. C'mon.'

Keira opened the front door and they followed Hal down the hill.

'I can't see which way he went,' Keira said disappointed. 'I think we waited too long.'

'No. Look. It's this way,' Jake said pointing to the damaged brush, and the foot worn pathway that led away from the house and in the opposite direction from the beach.

A few feet onwards the pathway ended with an abrupt connection with overgrown foliage.

'He can't have gone this way,' Keira said. 'And we shouldn't risk straying too far from the pathway either. Let's go back.'

Jake stared at the foliage for a while, then shrugged. 'Okay, but I don't want to go back to the house just yet. Let's walk down to the landing beach and back.'

Keira agreed: it would kill some time, making the long and lonely island days less boring for them both. There were only so many times you wanted to swim or wade in the sea or watch movies before you craved some different human company other than your own family.

The pathway to the beach was obvious on the way down, though it had seemed confusing on their arrival. As they approached the last line of trees Keira could hear the loud whirring of the helicopter rotors.

They emerged through the trees to see the vehicle lift off in a haze of swirling sand, with Hal in the passenger seat.

'Well, that explains it then. He doesn't stay on the island. He goes back to the mainland, and then returns early in the morning,' Keira said.

'Oh well,' said Jake. 'Shame he's not more interesting than that.'

'Let's walk along the beach for a bit before we go back. See where it leads,' Keira said.

For once, Jake's company wasn't too annoying and he was at least someone to explore with.

They turned left and followed the line of the beach for a mile or more until the sand terminated at a cliff wall which extended into the sea and effectively cut off any access to other parts of the island.

'It's getting late,' Keira said. 'We should go. Mom will have a meltdown if we aren't back before it goes dark.'

They made their way back to the helicopter landing area and followed the trail back up to the house.

'Where on earth have you been all this time!' Ella said as they came in.

'We just walked down to the beach to explore,' Keira

said. 'Chill, Mom. We didn't go anywhere dangerous.'

'I was worried. Thought I'd have to use that emergency phone to get a search party going,' Ella said.

'Give them a break,' Perry said. 'They should go and explore. And look, they found their way back, so everything is fine.'

'We'll go earlier tomorrow,' Keira said. 'As we both agreed we'd like to walk the opposite direction on the beach and see what's there. It's good exercise. You should come with us.'

'No long walks for me,' said Ella. 'I've a book to finish reading and my personal batteries to recharge. But your dad might …'

Keira glanced at Perry but her father's face said it all. No, he didn't want to do it either.

'Just don't take any unnecessary risks,' Perry commented.

The next morning Keira and Jake set off after breakfast and took the path back down to the landing area. This time they turned right and followed the beach.

'Look. You can just see the mainland from here,' Keira observed, cupping her hands over her eyes as she squinted across the shimmering, calm water.

Jake copied her and looked at the distant shape of the land many miles away from the island.

'What was that?' Keira said.

'What?'

'Not out there. Through the trees. This way. I thought I saw someone out of the corner of my eye,' Keira said.

Jake looked back frowning. 'This place is turning you crazy. There's no one here. Hal told us that the first day.'

Keira walked towards the tree line and looked through them. The woodland was denser than in the area that led to the house and Keira couldn't make out much because the light couldn't penetrate.

'Let's just look in here,' she suggested.

'Mom said to stay on the sand,' Jake said.

'Since when did you become such a wuss?'

Jake shrugged then ran towards the trees, plunging in amongst them before Keira had time to react.

Keira followed, glancing around to get her bearings for the beach. Though the wooded area was darker, the sunny beach was a beacon that would draw them back. She wasn't concerned that they would get lost when all they had to do was find the ocean again.

Once Keira caught up with Jake, they walked inland in silence. Pausing now and then to study the foliage, looking for any sign of a path which may have been made by human feet.

They emerged in a small clearing, and beyond that was grass that was over three feet tall. It rustled and moved gently in the hot breeze.

'Wait,' Keira said grasping Jake's arm. 'Should we be worried about snakes?'

'Now who's being a wuss?' Jake said. 'There's no poisonous snakes in this region, so I doubt any would be on this island.'

Keira frowned. 'We probably should go back. I made a mistake. No one's been this way, or we'd be able to tell.'

'Is that your Girl Scout training coming through?' Jake laughed.

'Survival 101,' smirked Keira. 'But seriously ...'

Jake glanced over at the grass. Although he was two years younger than Keira, he already towered above her by at least a foot. They could both see over the grass. But this was a tropical island, who knew what lay hidden here. Especially since the area was so uninhabited. Jake was torn between the urge to explore and concern for his sister.

Keira jumped as she again saw a slight movement from the corner of her eye but as she turned to see what or who was there, she found herself staring at more tall grass. This time though, the foliage was still moving.

'Let's go back,' she said. Her voice trembled but she tried to hide her irrational fear. 'It's almost lunchtime and I'm hungry.'

They turned back to the trees and weaved through, soon catching sight of the beach. Keira experienced an overwhelming relief as they emerged into the glaring midday sun but she hid it from Jake for fear of ridicule.

Later, after a long swim and a healthy lunch, Keira dozed by the pool under a parasol. She observed as she began to dream, how Ella's tan had developed and her mother was beginning to look more charred than healthy brown.

'Put some sun cream on, Mom,' she murmured.

Ella's response was lost on the wave of sleep that took Keira.

Keira woke to find herself alone by the pool. She looked around but none of her family were outside. She stretched and then sat up on the sun lounger. It was late afternoon and her parents were probably inside choosing the meats they'd barbeque for dinner and Jake was no doubt in the cinema room watching some slasher horror movie. She stood up and walked over to the bar area and retrieved a cool soda from the fridge. She popped the can and guzzled half of the drink as she felt dehydrated.

Keira was surprised that her parents hadn't woken her up. Her mother often worried about heat stroke and had made frequent comments to both Keira and Jake about drinking enough water.

Soda can in hand, Keira walked across the patio and into the games room. The door to the cinema room was open and the silence was palpable.

'Jake?' she said as she peered around the door.

The room was empty.

Keira left the games room and went into the hallway.

Normally at this time, she'd hear the chattering of her parents coming from down the hall while they decided what they'd make for dinner – though barbeque was usually the way everyone voted. Keira opened the kitchen door and went inside to find the room empty. Her parents were meticulous timekeepers and she would always expect them to be here at this point in the day, but the kitchen looked as it did after the housekeeper left in the morning. Everything was neat and tidy and not chaotic as it was when her parents started to pull meat and salad out read to prepare.

In the hallway, Keira experienced a moment of dizziness. She stumbled and fell against the newel post.

'Mom?' she called.

The banister wood felt hot and rough to her touch, as Keira looked at her hand, she saw a dark smear of charcoal. She sank down onto the stairs and stared at her fingers.

'Are you alright?'

Keira looked up to find Hal in the hallway.

'Where are my parents?' she said.

'Outside, I've just served breakfast,' Hal said.

'Breakfast? But it's afternoon!' Keira pulled herself up from the steps, she experienced a momentary dizziness.

Hal reached out a hand to help her. It was then that Keira noticed again how long his fingers were. He gripped her arm and steadied her.

Keira shook her head. She must have sunstroke after all. She was hallucinating that Hal's fingers stretched longer and wrapped several times around her arm. An ichor covered them and it dripped over her hand. His fingers seemed to have octopus-like tendrils emerging from them. She shuddered.

'Let me go!' she gasped.

Hal released her arm immediately.

'I'm sorry. I was trying to help. You looked like you were going to faint.'

Keira hurried away, rushing through the games room and out to the pool area. Her parents were on the patio as

Hal had said.

'Hey sleepyhead,' said Perry. 'You're just in time for breakfast.'

Confused, Keira sank down on her usual chair by the table. She glanced back at the house and saw Hal standing in the games room, looking out through the open bi-fold doors. Hal's long arms were down by his sides but Keira couldn't unsee those long, glistening, tentacular fingers. And now, the house behind him looked odd. Like the building was old and fire-damaged, as though it were nothing more than a charred ruin, still smoking with the heat that had destroyed it.

Keira put her head down on the table. 'I don't feel well,' she said and then she slipped away into a dark dreamless void.

Keira woke to find herself on the landing. It was dark and the large space looked very different from its daytime appearance. It was hard to imagine the bright clean walls, the sparkling chandelier hanging over the staircase and the polished wooden floors. For a second, she didn't remember the way back to her room. She turned on the spot, trying to get her bearings, all the time feeling disorientated and confused.

She swept her hand over the wall beside her as she searched for a light switch. A sickening dampness clung to fingers. The plaster moved, like a living organism taking a breath. She pulled her hand away and rubbed it down her nightdress.

She must be dreaming, for what she could make out, what she thought she'd touched, just couldn't possibly be right. She thought she was losing her mind.

Keira stumbled back along the landing. She passed the doors that the owners had locked, each one seemed strangely dark, as though the doors were black eyes that watched her progress. Damp sweat made the nightdress cling to her spine as she picked up speed and hurried past the rooms.

Trembling, Keira reached her bedroom and that was

when the heat hit her. Her hand connected with charred wood, still hot, still smoldering. With a yelp she stepped back, her fingers were scorched, the skin already blistering.

The house must be on fire!

'Mom! Dad!' she tried to yell, but her voice caught in her throat as she inhaled smoke.

The door opened in front of her. The room inside no longer resembled the clean and beautiful bedroom she'd been allocated, instead it was blackened and burnt. The mattress an inferno.

A figure emerged from the dark and moved towards her. Surrounding its head was a halo of burning light.

Shards of fire exploded into the room with the creature's every step. The heat was unbearable and Keira felt the tips of her hair singe as the burning figure drew closer, but she was paralyzed and unable to move.

Inside her head, Keira screamed, and somehow, through sheer will, the scream forced its way out from her terrified throat.

In the blink of an eye the illusion vanished: the room was back the way it had always been.

'Keira?' her Mom said. 'You were sleepwalking.'

'No. I … Mom the room was on fire. I felt the heat. I burnt my hand …'

Ella looked at Keira's fingers. There were no blisters and the skin was pink and healthy.

'Let's get you back to bed,' Ella said.

'I want to leave here. As soon as possible.'

'We only have two more days,' Ella said.

Keira let Ella tuck her back into bed in the way she had done when she was much younger. It was comforting, and the lingering dream slipped away as she lay down on the soft pillow.

How could she have ever thought the place was on fire? Or that there was something capable of walking amongst the flames. Something that could, by the height and size, have been Hal.

She'd had too much sun, that was all that it was. And, of course, the permeating alienness of Ma'an Du was playing with her subconscious.

The next morning Jake suggested that they explore some more of the island. Keira felt better again. Normal. Strong. And the silliness of the dark dream she had was oddly distant in the light of day.

'There's Hal,' Jake said.

Keira looked inland and saw Hal striding through the long grass. Without saying a word, she followed and Jake fell in beside her. They didn't speak as they shadowed Hal.

Hal appeared to be unaware of them as he continued onwards, never looking back. Wherever he was going he knew the way and he was carrying something in his arms. A large bundle that he held close to his chest.

The overgrown grass gave way to a clearing. Keira dropped to her knees, pulling Jake into a crouch beside her to keep from being seen.

The clearing was a perfect circle and in the center was a large building, the like of which Keira had never seen before. Though it was built from the island's resources of wood, the structure was complex and architecturally interesting. She could not in any way refer to this as a hut. And she didn't believe that any possibly indigenous race had built it even though it fitted its surroundings far more than the house on the hill.

'It's probably a storage building for the owners,' Jake said.

'It's a bit ... complicated ... to be just for storage. Storing what?' Keira said.

'Personal stuff, I guess.'

A taint was in the air, a waft of bonfire smoke and cooking meat. There was something in the smell that reminded Keira of her terrifying dream from the night before.

'Let's sneak around back and see if there are any windows,' Jake suggested.

Keira glanced at him and saw that rare amused and curious expression he had when something roused his interest. Keeping low, Jake went left, weaving through the grass as it curved around the barren circle. Keira had no choice but to follow. Besides, she was just as curious as her brother. She wanted to know what Hal was doing, and what was inside the building. Besides, it alleviated the boredom.

At the back of the building Jake and Keira found no windows and no doors. There was only one way in and out of the place and they couldn't risk going in the front as Hal would be there.

They agreed to wait until Hal left and they hid among the foliage at a safe but distant spot that overlooked the door.

Hal came out half an hour later. He no longer had the bundle in his arms: whatever he'd been carrying had been left inside.

Hal left the way he'd arrived, oblivious of their observation. They waited until they felt it was unlikely that he'd return and then, Keira and Jake scurried out of their hiding place and approached the door.

The entrance was large with big double doors held shut by a wooden beam that Hal had slipped across before he left. Keira couldn't help thinking that the building was not made to keep things out, but to keep something in.

'We shouldn't,' Keira said as Jake reached for the bracing beam. 'It's not our business and it's trespassing.'

'That's the future lawyer in you talking. But you haven't taken the bar yet Keira and this is probably the last summer in your life when you'll ever be able to take a chance and even screw up a bit.'

Keira paused taking in what Jake had said. She knew he was right. Once she started college she would have to be beyond reproach. 'Okay. Let's do it. Let's go inside.'

'Ow. It's hot,' said Jake. But even though he complained, he freed the beam from its restraining supports.

They hesitated for a moment and then Jake took hold of one of the wrought iron handles and tugged on the door.

The door had opened effortlessly for Hal, but Jake struggled and so Keira grabbed hold of the handle too and they both pulled with all their strength.

The door gave a little and then natural momentum as well as the body weight of both teenagers propelled the door open and both Keira and Jake let go and fell in a heap on the threshold.

Laughing, they recovered from the fall and climbed back onto their feet. Then the laughter died as the adventure at hand became more focused and they peered into the dark building.

Jake searched for a light switch but found nothing.

'How did he see in here?' Keira said.

Jake gave a shrug, and stepped over the threshold. He was swallowed by the dark as if a black cloak had been thrown over him.

Keira remained frozen for a split second and then she too entered.

As her eyes became accustomed to the gloom, he saw that she was in a large oval room. Her eyes fell on a small group of people huddling around something at the center.

'Nothing here,' said Jake. 'It's completely empty. Do you think Hal was fucking with us?'

The clustered group all stood, and turned to look at them but Jake didn't notice. It was as if he couldn't see them at all.

The group parted revealing a crib, with a silent baby laying inside. Keira saw the child move, reaching out to her with overlong arms and fingers. Keira gasped and stepped back.

'What is it?' Jake asked.

'Can't you see them?' Keira croaked and she pointed a shaky hand in the direction of the group. All of whom had the same malformed shape, over tall, elongated arms that dropped to the floor and hands and fingers that flicked and twitched like an angry cat's tail.

They shuffled towards her now, fingers lifting and lengthening as they reached out.

'What's the matter with you?' Jake said.

The group ignored him, focused as they were on Keira and when she turned and ran there was nothing else Jake could do but follow.

They burst from the structure and Keira plunged into the foliage leaving Jake to struggle with the door as he pushed it closed once more and placed the bar back behind them.

Then he sprinted until he caught up with his sister as she reached the trees and fell gasping and hysterical against one.

'What happened?' he asked again.

'You … couldn't see them … but they were there. They wanted to touch me. Oh God! I have to get away from this place …'

'Sis … you're not making any sense. The place was empty!'

'And the baby. It was like them. So alien and deformed …'

'Keira there was no one there!' Jake said. 'Look. You need to calm down. Mom and Dad will be mad we went exploring like that, and Hal … well I think he knew we followed him.'

Keira wrapped her arms around her body. She was shaking so hard that Jake frowned. He'd never seen his sister like this before. She was normally level headed and smart despite how he liked to say she wasn't. His eyes went back to the building – he could just make it out among the foliage now that he knew it was there.

'Okay. What did you see?' he said. 'Tell me in detail.'

They returned to the house, silent and subdued. Jake hadn't spoken after Keira described what she'd seen, and what she'd imagined the night before in the house.

'I think it's best that we don't tell Mom and Dad about this,' Jake said.

'They wouldn't believe me anyway,' Keira said. 'Like you don't.'

'I believe you believe this. And that you're really scared. But we leave tomorrow and if you're scared tonight, you can come and get me and I'll take care of you.'

'Thanks,' Keira said. 'That means a lot.'

The evening went by with no further incident and Keira began to believe that she had indeed imagined the whole thing. But as the night drew in the thought of spending one last night on the island began to terrify her. She couldn't shake the idea that it was important that she'd seen these creatures, but what horrified her more was the fact that they had taken notice of her. They had *seen* her.

'Let's stay up and watch one last movie,' she suggested to Jake.

As if he understood her concern, he nodded and agreed, 'Yeah, last time we get to have our own personal cinema room.'

When Ella and Perry went to bed, Jake looked through the movie library and rattled off the names of the films he wanted to see. They chose a comedy that they both agreed on and then Jake went out to the patio bar and fetched them both a bottle of beer each.

'Don't tell Mom,' he said.

'Do you smell that?' Keira said.

'No. What?'

'Like something's burning,' Keira said.

'Probably just the remains of barbeque smoke,' Jake said.

'I need to pee. Be right back,' Keira said.

Keira looked out onto the patio through the closed bi-fold doors. This place was about as secure as you could get. Even if all the doors and windows had been left open, the island was private and there was no risk of any crime. But yet, she was glad that the doors were closed and locked.

She turned to go back to watch the film and found Hal standing by the hallway door.

'What are you doing here?' she asked.

'You saw them,' Hal said.

Keira blinked. 'They were real?'

Hal looked past her and Keira's eyes were drawn back to the glass and the patio outside. There she saw the creatures gathering, the baby now crawling like a beached octopus towards the doors.

'And they saw you …' Hal said.

'Who are they?' Keira asked. Despite her fear there was a feeling that she was on the cusp of some great new knowledge.

Hal came to her side.

'A people that should not exist. A people that want to leave here, but can't.'

Keira looked at Hal.

His hands appeared over-long, and his face warped. For a second Keira thought she saw more than two eyes and then the vision was gone.

'You can see through the veil. You're a special creature.'

Keira looked back outside. The 'people' remained still, staring in at her, as though she were the curiosity and not them. Keira had the overwhelming sense of what it must be like to be a zoo animal in a cage.

'This island is theirs. Every week we have a new family here in the hope that one will have the gift. The owner has been searching for years for someone like you Keira,' Hal continued. 'Someone who might free us.'

'You're one of them too?' Keira said.

'I pass better than most,' Hal said.

The creatures outside began to sing. That was the only word Keira could find to describe the sound. A siren melody, warped and ethereal. An unusual calm washed over Keira, taking away all fear and doubt.

Hal unlocked the door.

'They need mercy,' Hal said.

'What do I do?'

'Fire. Cleansing and purifying. It's the only way.'

The creatures came into the house. They shuffled into the games room and Keira could smell the charred and burning odour that was forever in her nostrils since that awful, dark dream.

The singing continued.

Hal went outside. He fired up the barbeque and then returned with a burning stick, its end wrapped in oily cloth.

'It must be by your hand,' he said.

He passed the torch to Keira and then the creatures knelt before her as if she were some revered statue in an ancient church. One by one she touched their ragged clothing with the fire, and the burning shape would stand and exit the house, hurry towards the cliff edge and stumble away down onto the private beach. Burning, yet walking, and the singing continued until the last of the creatures was alight, a shape that vaguely resembled a female form, and holding the squirming form of the baby. Both went up in silent flames and then they too left the house the same as the others had.

As this last creature headed for the beach, so the song faltered and faded. When it was done and the song of the creatures was silenced, Hal took the torch, doused it in a bucket of water beside the barbeque and re-entered the house, relocked the door behind him.

'What about you?' Keira asked.

'I have to remain to take care of the others.'

'Others? But I thought——'

'There will be more. There are always more. Maybe not this year or the next or even in ten years. But more will arrive, born somewhere else in the world, they will be drawn here by the unknowable cosmic creatures that made them.'

Keira's mind was awash with confusion. But another vision swept behind her eyes, of the unspeakable creatures that Hal spoke of. The fathers of these poor souls and more. Of the human women who were soiled and used to make them. In the moments it took for this story to play out, Keira lost all innocence. She also realized who and what she was.

Keira returned to the cinema room. Jake was asleep in the chair; Hal was long gone. There was a strong smell in the air of burning flesh that stung her nostrils and sickened her stomach. She looked at her younger brother and for the first time she was relieved that he had been unable to see the creatures. She did not want him to know what she knew. For it was a taint on her soul that would always be there.

Leaving Jake where he was, Keira went back into the games room. Morning was breaking, and the room was already bright. There was no sign that the creatures had ever been there.

Keira opened the doors and went outside. She walked to the barrier, looking down at the private beach. She saw no evidence of burnt remains on the steps or on the sand. It was as if she had dreamed the whole thing. She stared out to sea, convincing herself that this was all in her imagination. What she believed to be true could be forgotten in time and her life could go on as planned.

As she turned around, she saw her father coming out for his morning swim. There was something off about Perry, something that she'd never noticed before and she found that she couldn't deny it now. His hands and fingers were longer than they should be. His face had a glow of ethereal light. He reminded her of the abominations she had released from this world only the night before.

Keira closed her eyes. The horror of the creatures' lives burned behind her lids, like the flame she had lit them with. Who and what was her father? What did that mean for her and Jake?

'You can give him mercy,' Hal said, appearing beside her as if he'd always been there. 'You can give it them all. Your mother is one of us too. Neither of them know.'

Her father finished his swim, climbed from the water and then went back inside the house oblivious of what his daughter was discussing with the peculiar servant of the house.

'If they knew what you knew, they'd wish for this too,' Hal told her.

Keira found her hands around the lit torch once more and as she entered the games room, she now smelt the strong tang of gasoline. She dropped the torch on the floor, and watched as the flames tore through the room and out into the hall. The fire lapped at her, but there was no pain. Only the deep desire for mercy too. Only the desire to go to her true home. And yes, the flame purified, but it did so much more. It was freedom.

Hal stood outside as the house collapsed and burnt to the ground. Rebuilding would begin within weeks. And as for the remaining tainted like himself, well, more could arrive at any time. And they'd wait on Ma'an Du for as long as it took for the next one with the power to send them home and relieve their suffering.

For the Old Ones' offspring was never meant to live on Earth.

About the Author

Samantha Lee Howe is the *USA Today* Bestselling author and multi-award-winning screenwriter of *The Stranger in Our Bed*. She is the author of almost 30 novels and many short stories, many of which are set in Lovecraftian mythos. Samantha is commissioning editor for Telos Publishing imprint, Telos Moonrise, and among other interests, is the Festival Director for The Sykehouse International Film Festival.

AFTERWORD

Samantha Lee Howe

In 2023 I went to my first Pink Ribbon gala. I'd been supporting smaller gatherings before that and I was introduced to the lovely Lisa Allen on many occasions by my friend, columnist and author, Steven Smith. Lisa is a dynamo and so impressive in her dedication to the cause that I was immediately interested in helping if I could.

Of course, there's more to my interest than just an altruistic urge to support. I'm the youngest of seven children. There's only five of us left now and my eldest sister, Kathleen, 15 years older than me, died many years ago of pneumonia related to her fight with Multiple Sclerosis. Kathleen had three daughters and her first born, Dawn, was the first among us to be hit by the blight. She sadly died, aged only 40 years old, of breast cancer. My other sister Sharna then developed breast cancer in November 2015 followed rapidly by her son learning he had lung cancer. You get the picture …

I learnt soon after that we had a serious problem and although not BRACA, they delved enough into our family history to confirm we were genetically at risk. Armed with this information, I opted for preventative surgery in 2017 and had a bilateral mastectomy and reconstruction. I wasn't brave. I was terrified because every day I woke up with a new lump and I was back and forth to the breast clinic being checked. I didn't want to face cancer. I wanted that risk gone and for me this was the only alternative. Even so, my scars are my battle wounds and I'm proud of them. I don't regret taking this step. It was the right one for me because I'm stronger knowing I don't have the sword of Damocles over my head anymore.

My sister Sharna is still fit as is my nephew Chace who are

both in remission. And my whole family, male and female, are vigilant about looking out for the signs.

But back to the first Pink Ribbon gala I went to, which was something very special. Not only was it a brilliant night full of entertainment but it was the first time I met some of the BOLD ladies – survivors still going through or recovering from chemo, who had taken part in a very brave campaign for Lisa and Pink Ribbon and had allowed themselves to be photographed still with their hair shaved or just starting to grow back.

The evening was glamorous, magical, not what you would expect to be honest as you might think it would be sombre. But no, it was more a celebration of life, but the whimsical theme of *A Mid-Summer Night's Dream* didn't take away any of the seriousness behind why we were all there.

During the night, a beautiful singer performed the song 'This Is Me' from *The Greatest Showman* musical, and the most incredible moment happened. Lisa and the BOLD ladies were gathered on the dance floor – I think just chatting. Then the music started up and we were all watching the performance. The ladies began to dance together in the way that only survivors, who know they are coming out the other end of a terrible traumatic experience can ever do. The music was so on point. *This is Me!* I'm strong! I'm a survivor. I remember looking at them, tears in my eyes and the moment, unrehearsed and so powerful hit everyone in the room at exactly the same time.

We surged onto the dance floor in support, some of us watching some of us surrounding them, some joining in.

It was one of those moments that affected everyone in the room and ran through like an electric current: a moment of awakening, elucidation, solidarity. A moment so powerful that I think none of us will ever forget it.

So – *This Is Me* is the only name I could have given this incredible *Criminal Pursuits* anthology.

I'm so grateful for the amazing and talented authors who took time out of their very busy schedules to donate a story to this book in support of Pink Ribbon. I'm incredibly proud of the content which is a stunning range of stories that will thrill, terrify and perhaps even have you cheering from the sidelines.

Thank you all! And I really hope, you dear reader, have enjoyed taking the individual journey of each powerful story, as much as I did.

Samantha Lee Howe, May 2025

Also Available From Telos Publishing

CRIMINAL PURSUITS: CRIMES THROUGH TIME
Ed. Samantha Lee Howe
14 short stories of dark and deadly crimes throughout varies
points in history. (in aid of PohWer)

SAMANTHA LEE HOWE Writing as SAM STONE

KAT LIGHTFOOT MYSTERIES
1: Zombies At Tiffany's
2: Kat On A hot Tin Airship
3: What's Dead PussyKat
4: Kat of Green Tentacles
5: Kat and the Pendulum
6: Ten Little Demons

MAXIM JAKUBOWSKI

JUST A GIRL WITH A GUN
Cornelia, a mesmerizing stripper is recruited by the enigmatic
organization known only as 'The Bureau'. She becomes an
unlikely assassin, caught between the dance floor and a life of
deadly precision.

PIPER'S DANCE
When two immortal children of Hamelin, escape from the
questionable clutches of the Pied Piper, they leave behind the
mysterious island that has been their prison for centuries.

SCOTT MONTGOMERY
THE LONG, BIG KISS GOODBYE
Hardboiled thrills as Jack Sharp gets involved with a
dame called Kitty.

TANITH LEE
DEATH OF THE DAY

GRAHAM MASTERTON and WILLIAM S BURROUGHS
RULES OF DUEL

EVGENY GRIDNEFF
A STINK IN THE TALE

TELOS PUBLISHING
Email: orders@telos.co.uk
Web: www.telos.co.uk

To order copies of any Telos books, please visit our website
where there are full details of all titles and facilities for worldwide
credit card online ordering, as well as occasional special offers.